MW00535349

Defy the Future

Also by Keira Andrews

Contemporary

The Spy and the Mobster's Son
Honeymoon for One
Beyond the Sea
Ends of the Earth
Arctic Fire

Holiday
The Christmas Deal
The Christmas Leap
The Christmas Veto
Only One Bed
Merry Cherry Christmas
Santa Daddy
In Case of Emergency
Eight Nights in December
If Only in My Dreams
Where the Lovelight Gleams
Gay Romance Holiday Collection
Lumberjack Under the Tree (free read!)

Sports
Kiss and Cry
Reading the Signs
Cold War
The Next Competitor
Love Match
Synchronicity (free read!)

Gay Amish Romance Series
A Forbidden Rumspringa
A Clean Break
A Way Home
A Very English Christmas

Valor Duology
Valor on the Move

Test of Valor
Complete Valor Duology

Lifeguards of Barking Beach
Flash Rip
Swept Away (free read!)

Historical

Kidnapped by the Pirate
Semper Fi
The Station
Voyageurs (free read!)

Paranormal

Kick at the Darkness Trilogy
Kick at the Darkness
Fight the Tide
Defy the Future

Taste of Midnight (free read!)

Fantasy

Barbarian Duet
Wed to the Barbarian
The Barbarian's Vow

Defy the Future

BY KEIRA ANDREWS

Defy the Future
Written and published by Keira Andrews
Cover by Dar Albert
Formatting by BB eBooks
Editing by Angela O'Connell
Sunset icon created by monkik – Flaticon

Copyright © 2024 by Keira Andrews

All rights reserved. This book or any portion thereof may not be reproduced or used in any manner whatsoever without the express written permission of the author or publisher except for the use of brief quotations in a book review.

ISBN: 978-1-998237-06-7

This is a work of fiction. Names, characters, businesses, places, events and incidents are either the products of the author's imagination or used in a fictitious manner. No persons, living or dead, were harmed by the writing of this book. Any resemblance to any actual persons, living or dead, or actual events is purely coincidental.

Dedication

For every reader who patiently awaited the end of Parker and Adam's journey.

Thank you for loving them so faithfully.

Acknowledgments

Huge thanks to Angela, Anita, Kathleen, Lori, and Mia for your invaluable help in making this book the best it could be. I also couldn't have done it without Leta Blake's friendship and encouragement.

Author's Note

Salvation Island and other locations are fictional and won't be found on any maps.

Chapter One

THE SHIP TRESPASSED on the edge of Parker's world without warning or welcome, almost obscured by the early morning haze.

Naked on the eastern shore of Salvation Island, Parker shivered as another cold wave washed around his knees. He squinted, though the rising sun was hidden behind a wall of clouds. The ship fucking up his morning swim was by far the biggest he'd seen since a former Coast Guard patrol boat carrying desperate, starving families had come to the island a year before.

Shit, maybe two years? Time didn't work the way it used to—at least not in Parker's mind.

Goosebumps rippled over his arms as he stared at the gray boat that almost blended into the gunmetal sky, willing it to disappear. It was a commercial fishing vessel, maybe? Trawler. Except it looked to have a full sailing rig with mainsail and headsail. Parker had never seen a hybrid like it.

He closed his eyes.

Opened them.

Still there.

He closed his eyes again.

Parker was teaching a class on nautical knots after breakfast. Then he had a weed-yanking shift in the south garden. He and Adam would meet for lunch before more garden duty, rain or shine—the latter seeming unlikely.

Then it was taco night, which was Parker's fave, especially

since the dairy team had started making sour cream. God, how he'd missed sour cream. It was thick and tangy and made taco night even better.

Adam had posted the after-dinner movie screening schedule for the week, but Parker hadn't peeked. He liked to be surprised. He'd made his guesses as to which movie Adam would choose for taco night, knowing their DVD/Blu-ray library was impressively vast yet finite. Adam had insisted that *The Fast and the Furious* had nothing to do with tacos—which was technically true—but Parker knew the vibe was right.

He opened his eyes.

Also, this boat could *fuck right off.*

Something crashed through the foliage, and Parker allowed himself a smile, his heart swelling as he waited for Adam to burst out from the overgrown path that led to the narrow strip of rocky, grainy sand. Everyone else swam on the western and southern beaches, which were softer under the feet and far bigger for families to spread out.

Parker retreated to the tiny beach—*his* beach—and tugged on his khakis, wet feet sinking into the cold sand, a rock under his heel. This February—their third on the island—had been surprisingly gray, but he'd grown up swimming off Cape Cod in spring when the Atlantic was still "bracing" as his mom had put it.

Salvation Island wasn't as far south as Miami and the Bahamas, but even when the water felt chilly, Parker swam. He'd learned the currents and tides and stayed very close to shore. More days than not in a year, the sun would warm his face and dry his skin as he sat cross-legged on a flat rock and cycled through the meditations Connie had taught him.

Meditation wasn't going to do shit this morning.

Adam exploded from between the zigzagging branches of the sweet acacia trees that would bloom again soon with puffy yellow flowers that smelled like grape Laffy Taffy. He'd been naked and murmuring in his sleep when Parker had left him with a lingering kiss to his scratchy, bearded cheek. At least he'd put on jeans before charging through the village.

"I know," Parker said, motioning to the horizon. "No one picked it up earlier with their super-duper werewolf vision? Must have been hull down."

Adam reached for Parker and scanned him for injuries, which Parker didn't protest anymore. Adam said, "Whatever you say, Captain."

"You remember—it's because the Earth is curved and you can only see the top. Maybe it was running without lights if they're being sneaky. Or the watch team was distracted."

His stomach flooded with acid as he thought of how easily he'd been taken by surprise that day years before on the *Bella Luna*. He'd been so stupid.

"Apparently, the fishing team radioed Connie a few hours ago when they spotted the ship."

"They were able to get through? That's good."

There'd been increasing signal interference on the radio for some time, and no one could figure out why. The best guess was an environmental cause, though again, why was a mystery. It wasn't like they could just Google it.

Adam said, "She didn't see the need to wake everyone up early. And we don't know that anyone is being sneaky." He smoothed his hand over the bruise on Parker's shoulder from where he'd caught a baseball by, well, not actually catching it. Adam kissed it gently.

The fucking new boat and the trouble it was probably bringing was nothing to smile about, but Parker allowed himself another one, soaking in Adam's love, which felt like the sun breaking through clouds. He pressed his cheek against Adam's and rubbed their beards together.

Okay, *fine*, Parker's facial hair wasn't quite a *beard*, but at twenty-one, he could finally grow a respectable amount of scruff. They'd both let their hair get longer over the winter and were due for a cut. In the meantime, Parker loved sinking his fingers into Adam's thick, glossy hair.

"I'm fine," Parker said. "No one's had time to kidnap me from my secret beach."

Adam held him close, running his hands up and down Parker's bare flanks and over his cotton-clad ass. "It's not secret. It's just a pain to get to."

"That's what makes it secret. It's not like we have actual secrets here, but at least everyone else swims at the easy beaches."

"You love to make things difficult." Adam inhaled deeply, and Parker lifted his arm so Adam could get his face right in there the way he liked. "I wish you wouldn't swim alone," Adam mumbled into his armpit.

"I'm fine," Parker repeated. Many mornings, he knew Adam lurked in the trees checking on him. But Adam also understood that Parker needed this ritual, and he needed to do it alone.

Reluctantly, Parker squirmed around in Adam's grasp so he could watch the water. "Any radio communication with the fuckers who are ruining taco night?"

"I'm not sure, and we don't know that they're 'fuckers.' They might be new friends."

"Hm." It was true that most of the people who had found their way to Salvation Island just wanted a safe haven. A home. Many of them werewolves who'd already visited over the years. There had been a few notable exceptions, though. All the Zen breathing in the world wouldn't change Parker's default suspicion.

He had a million questions, but Adam wouldn't know the answers, so he let them simmer for the moment. He'd used meditation to work on simmering instead of boiling over with varying degrees of success.

A flash of red on his fingers caught his eye. "Dude!" Parker spun and inspected Adam's skin, spotting a long cut slashed into his shoulder just before it healed and disappeared. "Careful with the acacias. Those leaves are sharp."

Adam shrugged dismissively. "It's already healed."

"Yeah, but it still hurt you." That Adam had been rushing because he was worried about Parker was both awesome and guilt-inducing. He tugged Adam down for a long kiss before sighing. "I was really looking forward to taco night."

"Me too. And the movie. I thought—"

Parker pressed his finger to Adam's slightly chapped lips. "No spoilers."

With a tender smile, Adam snagged Parker's hand and kissed his palm.

Parker pulled on his long-sleeved tee before they hurried back to the village. Leaves, twigs, and rocks dug into Parker's bare feet, but he barely noticed it now. On the beautiful summer days when he and Adam took *Bella* out for a spin, the polished deck felt luxurious under his callused soles.

In the clearing where the village's main buildings sat, they passed the school, which was a compound now of several one-story wooden buildings arcing around a grass playing field. One of the newcomers who'd arrived after Adam and Parker was a carpenter, and Alejandra had built an impressive jungle gym, seesaw, and swing set for the little kids. Instead of teeming with life and laughter, they all stood empty now thanks to this mystery boat.

Parker inhaled deeply for four counts, then held it for four, exhaled for four, and waited another four beats before inhaling again. Connie called it "box breathing" and said she'd learned it from YouTube back when the internet had been a thing.

God, Parker missed the internet.

The bell had been salvaged from an old ship, and on regular mornings, it rang twice five minutes before classes began, and once when class started. Now, Kenny, who'd been one of the first to greet them on Salvation Island, tugged the rope steadily, the bell chiming five times in a row. Then a pause before five more.

Adam winced as they approached, and Parker could imagine the clang was deafening to the werewolves, who didn't need it to know when something was wrong. Even for the regular humans like Parker and Kenny, the bell was undeniable.

"You see it?" Kenny asked. He was in his late twenties, Chinese, and had grown up in Orlando. He'd been one of the first humans to find their way to Salvation Island after the world had gone to hell. Slim and short-haired, he worked as Connie's assistant.

Parker nodded as they passed. "Trawler, I think."

The packed dirt pathways of the village snaked around various low buildings, including the new and improved hospital, which had recently been painted white. Salvation Island reminded Parker of Camp Weepecket, where he'd gone for two weeks every August until high school.

Connie would be waiting for everyone in the mess hall, which had a fresh coat of red on its wood frame. It was the heart of the village and had doubled in size since Parker and Adam had first arrived.

The roof was vaulted, and the kitchen and cafeteria-style buffet area gleamed with reclaimed stainless steel finishings. The tables were a mix of smaller round and long bench style, which were easier to build—especially before they had a carpenter on the island.

The long mess hall had a raised stage at one end that Alejandra had built in front of the smooth white wall they projected movies onto. She'd offered to make Connie a chair for when she took to the stage to address them, but Connie had refused, saying it would be far too much like a throne.

She was indeed standing on the stage waiting as they filed in, wearing one of her typical country cozy sweaters, this one with pink flowers in a yellow vase. She had olive skin, and her gray hair was the same no-nonsense bob it had been since Parker had known her. She was short and plump and wore tennis shoes instead of her Birkenstocks.

For a badass alpha werewolf, she looked strikingly like a grandmother who spent her time playing bingo, baking cookies, and maybe quilting—or whatever it was grannies did in the olden days before the creepers.

Craig waved them over to the end of a bench where he and Lilly had evidently been about to start breakfast. They were both African-American, and at eleven, Lilly had grown tall and skinny. She'd pulled her curly hair back with a headband and wore her usual capri pants, sneakers, and T-shirt.

Parker sat beside her and accepted the banana muffin she slid over. "Where's Jacob?" he asked through a bite.

Craig sighed. "He was gone early this morning with those new friends." His afro was cut close to his head, flecks of gray at his temples.

"That's good," Adam said. "At least he's not sleeping in and missing class."

"No, but he smelled suspiciously like…" Craig glanced at Lilly stirring her oatmeal and mimed inhaling a joint.

"He's sixteen," Parker said. "It could be worse." He joked, "Everything might be about to go to shit because of whoever's in this new boat."

No one laughed.

Parker's gaze met Bethany's where she sat next to Damian at one of the smaller tables, her fingers entwined with his. A new hand-poked tattoo snaked up her wrist—a daisy chain, which seemed far too innocent in Parker's opinion.

She smiled tightly as he stared, a brief lift of her pink lips, the shade of lipstick complementing her long red hair and pale skin.

Parker didn't smile back. He never did—not with her. But he could see her and usually not think about what had happened. He could tolerate her and live peacefully most days even if he didn't ever want to be pals.

Today was not one of those days.

Because what if the people on this new boat were like Bethany's old crew? Even though it had been years now, the terror of being helpless and alone and naked as he was robbed and hit and threatened with worse still made Parker sweaty and sick to his stomach.

Bethany had allegedly later killed the man who'd hurt Parker, but the world had to be full of more like him. Dangerous assholes and creepers were probably all that were left on the mainland. Parker was sure as hell never leaving Salvation Island to find out.

Peering around the mess hall now at his people, he swelled with love and a deep urge to protect his community. Whoever was on this new boat had better not try to fuck with Salvation Island, or Parker would make them sorry.

Granted, he had no weapons since they were locked up, and only Connie and her daughter, Theresa, could access them. Not that Parker needed a gun. He had Adam, and he knew without a shred of doubt that Adam would protect him and their home with every bit of strength he had.

And he had a lot.

Parker rubbed his hand slowly over Adam's denim-clad thigh, thinking about how strong and brave and sexy his boyfriend was. How damn lucky he was that when the world exploded into chaos without warning, he'd been arguing with Adam about his stupid grade.

Adam raised an eyebrow that silently said, "*Here? Now? Really?*"

Parker shrugged and dipped his hand to run his fingertips along the inseam of Adam's jeans, silently replying, "*Everywhere.*

Always."

Adam threaded their fingers together and firmly moved Parker's hand to the bench between them. He squeezed affectionately.

Parker leaned close and barely spoke, knowing Adam could hear him with his super wolfy senses. "What do you expect when you're shirtless?" he teased.

Adam rolled his eyes and whispered right in Parker's ear, his breath warm and ticklish. "I'm regularly shirtless. So is half the island."

This was true—some werewolves wore as little as possible. Some humans too, although Parker preferred shirts since sunscreen was a limited resource, and he'd always been pasty and prone to burning.

"Yeah, but—" Parker bit off the rest of his teasing words.

Connie must have made a small sound. If she so much as sighed, all werewolves in the vicinity fell silent and watched her with bated breath. The humans had learned to recognize this sign, aside from a few of the newer teenagers who were laughing and jostling each other in the back of the mess hall until their parents shushed them sharply.

Jacob was with them, hands in pockets and slouched against the wall, his brown hair flopping over his eye. His skin was as pasty as Parker's, but red with pimples. Parker pointed him out to Craig, who visibly relaxed as the hush settled over the citizens of Salvation Island.

The population was over five hundred now, and honestly, Parker felt like they had more than enough people. Why Connie insisted on continuing to broadcast her message over the radio, inviting strangers to mess up everything, was beyond him. Though now it seemed it likely wasn't reaching many people anymore, thanks to the deteriorating radio signals.

Connie gave them all a kind smile, and Parker exhaled a long breath. Even though he wasn't a wolf and biologically affected, her calming alpha presence still soothed him. Maybe it was also her grandma vibe? Not that his had been anything like Connie. His dad's mother had died before he was born, and his mom's had been kind of a bitch most of the time, if he was being real.

She *had* imparted on him to appreciate the little moments in life, and honestly, it had gotten way easier after the sort-of-zombie apocalypse. He squeezed Adam's fingers.

"Morning, folks. I know some of you have spotted the boat to our east," Connie said.

Alarmed murmurs snaked through the mess hall. It was still early, so plenty of people hadn't heard.

Connie's voice stayed steady and low. She never shouted, yet was able to project with seemingly no effort. "We've reached out to the newcomers by radio. They've told us they'd like to talk. We'll be welcoming them to the island later this morning after a launch party travels out to vet them."

Parker shifted on the bench, stretching out his legs and crossing his ankles one way, then the other. Folding his legs back under. Stretching out. Adam stroked his thumb along Parker's index finger.

"How many people?" Damian asked.

Connie looked to her daughter, Theresa, who stood from where she'd been sitting at the bench closest to the stage. She tucked a long, dark strand of hair behind her ear from where it had escaped her ponytail. "They say twelve. I'll be confirming that, along with other information we've been provided. Would anyone like to volunteer to accompany me?"

Adam's hand shot up, because of course it did. Parker choked down a surge of worry and playfully hissed, "Teacher's pet." If Connie or Theresa asked for a helping hand, Adam was always first in line.

Parker knew why Adam craved their attention. His parents and sisters had died horrifically when he was a kid, and he'd been alone for years. He craved that family connection, and though there were plenty of werewolves on Salvation Island, Connie and Theresa were special to him.

Parker hated the idea of Adam going anywhere near the potential fuckers on that boat, but he bit his tongue. A newish woman named Yolanda had volunteered, so there'd be at least one human in the greeting party. Connie and Theresa felt it was important that the humans knew their opinions were valued, yada, yada, yada.

Honestly, Parker was more than happy to let the werewolves make the hard decisions and protect them all with their super wolfy powers. Especially the part where they were immune to the virus that had turned most of the world into creepers. While there was no way to know anything a hundred percent, they'd heard it from multiple werewolves who'd arrived on the island.

Parker counted to four as he inhaled, drawing the box on a chalkboard in his mind as he went through the breathing cycle. The chalkboard visualization technique sometimes helped block the memories of Adam helpless and suffering in the basement lab at the Pines while that batshit scientist cut off chunks of his flesh for experiments.

Today was not one of those days.

"I'm fine," Adam murmured, stroking Parker's thumb.

"Just be skeptical, okay? Pessimistic, even. Channel me."

Adam chuckled. "Will do."

It was safe on the island. Unless Parker was at the helm, he detested Adam going anywhere. Adam had only done one supply run to the mainland not long after they'd settled on the island. Parker had actually puked he'd been so worried.

Adam hadn't left again.

There hadn't been scavenging trips to the mainland for quite a while now, presumably because the canned food and medicine and anything useful were permanently out of stock. Parker had always made himself scarce when a scavenging team returned. He didn't want to know what was going on out there.

After Connie told everyone to go about their day as normal, she left the stage. Conversations resumed, and the clink of cutlery on plates put Parker's nerves on edge. Adam kissed him sweetly and whispered, "See you soon."

Parker gripped his hand so tightly that it would have hurt a human. Adam only kissed him again, and Parker released him, not watching him go. He picked at the banana muffin, reminding himself that it wasn't an option to drag Adam back to their cabin and lock him inside.

"Who do you think they are?" Jacob asked without preamble, plopping onto the bench.

"No clue," Parker muttered. "But I wish they'd stay off our island."

Jacob laughed sharply. "For someone who was dead set against coming here, you sure have a hard-on for this place."

"*Language*, please," Craig hissed with a glare. He glanced at Lilly, who rolled her eyes artfully.

"I hope they're cool," Jacob said, ignoring him. "Not like the other newbies."

"I thought you were all getting along," Craig said, pausing with a spoonful of oatmeal halfway to his mouth.

Jacob shrugged. At sixteen, he'd grown and wasn't as scrawny, but slouched like it was his job. "They're fine, I guess. Ben's hooking up with Jessica from F Block."

Ah. Parker bumped Jacob's shoulder with his own. "You can do better than Ben anyway."

"Can I?" Jacob mumbled before leaving to join the line for scrambled eggs and lentils.

"He liked Ben," Lilly said.

No shit, Parker thought. Out loud, he said, "Yeah. It sucks for him."

Craig sighed. "A limited dating pool."

"Who am I going to date?" Lilly pondered, peeling the skin off a fresh orange from the grove Connie's father had planted decades ago.

"Whoever you want, as long as they're good enough for you," Craig said.

"Spoiler alert: your dad isn't going to think anyone is good enough for you," Parker stage-whispered to Lilly. She giggled. He added, "And they'll have to pass my rigorous standards too. It's not going to be easy."

Parker ate a segment of orange Lilly gave him, joking and teasing and pretending he wasn't counting the nanoseconds until Adam was back safe.

Chapter Two

"WOLVES," THERESA MURMURED as the motorboat neared the fishing trawler-slash-sailboat.

Adam's hair stood on end. He'd sensed it too, though he hadn't said anything in case he was wrong. He asked, "Do you think they know about us? Can they tell from the message?"

The radio message Connie had recorded welcoming all to Salvation Island had hooked into Adam's soul the moment he'd heard it, though he hadn't been able to understand why. He'd never known an alpha before—at least not to his knowledge.

"Possibly," Theresa said, her hands steady on the boat's wheel where she stood at the center console, her gaze steely as they neared the ship.

Damian sat in the front, with Adam and Yolanda on the padded seats in the stern. Given the potential threat from the newcomers, they were using precious diesel to power the motorboat in case a quick retreat was necessary.

"What?" Yolanda asked, shouting over the engine. She was a plump African-American woman with a wide smile and cropped hair. She wore a bright life jacket, and her knee knocked into Adam's in the tight quarters.

Yolanda had rolled her eyes when Adam, Damian, and Theresa had all rebuffed her suggestion of life jackets. Adam could admit that it was hard to look tough wearing fluorescent orange. He already regretted his choice of plaid shirt over his jeans. He should have grabbed his leather jacket.

Theresa raised her voice. "There are werewolves on the ship."

Yolanda tensed. "Have you had, uh, wolves you don't know come here before?" She was an older human—one of a group from Tennessee who'd arrived four months before on an overcrowded sailboat that had barely survived the trip across the Gulf Stream. She'd taken the news of the existence of werewolves largely in stride after Connie had deemed her group trustworthy. She added, "I mean, aside from y'all who were here before the end times began."

"Not as often as you'd expect," Theresa answered. "We were a minuscule population compared to humans before. Many packs were scattered to the wind in the modern world, growing up isolated like Adam did, with only a small, immediate family." She'd tightened her ponytail before getting behind the wheel, her attention laser-focused on the enemy ship.

Not enemy. Stop it.

As much as Adam adored Parker, his pessimism had verged on paranoia since they'd settled on Salvation Island. He'd been dead set against the island, but now that they knew it was safe, any outsiders where a threat.

Which they *were*, potentially. Still, Adam needed to keep optimistic. Most people were good and trying their best. He had to believe that. If they weren't, he'd deal with them. If any of them tried to hurt his people—hurt Parker—it would be the last mistake they ever made.

Yolanda eyed the ship nervously. "How do we know these are good ones like y'all?"

"We don't," Damian answered. He was a Latino wolf in his early fifties with muscled arms that could crack walnuts, to quote Parker.

"That means there *are* bad ones?" she asked, barely a whisper.

The image of Ramon's bright, welcoming smile filled Adam's mind. The memory of his strong, reassuring handshake. Waking in the basement lab of the Pines, drugged and powerless. How fooled Adam had been. It was a reminder that Parker wasn't wrong to approach newcomers with suspicion.

Damian shrugged. "Werewolves are like people. There are good and bad and in-between. We hope for the best and stay alert."

Yolanda glanced at Adam, and he gave her what he hoped was a comforting smile. Her lips lifted briefly, her heart thudding as she fiddled with the zipper on her life jacket.

Gray clouds hung low and heavy, threatening rain. The pack—Adam could see in an instant that it was—waited on the deck of the fishing boat, which was about a hundred feet long. Several rubber tires hung over the sides to prevent damage when docking. The bridge was an elevated boxy structure with windows set toward the stern. *60008* was written on the hull in black paint, along with the name *Diana* and the home port: *Plymouth.*

The eleven wolves on deck were various shapes, sizes, and ethnicities. Presumably one remained at the bridge, and Adam could see a shadow there behind the glass. Another stood ahead of the others, his legs braced wide, and Adam knew instantly he was the alpha. Adam longed to have his camera to document the meeting. He often filmed around Salvation Island, but it wasn't appropriate as part of the greeting party.

Just under six feet tall, the Asian man was around thirty and wore cowboy boots, jeans, and a leather jacket. He had longish dark hair, impressive muscles, and facial scruff—and would have looked far more at home on a motorcycle or even a horse than a modified trawler.

"Welcome," Theresa said after cutting the speedboat's engine, keeping her distance while trying not to look like she was. "We're glad to meet you. I'm Theresa, and I've got Damian, Yolanda, and Adam with me."

The alpha nodded, unsmiling. "I'm Sean." He spoke with a

crisp, posh-sounding British accent that didn't match his fierce aura.

Adam's heart skipped, and he scanned the other people aboard. Were any human? Could this boat have actually come from the UK? Could Parker's brother be among them? The odds were vanishingly small, but it wasn't impossible...

"You're not the alpha," Sean said to Theresa.

"My mother is."

This made his lips twitch into the ghost of a smile. "My mother was too."

When the silence stretched out, Damian asked, "Where you folks coming from?"

"Here and there," Sean answered. In the silence, he conceded, "Across the pond."

Theresa asked, "What's the situation?"

"Depends on who you ask."

Adam swallowed a surge of irritation at the vague answer. Sean's eyes were flecked with gold as all werewolves' were, his stare intense.

Part of Adam wanted to lower his gaze in deference, but Connie was his alpha. Still, Sean's presence made his skin hot and too tight. It was a strange attraction—not sexual, but powerful nonetheless. He imagined Sean transforming fully and was stabbed momentarily by jealousy.

Adam loved Connie, but her answers to his questions about transforming into a full wolf were frustratingly vague, even though she could do it. She didn't often, and he'd only glimpsed her in her true form once. Most of the time, he didn't even think about it, but there was something about Sean that brought it to mind immediately.

He refocused on the moment at hand.

"May I come ashore?" The question asked in Sean's English accent was incongruously polite given his aura.

"Of course," Theresa said with a measured smile. "You're all welcome."

"Just me for now," Sean said. He nodded to a woman of South Asian descent who also wore a leather jacket, her dark hair cropped short and a gold ring gleaming in her nose. Adam could imagine she had tattoos.

Sean turned back, and after a few moments of the two parties staring at each other, he asked, "Shall I swim?"

Theresa seemed to shake herself and laughed with a hint of nervousness Adam wasn't sure he'd ever heard from her before. "Of course not," she said, engaging the throttle and closing the distance to the *Diana*.

Yolanda shot Adam a worried glance, and he was reaching out to give her arm a reassuring squeeze when Sean landed between them on the deck with a controlled thud. Adam blinked back at the *Diana*, which loomed over the launch now that they were close.

"Wow," Yolanda blurted from her seat, gaping up at him. "Do you fly?" Then she clamped her lips together as if embarrassed.

Sean extended a hand to her with a sly smile. "I only leap tall buildings."

She shook his hand with a nervous laugh. Standing, Adam offered his hand. The heat of Sean's grasp emanated confidence and power. Adam resolutely kept his head up, not showing the deference he would to Connie.

After more handshakes, Theresa steered the boat home at full power, wind in their faces. Yolanda rubbed her arms, wrinkling her red blouse. Damian and Sean had a low conversation near the bow that Adam eavesdropped on. With the sound of the motor, Yolanda couldn't hear.

"How many ords?" Sean asked. As Damian's heavy brow furrowed, Sean added, "Regular humans. Ordinaries."

Adam had never heard the term before, and it didn't sound

like a compliment. He breathed deeply through his nose, gripping the buoy rope hanging by his leg. The boat skipped over waves with hard little slaps, and he wiped a spray of sea water from his clenched jaw.

Damian cautiously answered that their numbers were about half and half, but Sean's piercing gaze had zeroed in on Adam. Adam stared back, refusing to budge an inch. If Sean had the same ideas as Ramon about the purity of werewolf bloodlines, they were going to have a problem.

It had been three years since Adam and Parker had escaped from the Pines—since Parker had practically carried him to safety. Adam could still imagine Ramon in his shifted form—but not full wolf—chasing them down that two-lane blacktop with teeth bared in feral zeal.

Sean turned back to Damian. "Why so many?"

"I'm sure our alpha will be happy to talk to you about it."

Sean said, "Fair enough," with a careless shrug.

After a few moments, Damian added, "I assume you heard our message. Everyone is welcome here on Salvation Island."

"Mm. As long as the ords keep in line."

Adam gritted his teeth and peered out at the endless dark ocean. If this pack thought humans were lesser—thought *Parker* was lesser...

"Why does that make you angry?" Sean asked.

In the silence aside from the motor's rumble, Adam turned back to find Sean's gold-flecked eyes boring into him from the bow. Beside Adam, Yolanda looked back and forth, clearly confused. Theresa kept her focus on the water as she steered them home, but of course she was listening.

Damian answered with steel in his tone. "Adam and I are both in love with humans."

"Ah." Sean raised his hands briefly. "Apologies. In the UK these days, that would be quite a Romeo and Juliet scenario."

"Humans and wolves are fighting?" Theresa asked sharply.

"Some," Sean answered. As Theresa pulled back on the throttle as they entered the harbor, the motor only humming now, he added, "Not long after the change, many of us stopped hiding in the shadows. Some ord—" His gaze slid to Yolanda. "Some humans…objected."

Yolanda said, "Must be the stupid ones. Y'all are strong and organized. Anyone who doesn't want to hitch their wagon to that star needs their head examined." She snorted. "What did you call it? 'The change'? Sounds about right. Hot flashes, brain fog, and creepers out to get us."

Sean chuckled, and they all exhaled as the tension dissipated. When they docked, Adam leapt out of the boat, itching to see Parker. Unease permeated the island, which of course Sean would sense as well.

Amid the miasma of anxiety from wolves and humans alike, Parker's came sharp and near, like a finger poking Adam's kidneys.

Sean didn't betray any emotion as he offered a hand to Yolanda to step onto the worn wooden planks.

"Sorry." Adam hurried back, but he was too late, and Yolanda waved him off.

"I'm not made of glass, honey."

Theresa tied off the ropes methodically. "As you can see, we have quite a few watercraft for various purposes." She led the way down the pier at a stroll, and Adam almost stepped on her heels. He slowed his pace as they passed rows of boats bobbing in their moorings.

The *Bella Luna*'s hull had been badly scratched on that awful day when Parker had been attacked, but they'd painted over it. She was secure and stately, and Adam swelled with affection.

He and Parker had shared so much on her, and she was spic and span thanks to Parker polishing every inch of her by hand. Anyone could see the care and love in the gleam of her deck.

Particularly now, since Parker was aboard polishing the silver rail.

"Oh, hey!" he called, painfully casual and surely not fooling anyone.

He hopped onto the dock in his bare feet and started toward them. Adam could almost taste the sharp bitterness of his worry sweat, which was distinct from his sex sweat or exercise sweat or plain old heat sweat.

"Hello, Parker," Theresa said with a mild smile. She didn't ask why he wasn't teaching his course, thankfully.

Adam could understand why Parker wouldn't have been able to focus on anything else until he safely returned. Adam's hands twitched with the need to touch, and relief coursed through him as Parker reached out.

Their fingers entwined the way they had thousands of times, warm and reassuring. He caught Parker's mouth in a fleeting kiss before turning to Sean. "This is Parker Osborne." Last names seemed superfluous now, yet he felt the need to be formal with an alpha.

"Hey, man." Parker stuck out his hand—though Adam imagined he'd rather be giving the finger to the person who'd interrupted his safe routine.

"Hello," Sean said smoothly as he took Parker's hand. "Wonderful to meet you."

Wonderful seemed a bit much, and Adam slid his arm around Parker's shoulders.

Parker's gaze was locked on Sean. "You're from England?"

"Yes," Sean answered simply.

"As you can see, we have a fleet of boats of varying sizes," Theresa said, effortlessly pulling everyone's attention and walking on.

Adam kissed Parker's temple, wishing he could kiss away the tension in his body. Parker gripped Adam around the waist as they walked. Sean listened to Theresa with the occasional nod as she explained their farming system, which was twice the size it had been when Adam and Parker arrived.

"Damian, can you tell Sean about our solar energy grid?" Theresa asked.

He did, speaking in short, distracted sentences. The day grew humid, the mugginess only accentuating the cloying tension. They passed villagers who pretended not to be watching Sean, and others who openly stared. As Theresa led Sean to Connie's office, Adam ducked out, taking Parker's hand and heading toward their cabin. They needed to breathe and regroup.

Parker dug in his heels and tugged the other way.

Adam frowned. "Connie won't let us in the meeting. I know you want to find out more about England, but—"

"No, I don't!" Parker's nostrils flared. "I never said that. Don't put that on me."

"Okay." He stroked Parker's knuckles with his thumb. "Sorry."

Honestly, he'd have preferred it if Parker *had* been eager for news from the UK. He still spoke of his brother, Eric, from time to time, but he refused to entertain the hope that Eric might be alive. He didn't want to speculate on anything happening beyond Salvation Island.

Parker nodded, accepting the apology. "I need to swim."

"Can I come?"

"Yeah, if you get in."

Adam agreed, and they skirted the village toward the path. Parker didn't like it when Adam watched him swim from shore, but if he watched from the water, it was fine. He didn't pretend to understand why it made a difference to Parker. It did, and that was all that mattered.

Twigs snapped under their feet and a bird called in the branches. A warbler, perhaps? Wren? He needed to take another bird-watching seminar with Edwin, an older professor from Orlando who loved sharing his knowledge.

The *Diana* came into sight, still anchored in the distance, though closer now. Sean's pack would probably think it absurd to waste time identifying birdsong. Adam could imagine their judgment even though he hadn't even spoken to them yet.

He bent to tug off his boots when they reached the edge of the forest. Parker stripped off in a blink, already marching into the murky water before Adam had even unbuttoned his plaid shirt. He stopped to watch, admiring the way Parker didn't hesitate when he had confidence in a decision. When he wasn't gripped by fear.

There was never any dipping in a toe and squeaking about the water being cold. No fits and starts or back and forth, flapping hands or hesitating. Parker only strode into the water past the shore break, diving under as soon as it was deep enough.

Waiting for him to resurface, Adam smiled, relaxing.

But Parker remained agitated, swimming up and down as though he were doing laps in a pool. Normally, he'd mix up his strokes and tempos on new laps—freestyle, breaststroke, side-stroke. Not today. Today, he only powered through the water, feet kicking in tight motions, arms slicing through the waves in a determined front crawl.

Staying out of his way a bit farther out, Adam bobbed on the swells under the gray sky. Sidestroke was Adam's favorite, and he counted ten to his right and then ten to his left. His father's swimming lessons still echoed distantly.

"Pick the apple and put it in the basket."

He reached overhead with his right arm under the water, picking the imaginary apple as he brought up his left hand so they met at his stomach. At the same time, he jackknifed his legs, one forward and one back, before pulling them closed. He could swim much faster if he wanted to, but he was content.

The *Diana* loomed in his peripheral vision. Were Sean's pack watching him and Parker right now? Who were they, and what did they want?

He couldn't quite maintain his calm. Especially not with Parker churning through the water like he was at the Olympic trials desperate to make the team.

A flash of doing the wave with Tina at a Giants game reverberated through Adam's heart. Laughing and sharing nachos with orange-yellow processed cheese goop on top with ludicrously expensive cans of Bud. He hadn't been hugely into sports, but he missed baseball stadiums and peanuts and beer.

And of course Tina, the one close friend he'd made as an adult. The pain of losing her had dulled, but it would never go away. He knew that from the death of his family. Now he had Parker, which would never have happened if the world was still the same. He had Craig, Lilly, and Jacob, Connie, Theresa, and the people of Salvation Island.

Sometimes, it didn't seem right to have gained so much in the loss of civilization.

They were both still restless after splashing onto the beach. Adam picked his way over the rocks and realized they had no towels. Parker tugged on his clothes, not bothering to try drying off. He still breathed hard.

"Ready for lunch?" Adam asked, though it was too early.

Parker shook his head, droplets flying. He vibrated with coiled energy. "Need you. All of you."

In answer, Adam abandoned his shirt and scooped him off his feet, tongue already in Parker's mouth. Parker clamped his legs around Adam's waist and kissed him desperately, clawing at Adam's bare, wet skin.

Adam wanted to take him against a tree but couldn't risk hurting him. Keeping to the forest, he carried Parker with a burst of speed, zigzagging to their cabin while avoiding being seen. He didn't put him down until they were in their bedroom.

Adam had made the bed that morning, neatly tucking the yellow sheets and white duvet. Naked in a blink, Parker crawled across it, reaching for the bedside table. Adam knew without looking that it was what they called a "blue ribbon day."

The silk ties were baby blue, which perhaps was an incongruous color for a gag, but it wasn't as if they could swing by Joann Fabrics for options. Theresa had gifted it to them without a hint of embarrassment not long after they'd arrived on Salvation Island.

She'd explained that she'd always sewn in her spare time and had crafted any number of "intimacy aides," as she'd put it. Given the heightened hearing of the wolves on the island, it was considered a courtesy during particularly loud "activity."

Parker impatiently shook the gag toward Adam. While he could have tied it around his own head, Adam always did it. Kneeling behind Parker, he positioned the small black rubber ball, his cock swelling as Parker opened his mouth for him.

The ball was glued to straps that were covered in the silk. The blue complemented Parker's brown eyes and smattering of freckles, and Adam murmured, "So beautiful," even though Parker was impatiently squirting lube on his fingers before the gag was even knotted.

Parker fingered himself and moaned, muffled by the gag. On his knees, leaning on his left hand, he pushed his middle finger into his ass. He was shameless in his need, and Adam's mouth went dry watching, his cock throbbing.

First, he bunched the pillows under Parker's stomach, pushing him down in one sharp movement so Parker's ass was in the air and his shoulders on the bed. Parker fisted the sheets, his fingers shining with lube.

Leaning over, Adam whispered in Parker's ear. "You want me?"

Parker fidgeted, his damp back already hot under Adam's chest. He mumbled, and Adam would have known what he pleaded even if he was deaf.

"*All of you.*"

Just as they didn't always use the gag, Adam didn't always shift during sex—it depended on the mood. Today, his wolf howled and clawed to be freed, but he forced a breath.

Lips on Parker's spine, Adam stroked himself and eased back his foreskin. Holding his shaft, he teased the head of his cock along Parker's crack and around his hole as Parker whimpered beautifully.

"Want me to fuck your tight little hole?"

Parker growled a *hmmph* of frustration, and Adam had to laugh.

"You're so cute when you beg for my cock. You would beg if you could, wouldn't you?"

Nodding desperately, Parker turned his right cheek to the mattress. The ball gag wasn't huge, but it was big enough that he felt confined. The first time they'd used it, Adam had worried and fought stabs of guilt. The sex had been frustrating and unsatisfying for both of them even though they'd come.

Now, he knew it wasn't hurting Parker—that his usual flood of words would flow again easily. After his furious swim, he had to be tired. He needed to release the fear and grief that were distant most days on Salvation Island—specks on the horizon. Not today though.

"I've got you," Adam murmured, easing inside Parker and biting back a moan at the tight heat that enveloped him.

Parker squeezed and shoved back with his hips.

"Need more?" Adam's vision tinged yellow, his chest rising and falling faster.

"*Mmm,*" Parker whined, reaching back to clutch at Adam's thigh.

Controlling the shift had sometimes been a struggle before Salvation Island. Now, Adam could change back and forth at will. Fire washed through him, his fingernails on Parker's hips morphing to claws, hair thickening all over his skin, cock swelling inside his lover's body.

Parker's cry as Adam stretched him close to breaking point would have echoed across the island if not for the gag. He was impossibly tight around Adam's cock.

"*Fuck, Christ, Parker,*" Adam muttered around his fangs as he thrust in short, powerful movements.

It would be enough to see Parker with knees wide, his ass in the air split on Adam's cock. But to hear his cries and feel his heat—to know that he accepted Adam's true self—was a gift every time. The way he submitted as Adam pounded him, gripping his wrists to pull his arms back tautly so Parker was completely at his mercy, his claws so close to slicing the tender skin.

"If I turned into a wolf, you'd let me fuck you like that, wouldn't you?" Adam gritted out. He'd gotten used to speaking with his fangs extended.

Parker nodded, his face flushed against the blue silk.

"You'd let me come inside you, rub my scent into your skin so deep it would never go away."

Cheek against the bed, Parker moaned rhythmically as he jerked with every thrust. "*Yes, yes, yes, yes.*"

"You don't have to worry. I'll take care of you. I've got you."

Bending and pulling almost all the way out, Adam licked up Parker's spine, the salt of his sweat almost sweet as he neared climax. Then Adam slammed back in to the hilt, and Parker shouted around the gag.

Adam let go of one of Parker's wrists, though Parker didn't move his arm. Their flesh slapping, both of them grunting, Adam made a loose fist around Parker's cock, his claws millimeters from catastrophe.

Parker didn't flinch. He only whined and whimpered, begging, his eyes watering.

Sometimes, Adam made him wait, coming inside him and flipping him over, sucking him and teasing, holding Parker down until he flooded Adam's mouth with his sweet cum.

Today, Adam needed to be inside him when Parker let go. Parker writhed on his cock, drool leaking down his chin, face red and cries raw in his throat. He strained, needing to come so badly, and Adam stroked him beyond the point where he usually would have tipped over the edge.

Adam needed to help him. He flexed his muscles, desperate to give Parker what he needed. The golden haze in his vision deepened, and he growled.

Parker's scream reverberated through Adam's chest, and Adam swore his cock had swelled even bigger inside Parker's ass. Parker was coming, gasping around the gag, squeezing around Adam's shaft.

Adam felt like a balloon that had been blown up with too much air, bursting and pouring his seed into Parker, a white-hot fire of pleasure sweeping through his veins. Head back, he howled before he could stop himself.

He clamped his mouth shut and toppled onto Parker, retreating back to his human form. That had been as close as Adam had ever felt to fully shifting. He tugged the silk free and eased the gag from Parker's mouth, expecting a deluge of questions or exclamations.

Parker only panted with wide eyes, twisting his head to stare at Adam. Speechless himself, Adam pushed his finger into Parker's swollen hole, keeping his milky cum inside. Rising to his knees, he leaned over and kissed Parker gently, licking into his mouth slowly. They needed to clean up, but Adam couldn't stop touching him.

After a few minutes, Parker wriggled onto his back, and Adam stretched out on his side, rubbing Parker's chest with his palm. He enjoyed the rasp of hair against his hand and the rise and fall of Parker's slowing breathing.

"That was… Whoa," Parker mumbled.

Adam held his breath, his fingertips spread between Parker's nipples. "Too much?"

"Never."

He said it so simply—honestly—and Adam loved him more than ever. Every day, a fraction more.

As always, Parker's words returned, and he asked, "Who are they? All British?"

"I'm not sure. They're a pack."

"How many? Mostly wolves?"

"All wolves, apparently. Twelve."

Parker's heart stuttered. "No humans at all? That's new."

"Mm."

"What do you think it means? Does that mean something? Are they like that piece of shit Ramon?"

"I hope not. I don't know." He tried to think of something he could tell Parker. "He said that England—"

"I don't want to know. I don't want England to exist."

Adam brushed back Parker's damp hair. "You don't mean that."

"I do!" He huffed. "Not that I want everyone over there to be dead. I just don't want to know. I can't get my hopes up. Because there's no way I'll ever see Eric again. You know it, I know it, the universe knows it."

Adam couldn't argue. It was extremely unlikely that Eric was alive. Even if he was, Parker would surely never see his brother again. Still, now that a boat from the UK had arrived, he didn't want to ask more questions?

As if reading Adam's mind, Parker said, "I want the rest of the world to disappear. We're safe here in our bubble. We have food and medicine and electricity and the greatest sex on the planet. We don't need anything or anyone else. I wish it would all go away forever. I wish the world would just leave us the fuck alone."

They had gardening duty, but Adam pressed their lips together, kissing slowly until Parker's pulse was steady, and he slept, safe in dreams and Adam's arms. At least for now.

And Adam would do anything to keep it that way.

Chapter Three

TACO NIGHT WASN'T the same with the newcomers drawing everyone's attention, but the sour cream was still awesome.

Parker savored his last bite of grouper, cilantro, salsa, beans, and creamy, tangy, perfect sour cream. The taco shells were lettuce wraps since they were far easier than using their corn harvests for tortillas, but beggars couldn't be choosers.

Enjoy the little things, goddamn it.

Adam was setting up the projector, and Parker excused himself to Lilly and Craig, who were deep in conversation with Yolanda about... Actually, Parker had no clue. His gaze kept returning to the newcomers, who sat close to each other at one of the long benches with Connie, Theresa, and a few others. They seemed tense, which he supposed was totally reasonable.

After all, they were outnumbered. If they were on some stealth mission to disrupt Salvation Island, they would fail. Parker reminded himself of this as he circled his arms around Adam from behind, rubbing his chin on the soft flannel of Adam's shirt.

"Hey," Adam said, scribbling in his notebook.

Parker peered around Adam's arm, which took some doing given he had muscles for days. "*Real Women Have Curves?* Never heard of that one." He loved that there were still some movies in the collection that were new to him. One day, they'd run out. But not today.

"It's an indie classic from 2002 about a Mexican-American girl's coming of age. America Ferrera gives a standout performance. And I thought you didn't want to be spoiled?"

"It's almost showtime. Is that the first feature?" Parker rubbed his cheek against Adam's shoulder. Instead of flannel, he could imagine cool leather beneath his skin, his arms locked around Adam's waist as they sped across the country in the first weeks of the virus.

Now, they had full tummies and were surrounded by the hum of conversation from people in their community. They were safe and happy, and they were never going to ride Mariah on lonely, endless asphalt again.

He knew Adam missed riding her on the open road. Parker might have missed it too if the thought of going back to the mainland didn't make his skin clammy.

"What?" Adam asked, half turning and brushing a hand over Parker's hair.

"Nothing. What's the family feature?"

Adam turned back to his notebook. "*Spy Kids* by popular request." He leaned over and jotted a note. "This is the third time in three months."

It was adorable how Adam kept a neat log of the dates and movies shown. If it was the before times, he'd undoubtedly have a spreadsheet.

As Adam finished setting up, Parker stayed close to him like a barnacle. Adam didn't complain because he was the greatest. There were times after a particularly intense fuck that Parker needed to prolong that nearness. If he clenched his ass, he could still feel Adam inside him.

Adam turned his head to nuzzle Parker's cheek and whisper, "I know."

"Shit, did I say that out loud?" It was definitely on brand for him.

"No, but I can read your mind." He finished checking the projector's settings.

A sudden hush waved through the mess hall, and Parker gazed around in confusion. Sean was standing by his table, and soon all eyes were on him. Had he made some subtle werewolf noise like Connie did? Was that an alpha thing?

"Thank you all for welcoming us today," Sean said in his smooth tenor and fancy accent. He'd taken off his leather jacket, and his black tee clung to lean muscles. Dark jeans hugged his toned thighs and somehow the cowboy boots worked. "We haven't had such good food in a long, long time. And now a movie? It's more than we could have imagined."

"We're delighted to have you. Sit back and relax," Connie said.

Sean did, but most eyes stayed on him, and understandably so. "Whoa," Parker murmured.

"'Whoa' what?" Adam glanced up.

"Dude, come on. You can admit he's hot."

"... Can I?"

Parker laughed. "Will it help if I say he's objectively smokin'?"

"Not really." Adam slipped his arm around Parker's shoulders, nudging him closer.

Chuckling, Parker whispered into Adam's neck, "Don't worry. You're the only big, bad wolf I want."

"Damn right." He caught Parker's lips for a fleeting moment. "I think the opinion that Sean's hot is certainly shared."

Parker followed his gaze to Jacob, who sat with the new kids at a round table but stared intently at Sean. "Uh, yeah, you don't have to be a werewolf to sense Jacob's boner. I guess I've finally been replaced in his affections." Parker dropped the joking tone. "Poor kid. I wish there were a bigger dating pool for him. Or any, really."

"That's one of the reasons newcomers are a good thing."

"True," Parker admitted. "They're still on notice until I'm sure they aren't plotting to overthrow us." He picked up Adam's pen and twirled it between his fingers. "It's weird to have another pack here. Surprised it took this long for one to show up."

"Mm. If there's one thing werewolves understand, it's caution."

"But you're all way stronger than us. And immune to most of our human viruses." He dropped the pen, picked it up, and started twirling it again.

"We were still incredibly outnumbered in the past. Maybe now after a few years of the new world, we'll start to see more packs coming out of the shadows."

The new world. God, Parker hated being reminded of it. "I guess."

"Sean mentioned it's happened in England. Werewolves aren't hiding, and some humans don't like it."

Parker gripped the pen. "Seriously? Like we all don't have enough to worry about with the creepers?" His voice rose. "Not to mention the collapse of infrastructure and society? We can't just all get along?"

"Hey, hey," Adam murmured, rubbing up and down Parker's back. "We get along here. There's nothing to worry about."

Exhaling, Parker nodded. The lights dimmed, and Adam gently reclaimed his pen. During the first movie, he pulled out his video camera and shot a few minutes of everyone watching the screen—or wall in this case. Parker followed the camera's gaze. Kids laughed at jokes they'd heard before, light flickering on happy faces. Cinematic comfort food.

Parker tried to keep Sean and the newcomers out of his mind, but did they have to be from *England* of all places? He'd meant what he'd told Adam—he didn't want to know. What was the point?

Of course, while he really did mean that, he was also freaking dying to know. The outside world was terrifying, but he couldn't quite silence the *what if...*

After the movies, he and Adam returned the DVDs to the library, a cabin with each room—even the bathroom—crammed with bookshelves holding books, movies, CDs, and vinyl. Adam had cataloged every piece of media using the Dewey Decimal system, which was so geeky and sexy.

While Adam logged the movies back in, Parker wandered into the former bedroom that housed the CDs. It was dark, but he could see by the moonlight spilling through the window. He ran his fingertip over the rows of jewel cases.

He'd ditched all his CDs years ago when streaming had come along, but his dad had insisted on keeping a massive collection. Parker and Eric had laughed and rolled their eyes, telling him the internet had changed everything.

God, he really, *really* missed the internet.

"I said *no*."

Frozen by the extensive collection of folk music, *Complete Greatest Hits* by Gordon Lightfoot under his fingertips, Parker strained to listen. That male voice had spoken with an English accent.

A woman replied, but Parker couldn't make out the words. He tiptoed to the window. Under trees on the shadowy path lit by low solar-powered moon lights, he could make out two people— Sean and one of the newcomers, a woman with a nose piercing and a fierce stare. The one Adam had said seemed to be Sean's second-in-command.

She said, "If we tell them—"

"*No!*" It was a growl this time, making Parker's heart kick.

Which of course they heard because of the whole werewolf thing, their golden eyes skewering him in the window.

"Um, hey!" He waved like a dork. "Sorry. Didn't mean to..." He backed into Adam, which made him yelp, and this was going *awesomely*.

They went outside to face the music, and Adam held Parker's

sweaty hand because he was the greatest boyfriend in the history of boyfriends. Sean and the woman waited with tense expressions, her arms crossed tightly. Sean seemed to relax when he saw Adam, and Parker didn't know how to feel about that.

"Evening," Adam said smoothly.

"Sorry I interrupted," Parker said. "I heard a noise. I didn't realize what it was."

Sean smiled, his voice as smooth as Adam's. "Not a problem. We should have realized you were there. Too distracted. It's been a busy day."

"I didn't hear anything if that helps," Parker said.

Adam asked the woman, "I'm sorry, what's your name?"

"Gemma," she answered in the same sort of fancy British accent as Sean. She smiled for a nanosecond.

Adam and Parker introduced themselves before saying goodnight and taking the path snaking off toward their cabin. Adam whispered, "So, what *did* you hear?"

"Not much." Parker relayed the little he knew. "What do you think it means?"

"Nothing. It's none of our business."

"Unless they're up to no good. Then it is a thousand percent our business."

"Don't borrow trouble."

"*Moi?* Never."

Adam chuckled. "Of course not, sweetheart."

Raised voices ahead cut through the familiar peace of cicadas singing in the darkness. Craig said firmly, "It's a school night."

Parker sighed as they rounded the bend and came upon Craig and Jacob in front of their cabin. Craig stood tall on the top step of the little veranda, Jacob glaring up at him from the path.

Jacob barked out a laugh. "Give me a break. Why do I even have to go to school? It's bullshit. You're all pretending the world is still normal when it never will be. What's the point?"

Craig spoke calmly, his low voice resonant. "The point is that this life is all we have. We all know the world out there is a shit show. Right, Parker?"

Craig swore so infrequently that Parker didn't want to answer. "Um, yeah." His stomach gurgled with acid. He hated this.

Jacob rolled his eyes as Craig added, "We should make our lives here on the island the best, most normal we can." He lifted his hands. "Because this is all we have, J."

"Fine. And normal teenagers get to hang with their friends."

"At ten o'clock on a school night?" Craig asked dubiously.

"Why not? I'm not tired."

"That's because you'd sleep 'til noon if I let you," Craig muttered.

Parker wanted to argue that sleeping in actually *was* normal for teenagers, but he didn't think Craig would appreciate his input. And when did he start feeling so much older than teenagers? He did, though. God, he really, really did.

He said, "Hey, I'm not tired either. Adam's hitting the sack. Want to keep me company, Jacob?"

Adam yawned on cue—best boyfriend ever—and Jacob grudgingly agreed to walk with Parker. They veered onto a trail that passed the field of growing potatoes. Shoulders rounded, Jacob shoved his hands into his hoodie pockets.

"I get why you're frustrated," Parker finally said.

Steam practically shot from Jacob's ears. "He doesn't understand anything."

"That's not fair." Parker forced a breath and blocked the flood of words he almost let out. He needed to tread lightly. "We're friends, right?"

"Yeah," Jacob muttered. He sighed loudly. "I'm sorry. I know I'm being an asshole. I just hate it here sometimes."

Parker boggled. Salvation Island was the *best*. "But we're so lucky to be here. It's a hell of a lot better than the alternative."

"How would you know?"

"Uh, I remember what it took to get here."

Jacob kicked a rock. "At least we had, like, freedom."

"The freedom to die horribly?" As soon as the words were out, he regretted them.

Story of my life.

Jacob trudged along silently, and Parker quickly added, "I'm sorry. I didn't mean to—" He squinted at Jacob and the collar of his hoodie. "Where's your necklace?" The delicate silver dove Jacob's mother Abby had left him was missing from his throat.

Jacob's face flushed. "Chris said it was too girly. He's probably right."

Deep breath. Deep breath!

"Is Chris one of those new kids that arrived with Yolanda's group?" At Jacob's nod, Parker continued. "Chris is wrong. And so what if it's feminine? We live in the zombie apocalypse. Do we really need to be policing each other's jewelry for gender stereotypes?"

Jacob cracked a smile. "I guess not."

"Definitely not. You should wear that necklace. If you want to. It's up to you. Your mom—" Parker broke off with a sudden swell of emotion clogging his throat. The memory of Abby's blood pumping out between his desperate fingers as she gasped and died would never, ever leave him, but most of the time it was in small print.

Not all caps bold with exclamation marks like it was now.

"You think she'd want me to wear it?" Jacob whispered.

Parker cleared his throat. "I think she'd say that was up to you. And that you should listen to Craig and not stay out too late with douches like Chris."

That got a laugh, at least. "Yeah, probably."

A slim figure appeared ahead. Theresa's son, Devon, called softly, "Hey," and gave them a wave. He was fifteen and didn't look the part of werewolf royalty with his golden curls and willowy body. He'd shot up recently, and Parker was surprised to realize Devon and Jacob were as tall as he was.

"What are you doing here?" Jacob asked bluntly. No smile.

Devon shrugged. "I was checking out Chris's thing."

"Won't your mom get mad?" Jacob eyed Devon suspiciously. "Or are you still spying for her and your grandma?"

"No!" Devon's voice cracked. "That was two years ago. I was a kid. I didn't know better."

"If you say so," Jacob muttered.

"Give him a break," Parker said. "We've all fucked up. Ask me how I know."

The boys laughed at this, thankfully. Hands in the pockets of his skinny jeans, Devon said to Jacob, "I thought you might be there."

Hmm. Maybe the dating pool wasn't empty after all?

Jacob seemed genuinely confused. "Why would you care if I'm there?"

Parker jumped in to save Devon, who didn't seem to know what to say in the face of Jacob's cluelessness. "Is it a cool party?"

Jacob snorted. "Now *you* sound like a narc."

"The party's definitely uncool," Devon said. "They were going to tip cows."

"Oh, hell no!" Parker exclaimed. "That's cruel bullshit." He squinted in the direction Devon had come from. "Are they still out there? I'll go rip them a new one."

"No need." Devon's eyes glowed gold in the night, and he growled before smiling like one of those little Valentine's Day angels. "People forget I'm a werewolf."

Parker raised his hand for a high five. "I like your style."

Devon ducked his head. He might have been blushing. "Thanks."

"That's cool you stood up to him," Jacob said. To Parker, he added, "I still don't want to go home. Can we walk more?"

"Yeah, totally." He motioned to Devon. "Unless you guys want to hang instead."

Jacob's brows met, and before he could say anything, Devon was already walking. He called, "I've got to get back. Early mess hall duty. Later!"

Parker and Jacob kept walking, and Parker did his very best to sound casual. "Devon's pretty cool."

"Huh? For an annoying kid, I guess."

"Why is he annoying?"

"He always wants to tag along to stuff." Jacob kicked another rock as they approached the pasture. Fortunately, all the cows were standing and there were no douchebags in sight.

"He's only a year younger than you. I know, I know, that seems like forever at your age." Parker grimaced. "God, I sound like my parents. I just don't want you to—" He stopped. "Did you see that?"

Jacob squinted at the trees beyond the edge of the pasture. "What? Oh, shit!"

A black-haired wolf raced along the tree line. Cows mooed and stamped their hooves, but the wolf didn't approach the pasture fence. It disappeared into the forest, and the cows settled. Cicadas sang, and it was like the huge wolf hadn't been there at all.

Parker had learned after coming to Salvation Island that *holy shit*, werewolves were enormous when fully shifted. He'd seen normal wolves at the zoo once, and he was pretty sure he remembered they were average-sized.

"I guess someone needed to burn off energy," Jacob said. "That wasn't Adam, right?"

"No." Parker didn't mention that Adam didn't know how to fully shift. It wasn't a *secret*, but he knew Adam was insecure about it. "Come on. Let's head back."

The trail toward the cabins snaked through more forest, and it wasn't lit by moon lamps so far out. Still, the real moonlight was plenty to glimpse the completely naked man ahead.

Sean turned, and Jacob made a choking sound beside Parker. Parker plastered on a smile, ignoring the fact that Sean was letting his massive dick hang out. "Evening!" Parker called. "You, uh, need something?" What the fuck? Were Sean's pack nudists or something?

Sean said, "I'm afraid I got turned around. I went for a run, and I can't find where I left my clothes."

Jacob was silent, probably fighting the biggest boner of his life. Keeping his gaze up, Parker said, "That was you all wolfed out? I guess you needed to stretch your legs after the journey. Did you come straight from England?"

Why did I ask that?

"We've traveled down from Canada. Been on the move for a while. But yes, it's been too long since I was able to run freely." Sean's chest was smooth and buff, and he scratched himself idly.

Totally normal, just having a conversation with a naked dude.

"I'll help you look," Jacob blurted.

Sean smiled at him, dimples appearing in his cheeks, his teeth gleaming. "Cheers."

"Actually, Jacob needs to get home," Parker said, because nope, not appropriate. "I'm sure we can find your stuff in the morning."

"I need my boots." Sean's smile had disappeared. "It's fine. I'll keep looking."

"We'll help you. It's only polite." Jacob glared at Parker. "Mister, um, new werewolf's, like, our guest."

"Call me Sean."

"Sean," Jacob repeated breathlessly.

"Okay, let's find those clothes!" Parker clapped his hands. "Did you take the other path southeast from the village?"

It turned out, yes, he had, and once they skirted the village—Sean walking with them with his big dick swinging like it was totally normal—there were his clothes folded neatly on a rock.

"I guess it's not like the Hulk where you still wear pants," Parker said because he was an idiot. "When you shift fully, I mean."

Sean raised an eyebrow. "Haven't you seen Adam shift?"

"Oh, yeah, I just—it was a joke." While other wolves on the island shifted fully, Parker had never witnessed it. It had always seemed a private sort of thing. Not to Sean's pack, apparently.

"Ah." The black cowboy boots stood side by side. Sean picked them up, running his hands over the leather.

"You don't seem like a country and western sort of guy," Parker said as Sean mercifully pulled on his jeans and put his hands in his pockets. He apparently went commando, and Jacob was watching his every movement so obviously that Parker finally elbowed him.

Sean's lips twitched. "I'm not. They were a gift."

He didn't say more, so Parker nodded. "Cool. You know the way back to your cabin?" Before Jacob could offer to show him, Parker nudged him toward the other path. "Have a good one."

"I shall. Thank you, Parker. Jacob. I'm grateful for your assistance."

Parker saluted. "Anytime." He steered Jacob away.

"Wow," Jacob whispered. "That was... He's..."

"Yeah, he is." The poor kid didn't have porn like Parker did as a teenager. He couldn't blame Jacob for enjoying the view. They reached Craig's three-bedroom cabin. "Now go to sleep. That's enough excitement for today."

Jacob asked, "Do you think they all go around naked like that? He didn't seem to care. I guess if I looked like that, I wouldn't either."

Parker laughed. "No lie detected. Okay, hug it out." He

opened his arms.

Jacob embraced him. "Why are you my friend even when I'm a dick?"

"We're family." There was no question about it.

With a watery smile, Jacob ducked inside. Parker returned to his cabin, knowing Adam would be waiting up like always.

Chapter Four

"WHAT ARE THEY saying?"

Adam followed Parker's narrowed gaze across the orange grove to where Jacob stood halfway up a ladder. He passed down the cotton sling he wore to Sean, who emptied the oranges into a crate at his feet.

Sean still wore the cowboy boots even though the weather had turned suddenly hot in the two weeks since he and his pack had arrived. His red T-shirt hung from the back pocket of his jeans.

"And why isn't he wearing a shirt?" Parker muttered, wiping sweat from his brow with his forearm before tugging his Marlins baseball cap back on. Kneeling in the dirt in the shade of a tree, he freed a low-hanging orange.

"I'm not wearing a shirt," Adam reminded him.

"That's different."

"How is that different?"

Parker waved his hand toward Sean and Jacob. "It's inappropriate!"

Adam pushed up his sunglasses. "Would you be wearing a shirt in this heat if you didn't burn so easily?"

"That's not the point!" he hissed. "I'm not the object of Jacob's affections. Sean shouldn't be toying with him."

"We don't know that he's doing anything of the kind." Adam tugged an orange free and placed it in their crate. Still, he peered a little more closely. Jacob and Sean didn't seem to be doing anything differently from Bethany, who was up a ladder at another tree with Yolanda spotting her.

"Well, if you would turn on your wolfy powers and listen to what they're talking about—"

"*No.* You know the rules. *That* would be inappropriate."

Parker rolled his eyes and took off his hat again, grimacing at the sweat-soaked interior. "This is why you were such a good TA. Always a stickler."

Chuckling, Adam brushed a hand over Parker's damp, messy hair. "If you'd actually watched the assigned movie, I know you would have written a brilliant essay."

"Duh." Parker leaned into Adam's leg, running his hand over Adam's bare knee and calf below his cargo shorts. Neither of them wore shoes. Adam stretched his toes in the dirt.

For a minute, they only petted each other. The memories of being on campus at Stanford could have been scenes from one of the island's DVDs. Adam could play them in his mind—Parker's entitlement when he marched into Adam's office to demand a better grade. His indignant huffs when Adam refused. His tight, sexy ass that Adam had tried very hard not to appreciate when he'd stormed off.

Of course, the memories almost instantly turned horrifying. Blood-soaked montages of death and terror. But what stuck stubbornly in Adam's mind the most was Parker's sob of relief when Adam had gone back for him in the chaos. The pressure of Parker's fingers digging in as he held on for dear life on the back of Mariah as they'd zoomed away to safety.

Safety had always been fleeting, never certain, until Salvation Island. Adam tried not to think about how swiftly that could change. If he could go to the mainland and see for himself the state of the world—or at least the Florida coast—perhaps it wouldn't feel so threatening. It would be known.

But then he remembered returning from the single scavenging trip he'd made after coming to Salvation Island and finding Parker curled on the bathroom floor. The petechial hemorrhaging around his eyes from vomiting so forcefully, pinpricks of blood under the skin that had felt like jagged knives to Adam's gut.

So, Adam stayed. The scavenging trips ended when supplies had been thoroughly looted. The world remained unknowable beyond snatches of information here and there. Connie reported the occasional conversation with distant survivors, though fewer than Adam would have thought. There had to be more communities like theirs, but it seemed most had turned insular.

He wondered if the Pines in Colorado still existed or if it had been overrun. Was Dr. Yamaguchi still conducting experiments to create a vaccine? Were his werewolf subjects willing? Or had the Pines descended into chaos?

It probably should have bothered Adam more—what Yamaguchi had done to him. He recalled waking helpless, but not the harvesting of his flesh. As time passed, the overwhelming memory he had was the relief and gratitude for Parker saving his life.

Parker remembered all of it, though. He had to witness it all. When he woke thrashing and crying out from nightmares, Adam could only hold him.

"We should take Mariah out sometime," Parker said quietly. "Give her some love."

Adam didn't let his surprise show. He'd maintained his motorcycle faithfully with help from Barry, an older werewolf who'd engineered the island's solar farm. They'd transformed her to be able to run on a solar-powered battery. She wasn't as powerful as she'd been on the old gasoline, but what they never told you in zombie movies was that most regular gas was unusable and contaminated within a year. Diesel lasted longer, and the island was stocked with fuel stabilizer, but long term, solar was the best option.

He'd occasionally ridden along the path by the pasture so Mariah didn't rust. But Parker had always too-casually turned down offers of a ride. As grateful as Adam was for the safety and community of the island, once in a while he did miss the wind in his face and Parker's thighs wrapped around his hips as they roared along the open road.

Bending, Adam kissed Parker's head, inhaling his scent.

"Dude, I'm so gross right now. This humidity is killer."

"Mm." He inhaled more deeply.

"I really don't want Jacob to get hurt. Why can't he notice that Devon is super into him?"

"Because he's young, and Sean is an exciting fantasy."

"Yeah. Seeing him naked definitely didn't help."

Adam straightened. "What are you talking about?" Had Sean actually crossed a line?

Parker tensed—just for a split second—and dropped his hand from Adam's leg. He pulled on his cap and reached for another orange. "Oh, nothing. Can you pass the water?"

The bottle was well within Parker's reach, but Adam held it out for him. "What happened?"

"It's no big deal, seriously." He gulped from the bottle before leaning closer to an orange. "Hmm. Nah, this one can wait a couple more days. Man, I miss fresh-squeezed OJ. I know it's a waste of too many oranges to juice them now, but do you remember how good a glass of cold, fresh juice was at brunch?"

"The more you don't answer me, the bigger deal this becomes."

Parker sighed. "That first night Sean and his pack were here? Jacob and I saw him running out by the pasture."

"Naked?" While some werewolves were often shirtless on the island, not wearing pants was certainly frowned upon.

"Yeah, but, you know. Furry." Parker pulled an orange off the tree. He shrugged. "He was a full wolf. Then he wasn't, and he was butt naked. Jacob got an eyeful."

What did his pelt look like?

Adam peered at Sean, trying to imagine. He'd often wondered how his own would look. His mother's had been dark brown and his father's tawny. Would his be some combination of the two? Or dark like his own hair?

His chest had tightened painfully, and he blew out a breath. "Why didn't you tell me?"

"It's no big deal." Parker's eyes were on the water bottle as he fiddled with the lid.

Adam had to pace a few steps, frustration simmering quickly to a rolling boil. "Stop saying that when we both know it's not true."

"*Fuck*," Parker muttered. "I know. I'm sorry."

"Then why didn't you tell me?" He hadn't intended for his voice to *boom*, but he was immediately aware of eyes on him.

Parker pushed to his feet and called out, "Everything's fine," giving a fake smile.

Yolanda's brow was still furrowed. "You sure?"

"Yeah. I was a dick, and Adam's calling me on it." He motioned toward Jacob and Sean. "Ask Jacob—I can be a dick sometimes."

"So can I," Adam said, skin prickling with embarrassment. Jacob laughed, but Sean only watched them with his usual inscrutable alpha expression.

"So can we all," Bethany added, pushing up her sunglasses and reaching for an orange on a high branch, standing almost at the top of her ladder.

Part of him appreciated the understanding while another part wanted to growl that Bethany had done far more in the past. Adam would never go along with hurting innocent people the way she had when her old crew had assaulted Parker and God knew who else.

That old fury and sickening guilt resurfaced like a tsunami, and Adam had to walk away. Bethany had gotten a second chance, and he knew she deserved it. Still, the memory of not being there when Parker needed him *roared*. Parker was saying something else to the others, but Adam couldn't focus. He ducked across the rows of the orange grove, marching toward the solar farm.

Even with his sunglasses, the sun's gleam on the towering solar panels made him squint. Behind him, Parker's footsteps hurried close.

"In case you're wondering why I didn't tell you, this is why!"

Fresh irritation slashed through him, and Adam wheeled around. "That's bullshit."

"No, it's not." Parker faced him with shoulders squared and hands on hips. "I mean, fine, yes—I get why you're mad right now. And I'm sorry. But the way you yelled back there? That's why I didn't tell you. Because it upsets you. I don't want you to hurt. You'll deny it—you're about to right this second!"

Adam snapped his jaw shut.

"You're going to say it doesn't bother you, it's no big deal, and you don't want to overstep by asking Connie too many questions. You'll shrug and change the subject. Yes, I realize I just did the same thing back there. I never said I wasn't a hypocrite."

A laugh punched out of Adam. He took off his Aviators and rubbed his face. "It's not..." That it was so hard to talk about was proving Parker's point.

Parker was suddenly there, looping his arms around Adam's waist, his warm fingers spread over Adam's bare back. "Baby, it's okay that it bugs you. I remember when I suggested we try to figure out how you can shift fully. I get why you kind of backed off from that. We had a lot of shit going on. The whole zombie apocalypse thing."

"It's time-consuming." Adam ran his hands over Parker rhythmically, rubbing circles over the knobs of his shoulders.

"Less so on the island, though. It's been three years. We're living in a werewolf commune. No time like the present to delve deeper."

He was right, yet the knot in Adam's stomach didn't loosen.

"See, but then you make that face." Parker smoothed his thumb over Adam's forehead. "Oh shit, my hands are dirty." He rubbed harder at Adam's skin.

Laughing, Adam caught Parker's hand and kissed his dirt-dusted knuckles. "It's okay. I don't know what I'm afraid of."

Parker pursed his lips. "I'll be generous and not argue with that." He drew down Adam's head for a kiss. "I hate how tense it makes you."

"I'm okay." He nuzzled Parker's nose.

"We could take out the boat. Release that stress."

His heart swelled at the idea, desire blooming through him like petals unfurling in the sun. This desire was gentler than the fierce fire that burned when he fucked Parker, but no less deep. Parker's fingers danced over Adam's lower back, about to dip below his waistband…

"We need to finish our shift at the grove," Adam forced himself to say.

Parker groaned but withdrew his hands. "See? A stickler."

"Maybe I'll give you an A for your work later." He slung his arm over Parker's shoulders as they made their way back.

"Not an A+? Rude!" Parker elbowed Adam in the ribs.

That afternoon while Parker was teaching marine navigation to the middle school kids, Adam wandered to the western beach. The sand was a little softer there, and it was where most islanders came to swim.

He eased his camera from the pocket of his cargo shorts and zoomed in on Connie at the water's edge, waves washing around her bare shins. Her Birkenstocks were safe farther up the sand, and she wore capri pants. She didn't seem to mind that the hems were getting wet.

"Hey there," she said after a minute, not looking in his direction.

He'd known she was aware he was there—of course she was—but Adam's face still heated as he managed to hold the camera steady and walk closer. "Any words of wisdom?"

Grinning, Connie turned her head to look straight down the camera lens even though she was twenty feet away. Her pink T-shirt read: *If opportunity doesn't knock, build a door.* She glanced down. "Besides this?"

"Sure. Can't have too much wisdom." He pushed in closer on her round, lined face.

"Never pass up the opportunity to dip your toes in the ocean."

Adam pressed stop and pocketed his camera. His feet were already bare, so he walked right over as another wave washed ashore, sinking him to his ankles in the wet sand.

"Ain't it just the best feeling?" Connie asked. "I know Parker would agree. That boy loves the ocean."

"He does."

"Everything okay with you two?"

"Absolutely. It was a silly argument." Maybe "silly" was the wrong word, but he didn't want to go into it with Connie. Although Parker was probably right, and Adam should ask her more questions. Before she could probe any deeper about Parker, he asked, "What do you think of Sean and his pack?"

"They're interesting." Her gaze remained on the horizon where the blue sky met the water, only a faint line of pale white differentiating them. "What do you think?"

"Parker doesn't trust him. Them."

"With all due respect, Parker has trust issues. And rightfully so." She gave Adam's wrist an affectionate squeeze. "I don't blame him. But I asked what *you* think."

"Honestly, I don't know. Sean's been respectful." He didn't share the info about being naked in front of a teenager. He was giving Sean the benefit of the doubt that it had been accidental.

"Willing to work. Not overly friendly. Reserved."

"Agreed. Could be a British thing."

"Could be." Adam spread his toes in the wet sand. "Has he told you anything else about what it's like over there? He said some humans and wolves were fighting?"

Connie nodded grimly. "There's conflict between packs over it as well."

"Why haven't we heard of anything like it happening here on the mainland? I know the radio's not reliable anymore, but Yolanda and her group didn't know about werewolves until they came here."

"England's tiny in comparison. It's what, two or three percent of the US land mass? It makes sense that conflict happened quickly there."

"True."

"Some wolves think humans should be subjugated. There are rumors of cruel treatment of humans. And worse."

Adam swallowed hard. How long could he protect Parker if it came down to it? Or Lilly, Jacob, and Craig? Yolanda and so many others?

He said, "Parker's right. As if we don't have enough on our plate with creepers and the end of life as we knew it."

Connie smiled humorlessly. "You can *almost* understand where the Zechariahs were coming from. If they even exist. My dad often saw the worst of humans in his business. Extremely wealthy people don't often get to the top by being kind and decent."

Putting aside the question of the Zechariahs—which they were no closer to answering—Adam asked, "How did your father succeed?" He quickly added, "Not that he wasn't kind and decent."

Her eyes crinkled as she smiled genuinely. "He was, though he had his moments of being cutthroat when necessary. He was lucky. He made the right product at the right time and became a billionaire."

"You said you became the alpha when he died. Did you take over the company too?"

Connie chortled. "Oh, heavens, no thank you. Corporate boardrooms weren't for me. I left that to Edward. My husband— Theresa's father."

"You've never talked about him before." Adam tried to ignore the skitter of excitement that Connie was trusting him with private information.

"I haven't, no. Edward was a human. The biggest disappointment of my life." She chuckled. "Not *because* he was human, to be clear. I look back, and I just can't imagine what I was thinking. What's that saying? The heart wants what the heart wants? Let me tell you, the heart isn't always the shiniest coin in the collection plate."

Adam smiled briefly. "He accepted that you were a wolf?"

"Oh yes, and he knew any children born to a werewolf would be wolves themselves. Honestly, with my father's money, he'd have married me if we were three-eyed leprechauns with horse tails." She gazed at the horizon. "He started spending too much time in those boardrooms and at private clubs with the rich and frankly terrible. He disconnected from the pack. From me and Theresa. I finally told him to choose between us and his billionaire cronies. He chose poorly, and he paid the price."

Adam could imagine Parker hissing excitedly in his ear: "*Did she kill him? Hire a hitman? A werewolf assassin?*"

As if reading his mind, Connie said, "I didn't bump him off if that's what you're thinking. Daddy had warned me about him when we married, but as I mentioned, I was young and unbearably foolish. Still, Daddy'd never completely trusted him, so even when Edward took over as CEO of the company, our prenup was ironclad. Oh, the fuss I'd put up about signing it. But I did, thank goodness."

"So, you divorced?"

"Yep, and Edward got nothing. He turned his back on Theresa. Never even met Devon before he died. Stupid, stupid man. It was his loss. We were all better off without him."

"Are you sure you didn't bump him off?" Adam joked, relieved when Connie's full-chested laugh boomed.

"It was a plane crash that did him in. One of his CEO pals had gotten his pilot's license but shouldn't have been flying without an instructor. Went into what they call a 'graveyard spiral.' He wasn't licensed for flying in low visibility, but rules weren't meant for jackasses like them." She winced. "I must sound heartless."

"No." Adam took her shoulder, relieved when she reached up to squeeze his hand. "For you to turn your back on him, Edward must have earned it."

"Still. It's unkind. And we should be kind. I have a T-shirt and everything." She patted his hand, and he let go of her shoulder.

Adam could picture the shirt—purple with a yellow bumblebee. Cool water washed around their ankles, remaking the sand in new patterns. Was Connie waiting for him to say something else? She was so comfortable with silence.

He smiled to think of how antsy Parker would be getting if he were with them, the words lining up to trip off his tongue. He and Parker shared moments of silence sometimes, but with other people, Parker found it nearly impossible.

Channeling him, Adam blurted, "I've only seen you in your true form once."

Connie contemplated that for so long Adam was about to apologize for being nosy.

Then she said, "That's interesting. The way you put it. Why is being a wolf 'truer' than your human side?"

"Oh. Uh… I don't know. I've just always thought of it that way."

"Even though most of us spend the majority of our days like this?" She motioned between them. "No claws. No fangs. Aren't we just as human as anyone?"

"I suppose so. I just wish I had the skill to fully transform. The control."

Connie's forehead crinkled. "Who says you don't?"

"My parents warned us not to even try until the time was right. They told us it could be dangerous to lose control."

"Hmm. Well, they weren't wrong." Connie bent and picked up a stone as a wave receded. "You're all grown up now, though." She flicked her wrist, and the stone skipped over the water before disappearing below the surface.

"Then why won't you tell me what I need to know?"

"I'm sorry, hon. I genuinely didn't mean to be mysterious about it."

Adam couldn't stop himself from arching a skeptical eyebrow. Fortunately, Connie chortled—a belly laugh that lit up her face.

"All right, you've got my number. Alphas do love to be mysterious. Part of our aura."

He smiled. "You're very good at it."

Connie took his hand, sending a wave of warmth through him. "The truth is, you'll shift fully when the time is right. When you need to. Stop trying to force it. Ease into it when you're ready."

"I've been ready for as long as I can remember!" He cleared his throat and lowered his voice. "I can't imagine being more ready."

"I understand. Now c'mere." She tugged him close and wrapped him in a cinnamon-scented hug. Stooping, Adam embraced her gratefully. Despite his lingering frustration, the comfort she radiated made him feel like the innocent little boy he'd been so very long ago.

A group of young kids arrived for their swimming lesson, and Adam headed back to the cabin. He jerked to a stop as he rounded the bend in the path and spotted Sean waiting on the porch.

Sean sat on the top step, still shirtless and wearing his jeans and cowboy boots. He was flipping a coin, and Adam realized with a jolt that he hadn't seen money in years.

Without looking up, Sean said, "Hope you don't mind me dropping by."

Alphas really did love to be mysterious.

"Course not. Can I offer you a drink?" He peered closely and saw that the coin was an American quarter, which struck him as odd given Sean had just come from the UK and Canada. Still, he could have picked it up anywhere.

Sean's full lips twitched. "So civilized here. I'd ask for tea, but I've made that mistake before in America. I'll have whatever you're having."

Adam ducked inside, relieved when Sean didn't try to invite himself in. Parker would definitely not like that, which was fair enough. Adam poured two glasses of water from the pitcher in the mini fridge, grinning at the scrawled note Parker had stuck to the fridge with a NASA magnet of a space shuttle:

BBW,

Blow my house down later?

P

Adam would never have thought he'd feel so loved being referred to as a "big, bad wolf," but Parker made it work.

Outside, Adam sat beside Sean on the porch. Not too close, but not too far away either. He couldn't seem intimidated.

Sean had apparently pocketed the quarter. After a sip of water, he said, "I understand you can't complete a full shift."

Adam gripped his glass, fingers slipping in the condensation. The old trees shaded them from the relentless sun, but the humidity was impossible to escape. "You shouldn't have been listening to me and Parker. That's the rule here."

Sean lifted a hand. "Apologies. So many rules. I don't make a habit of eavesdropping, but you were having a rather loud disagreement."

Adam nodded to acknowledge that.

"I admit I'm puzzled as to how you haven't completed this step. It's vital. You must feel the loss of it. The aching void."

"I wouldn't go that far." Yes, there was an ache, but a *void*?

Sean didn't argue. "Your pack never taught you?"

"I didn't grow up with a pack. Only my immediate family, and they were all killed in an accident when I was young."

"I'm sorry," Sean murmured. For a moment, he laid his palm on Adam's bare shoulder.

The urge wasn't as strong as with Connie, but Adam still wanted to lean into Sean's touch. Guilt seared him even though he reminded himself it wasn't sexual. Still, it wouldn't seem as innocent to Parker as Adam's connection to Connie— understandably.

Not that he had any reason to think Sean was hitting on him. The touch had only been for a moment, and Sean now simply watched him, waiting.

Adam cleared his throat. "I never even spoke to another were-wolf until Parker and I came here."

Sean's eyes widened. "And that was…?"

"Three years ago."

"Christ. You lived most of your life with no pack? No wolves at all?"

Adam nodded and gulped his water.

"That's monstrous. You must have felt incredibly isolated. Alone. It's one thing to date an ord, but to live completely among them with no pack? Unimaginable."

"*Don't* call Parker that."

"I mean no offense."

Adam glared.

Sean chuckled. "All right. I do apologize sincerely. I'm not used to so many ord—regular humans around."

"You have a problem with it?" Adam asked through a clenched jaw.

He seemed to consider it. "No. It just wasn't my pack's way. I'm not sure if that was a good thing or not."

"Your pack must be bigger than the group you came here with?"

"Oh, yes. Much bigger. I had to be sure everyone was safe and settled before I could make the journey with a select few."

Safe. There was that word again. Adam and Parker were safe and settled, but for how long? "Why did you? Make the journey?"

"Good afternoon!" Theresa called cheerfully as she walked into sight with Devon trailing behind. "Hot one, huh?"

"*Mom,*" Devon muttered.

"What?" Theresa wiped sweat from beneath her ponytail. "Are you saying it's not hot as hell?"

Devon rolled his eyes. "I'm saying everyone is extremely aware of how hot it is."

Ignoring him, Theresa said to Sean, "I don't think you've officially met my son, Devon."

"I don't think I have." With a charming smile, Sean stood and offered his hand. "A pleasure."

"Um. Yeah." Devon seemed reluctant to shake Sean's hand, but did. "Jacob says you're cool."

"Does he? I'm flattered."

"Anyone who can impress Jacob is a great addition to our community," Theresa said. "See you at dinner."

When they were gone, Sean asked, "Were you and Parker here when everything changed?"

"No. We were at Stanford. Near San Francisco."

Sean leaned closer, his brown gaze intense. "You traveled across the country?"

"We did."

"What did you see?"

Adam frowned. "Chaos. Death. Creepers everywhere. The infected, I mean. I imagine it was the same in the UK?"

"It was. Still is." He sipped his water, though the movement seemed forced. "Did you see any planes?"

"Planes? Military, you mean? No. A helicopter or two early on, I think. That was it. If this was terrorism, they knew what they were doing. Or arguably they didn't because I'm not sure this was the Earth the Zechariahs wanted to inherit."

Sean scratched idly at his neck. "You heard that rumor too? I don't know if I believe it. I suppose it doesn't matter at this point."

"Not really. Even if they were real, how many are left now?"

"Don't suppose we'll ever know." Sean's gaze had gone distant. He rhythmically flipped the coin again.

Adam smelled Parker approaching before he heard him. He resisted the urge to shoo Sean away. There was nothing going on. After all, Parker had apparently seen Sean naked, so he had nothing to be jealous about.

Then Sean squeezed Adam's bare shoulder again, and Adam could have sworn he did it exactly when Parker would spot them. "Again, my apologies for eavesdropping. But if you have questions, you can come to me."

Adam nodded stiffly, and Sean stood as Parker called, "Hey!" far too loudly. "What's up?" That plastic, tense smile cracked his face.

"Just taking a break," Sean said smoothly before draining his glass. He handed it to Adam. "Thank you for the hospitality." He smiled at Parker before sauntering away.

"What did he want?" Parker whispered.

"I don't know." It was the truth.

"Whatever it is, I bet there are strings attached."

Adam stood and brushed off his shorts. "Agreed." He pulled Parker close and kissed him long and slow, trying not to think about what kind of answers Sean might have that Connie hadn't shared.

Chapter Five

"HE'S IN THERE again."

Adam glanced up from a deepening hole in the ground as he threw another shovelful of dirt onto a pile. "Who?"

Parker internally rolled his eyes. He bit back a retort but stopped pacing to give Adam a withering look. "You know who, and you know where."

Returning to digging, Adam said possibly the most annoying thing he could have said. "It's none of our business."

"*Yeah*, but why are Sean and Connie having so many secret meetings?"

"If they were secret, you wouldn't be obsessing about them." Adam's bare back flexed as he powerfully dug the hole.

Parker tossed an orange from one hand to the other. "At least we won't die of scurvy."

Adam barely blinked at the abrupt change of subject. "Nope. All the vitamin C we can handle and then some."

Parker's gaze returned to Connie's office across the open common area near the mess hall. The office was a one-room cabin with a multicolored sign on the door reading *Wipe your paws*, which Parker had to admit was cute. "If we got a little closer, you could—"

"*No*." Adam glared at Parker, his nostrils flaring. "Stop. Please." His expression softened. "Why don't you go for a swim? Work through your meditations."

In the month since Sean and the newcomers had come, Parker

had been too keyed up for his morning swims most days, and no way did he have the concentration to meditate. What if everything went to hell when he wasn't watching?

Sean's pack had moved into the last empty cabins in C Block on the east side of the living area. They were helping with chores and being polite. They asked a lot of questions and didn't make waves. Though Parker noticed they didn't *answer* many questions.

They still made trips out to their ship, which had dropped anchor outside the harbor. Parker didn't think it was too big to come closer, but it wasn't his decision. (Why *did* they stay so far out, though?) Of course, the ship had been searched as a precaution, so there was probably nothing to worry about.

Probably.

He'd asked Connie if they were staying for good, and she gave one of her annoyingly vague, cheery answers like, "*Time will tell!*" or "*Tomorrow will take care of itself.*" Did all alphas speak in clichés?

She'd also insisted that all newcomers were given the benefit of the doubt and the chance to prove themselves through actions and attitude. That Salvation Island was a sanctuary, blah, blah, blah.

He could have talked to Sean more to find out, but…nah. While no one else seemed to see it, there was something about Sean that Parker sure as hell didn't trust. Of course, when he mentioned it to Adam, Adam sighed affectionately and told him he was being paranoid.

Sure, but that didn't mean Sean wasn't out to get them.

"*Parker.*" Adam was squeezing his hand.

"Huh?" He jolted to attention. "Yeah. Sorry. Don't feel like swimming. Besides, I'm helping you."

Adam glanced around at the waist-deep hole in which he stood. It was for a post of the new cabin that would host a dentistry practice. The dentist had arrived with Yolanda and had their work cut out for them. "Right," Adam replied dryly. "I couldn't do it without you."

One of the knots clustered inside Parker loosened. "I'm offering moral support." As Adam snorted and continued digging, Parker resumed pacing, nodding and smiling to people as they passed by, going about their chores like everything was totally normal.

"How does that even work?" he asked Adam. "Having two packs and two alphas in the same place."

"I have no idea. I didn't grow up with a pack, remember?"

"Right. Sorry." *Ugh.* Now Parker felt like an asshole. "I wish they'd just go away and leave us in peace."

Adam's shovel made a rhythmic scraping sound in the earth. "Are we not living in peace now? Why are Sean and his pack different from Yolanda and her people?"

"Super valid question. I don't know. They just are. I felt it as soon as I saw their boat out there." He tossed the orange back and forth, back and forth, back and forth.

Adam stuck his shovel in the dirt and jumped out of the hole without using his hands, which was *hot.* He cupped Parker's cheek and forced Parker's gaze away from Connie's office.

"Don't you have an assignment this morning?"

"Hmm? Yeah, I'm on laundry. I'll go in a sec."

"You'll be late. And aren't you going to help Craig decorate for Lilly's party?"

"Yeah, I will." At Adam's raised eyebrow, Parker sighed. "I will. I know, I'm being crazy."

"I don't like that word. You have anxiety. Very understandably. But you know you'll feel better if you swim and meditate."

"I know, but there's no time now." He kissed Adam and pocketed the orange. "Gotta go bleach some sheets."

He escaped, and Adam let him go. He knew Adam was right, but he was too keyed up. He'd swim and meditate tomorrow. There was way too much to do.

As Parker hurried to the laundry cabin to crank up the old washer and clean the infirmary sheets, he passed Connie's office and stopped to tie the laces on his worn sneakers. What he wouldn't give for supersonic werewolf hearing.

THEY DIDN'T HAVE balloons or streamers, but Parker had collected flowers from multiple gardens—with permission—and borrowed an impressive collection of colorful scarves to drape everywhere. They belonged to an older female werewolf who'd been coming to the island for years before the world went to hell.

"You should really get a werewolf to churn that butter," Parker called to Craig, who was using an old hand-cranked mixer in the yellow linoleum kitchenette to transform fresh cream into butter for the icing. "Doesn't the kitchen in the mess hall have one of those stand mixers like my mother had on the counter and literally maybe used once?"

"Yeah, but I want to make it myself." Craig wiped sweat from his brow. The beaters clinked against the sides of the metal bowl as he turned the handle. "They made the cake for me since I don't have an oven, but I'm churning this butter if it's the last thing I do."

Parker finished decorating the living room, draping scarves over the old watercolor seaside paintings on the wooden walls. There was no dining room, but they could eat Lilly's favorite—hot dogs—easily enough on their laps. They did need another chair, so he checked Jacob's room, remembering there was a battered desk in the corner.

The closed door swung open with a creak, and Parker flicked on the overhead light. The window blind was down even though it was daytime, and the musty air made him sneeze. The floral wallpaper was covered almost to the ceiling with ads and pictures cut out of old magazines that must have been in the island's library. Even in the zombie apocalypse, teenagers wanted to make spaces their own. It was weirdly reassuring.

Like many of them, Jacob didn't own a huge wardrobe of clothing options, but somehow his floor was still strewn with dirty laundry. The duvet was crumpled at the bottom of the double bed, and Parker straightened it, thinking of his mother nagging him about the "*disaster area he called a bedroom.*"

"Jacob needs some fresh air in there!" Parker called as he dragged out the desk chair.

"What?" The mixer still clacked and whirred.

"Nothing!" Repeating it would make him feel even more ancient than he already did.

Adam arrived with the countertop grill on loan from the mess hall. At breakfast, everyone in the hall had sung "Happy Birthday" to Lilly, and she could have had a big party if she'd wanted, but she'd requested a family dinner.

"It looks great," Adam said, giving Parker a kiss. "Any ideas for wrapping paper?"

Parker grabbed the scarves he'd held back. "Voilà."

As Craig bitched to himself about pioneers over the clatter of the mixer, Adam carefully pulled a gold bangle from his cargo shorts pocket. "It was Theresa's when she was a girl, so it should fit."

"Wow. That's generous of her."

Parker wrapped a pink scarf around the comic he'd drawn of Super Lilly, a crime-fighting astronaut. It was only several pages, but he'd worked on it for days. Though he wasn't the best artist in the world by any stretch of the imagination, Lilly didn't seem to mind.

He'd created the character for her first birthday on the island, and he hoped she wasn't too old for it now. She'd loved last year's incarnation with Super Lilly fighting one-eyed aliens on Mars, so fingers crossed. He'd decided to set the stories in space since Earth was…problematic.

Craig shouted his triumphant victory over the cream that was now butter, and they applauded. Before long, Lilly burst through the door, all smiles, and they played a game of Monopoly sitting cross-legged on the living room floor while waiting for Jacob.

And waiting.

And waiting.

"School was out an hour ago." Craig checked his watch and pushed to his feet with a small groan, muttering under his breath about getting old. "I'll round him up."

"I can go," Adam offered.

"Uh-uh. You just landed on my railroad." Lilly held out her palm. "Pay up, sucker."

Parker whistled under his breath. "No-prisoners Lilly is in the house."

She giggled. "You just did a happy dance when Dad landed in jail."

"What can I say? Capitalism is a harsh mistress."

They played on, Adam trying to appeal to Parker's mercy when his little top hat landed on Pennsylvania Avenue. Parker twirled his villain mustache and bankrupted him while Lilly laughed in delight.

"This game really is fucked up," Parker said, laughing so hard he was wheezing. "Shit. I mean—sorry. It's *messed* up."

Lilly rolled her eyes. "Dad's not here. You can swear. It's only words for fuck's sake."

"Lilly!" Parker and Adam exclaimed in unison before they all broke down laughing.

Footsteps sounded on the porch, and Lilly jumped up and exclaimed, "I'm winning!" As Craig reappeared alone, her smile faded. "Where's Jacob?"

"I'm not sure, baby." Craig kept his tone light, but Parker's stomach clenched. *Shit.*

"Oh. Okay." She sat back on the gingham area rug, shoulders slumping.

It was Parker's turn, and when Lilly was looking toward the door as if willing Jacob to walk through it, Parker fudged the dice so he'd land on her property. That only made her smile for a moment, though they finished the rest of the game, trying to be cheery.

"I'm sure Jacob's on his way," Adam said. "I'll just go give him a hand with whatever's keeping him."

"*No.*" Lilly's jaw was set. Parker wasn't sure he'd ever heard her so forceful. He, Adam, and Craig blinked at her in surprise. She finished packing up the game. "If he doesn't want to come to my birthday party, then I don't want to make him."

Parker's heart *hurt.* They cooked the hot dogs and put on big smiles, and after a little while, Lilly seemed to enjoy herself. Adam filmed her opening presents and blowing out her candles. She hugged Parker so tightly after unwrapping the comic, the new bangle on her slim wrist.

"I love all my presents," she said. "Even if I didn't get a puppy again."

Craig chuckled. "You know there are no dogs allowed on the island."

"I know," she muttered with a dramatic sigh. "It can be dangerous for them because they get confused when people shift into wolves," she parroted.

"And you wouldn't want a sweet dog to get injured mistakenly trying to protect you," Parker said.

"No." Lilly eyed Adam. "But you're still *you* after becoming a total wolf, right? You can still think and stuff?"

He smiled stiffly. "From what I understand. I've never completely shifted, so I'm not sure what it's like."

Parker wanted to assure Adam that it was okay, and he'd figure it out eventually, and it wasn't a big deal, but would that be annoying and condescending?

"Hmm." Lilly seemed to ponder it. "And I know they say dogs can give you disturbance or something?"

Craig laughed. "*Distemper*, baby. Humans can't catch it, but werewolves can." He looked to Adam. "It wasn't a big concern in the before times because there weren't a lot of dogs running around with distemper and rabies and that sort of thing, right?"

"Right," Adam said. "My parents were very wary of it when I was a kid. It's one of those viruses that can be fatal for the old and young. Now, without vets and with so many people gone and dogs roaming, the risk is higher. I was always taught to avoid wild animals and domestic dogs when I could, but it wasn't a big worry back then."

Lilly sighed. "We have to worry about *everything* now."

Parker's heart squeezed, imagining having to grow up in this terrifying new world. He gave her a smile. "Not here, though. We keep dogs off the island, and presto! Nothing to worry about."

She nodded. "I still miss Lola though."

Craig kissed her head. "Me too, sweetheart. She's playing around up in Heaven, stealing the smelly socks out of angels' shoes."

Lilly seemed to ponder it. "Do angels wear shoes and socks? Or just gold sandals or something?"

"All I know is if it's Heaven, they have stinky socks for Lola," Craig said.

Later, as the sun set, Parker found the cows standing in the pasture, alone and content under the pink sky, lowing softly. Why hadn't he let Adam be the one to search for Jacob? With his wolfy speed and hearing and smell, he'd have found him in two minutes.

"Because I have to be stubborn," Parker muttered as he headed to the orange grove.

He'd asked Theresa once why she and Connie let the teenagers sneak around to party when they could bust them so easily. She'd said it was a normal part of growing up, and they'd only step in if someone was in danger. Which made sense, but it made him feel like a dick since his first instinct was to go old-school authoritarian like his parents.

Snatches of laughter and weed caught on the wind, and he squinted beyond the orange trees to the hulking skeletons of the solar farm. He'd tried pot a few times when he was younger, but it had made him paranoid. He sure as hell didn't need any help in that department.

Those little assholes better not be climbing them and fucking up our power source.

Parker marched over, peering into the gloom under one of the panels. "Hey! Jacob?"

The pimply leader, Chris, unfolded from where he leaned against a metal post. "What do you want?"

"Three guesses, and the first two don't count."

"He's not here," one of the girls said. Parker blanked on her name.

"Probably sucking his boyfriend's dick," Chris sneered. He wore a backwards baseball cap over his greasy hair.

Parker breathed through gritted teeth, though his anger eased. Had Jacob given Devon a chance after all? "Where are they? Devon has a curfew too." Maybe he could sneak them back into the village and help give them an excuse...

Chris snorted. "Not that little loser. The weird British guy."

For a second, Parker could only stare, waiting for the words to make sense.

"He's hot though," another girl piped up as she passed a joint to Chris. Her name was Heather, Parker thought.

"Whatever," Chris scoffed. To Parker, he added, "Guess you're not the only freak who wants that werewolf dick."

While part of him *really* wanted to kick Chris in the shins and tell him to go fuck himself because no one else would, Parker kept focused. "You're talking about Sean?" His throat was painfully dry.

"Yeah," Heather answered, stepping closer, her face pinched. "I saw Jacob sneaking out of his cabin a few nights ago. I know I should have said something, but I didn't want to be a narc."

Parker nodded. "Okay. Thank you for telling me now." He strode away, waiting until he was back in the forest to run.

He stormed into C Block, and there was Jacob ahead on the path in his familiar baggy jeans and hoodie. Which cabin was Sean's? Had Jacob been there again? Parker barked his name.

Jacob spun with a scowl. "What's your problem?"

"Did you seriously forget Lilly's birthday?"

He blanched, his eyes widening. "Oh, fuck. What time is it?" He looked up at the darkening sky like he was only just noticing it. "I lost track of time. I was just—fuck. I'm sorry!"

"Tell her that."

"Is she pissed?"

"She's *hurt.* Jesus Christ, she's twelve, and you couldn't get your head out of your own ass long enough to come to her birthday party? It was just us, so you were a major part of the guest list. How could you *forget*? You're too old to be pulling this shit. It's time to man up."

"I'm sorry, okay?" Jacob huffed defensively. "I didn't mean to. I'll go now."

"Wait. We need to talk."

Jacob's expression hardened. "So you can tell me more about what a fuckup I am? Trust me, I know."

"No. Come on." Parker led him away from the cabins toward his private beach, ignoring the curious glances from people as they passed. The gossip would be flying.

"Where are we going? Ow." Jacob followed along the overgrown trail, batting branches away.

Heart thudding, Parker tried to gather his thoughts. He wanted to tell Craig and let Craig do his dad thing, but there was no way Jacob would want to talk to him about this. Parker wasn't *that* far removed from teenagerdom.

Once they reached the gritty sand, Jacob held out his hands. "Okay. What do you want?"

"I'm worried about you. We need to talk about Sean."

Jacob blinked, looking around nervously. "Why?"

There was no good way to ask, so Parker just said it. "Did he touch you?"

"*What?* I fucking wish. Don't be crazy." He spun on his heel.

Parker grabbed his arm before quickly letting go. "Wait. Talk to me. Please."

"There's nothing to talk about!" Spittle flew from Jacob's chapped lips. "Unless you want to dive into how much my life fucking sucks."

"You have food and a home and people who love you—"

"Yeah, but it still sucks, okay? I hate it here."

Parker tried to keep his cool. "Do you remember the alternative?"

"Obviously, duh. But we don't know what it's like now. There could be places where it's better. My dad might still be alive. It might be good where he is."

"You can't be serious." Parker fought to remember. "Wasn't he in the Bay Area?"

"Yeah, Oakland. Mom wouldn't even consider finding him."

"Adam and I came from there. Trust me, it was a bad, bad scene. Your mom did everything she could to keep you safe. That was all she cared about."

Tears sprang to Jacob's eyes even as his pimply jaw clenched. "Bullshit. She wouldn't have left me if she'd really cared."

Parker swallowed hard. "You know that's not true. It wasn't her fault."

He could hear the creepers and their chattering teeth, that awful sound filling his mind so completely he had to look behind him. There was only the shadow of trees, though he could see Abby's pale face as she died, the terror in her eyes not only for herself but for her son she was leaving behind.

Parker had to clear his throat. "I know it's hard for you growing up here. Growing up in this new world. It's not how any of us imagined our lives. But we're safe here. That's what matters."

"Is it?" Jacob wiped his eyes angrily. "Sean says—" He broke off.

"What? What does *Sean* say?"

"Forget it. You hate him for no good reason."

"I have plenty of reasons. For example, what were you doing in his cabin at night?"

Jacob scoffed, but he looked at his feet immediately. "What are you talking about?"

"Heather saw you sneaking out. What were you doing there?" Parker lowered his voice with effort. "If there's something going on, you can tell me."

"Oh, how freaking generous of you. So what if there was? Who cares about rules? You get to fuck a hot werewolf. Why shouldn't I?"

"Because you're a kid!" Anger and worry boiled through Parker's veins. Fuck, was it seriously true? "I'm not going to stand by and do nothing while you're at risk."

"A minute ago, you were telling me I'm too old for this! Now I'm a dumb kid. Make up your mind!"

"You know what I mean. Tell me the truth. What were you doing in his cabin?"

"Nothing! I'm just talking crap. You think a hot guy like that would want *me*? As if."

If someone was a pervert who got off on the power imbalance, it wasn't about looks. "I know you're scared and hurt and maybe embarrassed, but you can tell me anything, okay?"

"There's nothing to tell. I swear."

Then Jacob scratched his ear—and Parker's heart dropped. He was lying. That was his biggest tell. Parker took a deep breath. He was messing this up. He couldn't shake the truth out of him. He had to focus on what he could manage right now.

Parker said, "Yes, we live in the shittiest timeline our planet has ever known, although honestly, I don't think the Middle Ages were all that fun by the sounds of it. But we're here, and we have to make the best of it. We live on a beautiful, safe island. You need to embrace it. Stop fighting everything."

"That's rich coming from you. You haven't 'embraced' Sean and his pack. You hate change. But I need it. I can't just sit around here with my thumbs up my ass! God, it's so boring!"

"Boredom is a privilege!" Parker inhaled through his nose and exhaled through his mouth, counting in his head. "There's plenty to do here. Survival, for example. It's not the life any of us imagined, but we're *safe*. We have family. Community. Lilly and your dad are—"

"He's not my dad! I'm sick of him telling me what to do."

"The hell I'm not."

Parker and Jacob jolted as Craig appeared, striding toward them, saying, "I promised your momma I'd take care of you. I know if it was her here instead of me, she'd be raising Lilly like she'd borne her. I'm your father whether you like it or not. Now come home. It's time for bed. Lilly already cried herself to sleep."

Jacob's shoulders drooped, shame creasing his face. He stared at his feet. "I really didn't mean to forget her party."

"I know," Craig said softly. "You can make it up to her tomorrow." He nodded to Parker, and Parker nodded back.

"Jacob, we'll talk tomorrow too, okay?" Parker called after him as he slouched away with Craig. Jacob didn't respond.

Parker walked random paths, trying to envision the blackboard in his head to draw his chalk breathing box. It was useless. His brain kept supplying the image of Jacob tugging his ear. What was he lying about? What had he been doing in Sean's cabin? At any time, but especially at night?

That little punk Chris's nasal whine echoed through Parker's mind.

Probably sucking his boyfriend's dick.

Anxious and keyed up, Parker prowled the cabin blocks and village. Why couldn't anyone else see it? Why were the people still up sitting on their porches or playing cornhole by the mess hall?

There's something going on. I'm not wrong. I know it!

His heart pounded, his face hot and sweaty even as a terrible chill coiled around his spine.

Abby's blood slowing between his fingers after her heart stopped pumping. The way she was already going cold when he wrapped her body in plastic.

Parker was running now.

He'd promised Abby he'd keep Jacob safe. He couldn't let her down. Jacob was hiding something about Sean, and what the hell else could it be? No matter what it was, Parker wasn't going to break his vow.

As he reached the harbor, he spotted Bethany on the dock. A barrage of memories of Shorty and his crew on *The Good Life* punched and slapped and tore at him before Parker was able to shove them away.

Sean's perfect teeth gleamed in the moonlight as he said something to Bethany, and wow, he was actually wearing a shirt for once. A jacket, even. Parker's whirring brain clocked these details as he strode down the pier, the worn wood thudding under his sneakers.

He was being so loud that Bethany turned with a frown. "Parker?"

Ignoring her, he shoved against Sean's chest as hard as he could, the leather soft under his palms. Sean didn't move an inch, because of course he didn't, but his eyes glowed gold.

"Parker!" Bethany gasped.

"Stay the fuck away from him!" Parker shouted in Sean's face, dropping his hands because he felt like a dumb kid pushing against a concrete wall.

"From who, precisely?" Sean asked with infuriating calm.

Bethany tugged Parker's arm. "What's going on?" she hissed. "Are you outta your mind?"

He shook her off. "You stay out of it!"

She backed away, eyes wide, and that memory of holding a gun on her on this very pier—of wanting to pull the trigger—slammed into Parker with full force, shame and fear and fury clamping around his lungs.

No. This was about Jacob. He refocused on Sean, who had the nerve to *smile*.

"If your boyfriend wants me to help him with his shift, it's really none of your concern."

Wait, what?

Parker's mind spun, but he focused. He had to protect Jacob. He had to take care of his family. "Stay away from Jacob," he gritted out.

A furrow appeared between Sean's smooth brows. "Why?"

"You know why."

"I assure you, I don't."

"Because he's only sixteen! He doesn't know what he's doing. You're a fucking pervert."

It wasn't so much that ripples appeared below Sean's calm facade, but a tsunami. The gold of his eyes flared bright, his fangs suddenly out, hair spreading, and holy shit, was he taller somehow? The air around them charged with danger, and Parker couldn't breathe.

"Shut your mouth," Sean snarled. "Don't you dare talk to me like that."

His knees trembled, but Parker stood his ground. "Oh, I dare! You think I don't see you whispering with him? Getting him to trust you? You could fuck almost any adult here, yet you're hanging around a kid. It's sick."

"Are you out of your fucking mind?" Sean growled. "I've been nice to a lonely boy. That's all."

"That's not what I heard."

His golden eyes narrowed. "Who told you that?"

As much of a little shit as Chris was, Parker wasn't going to sic Sean on him. "It doesn't matter. I know he was in your cabin the other night."

Something flickered in Sean's feral expression. "That was a misunderstanding."

See? Jesus Christ, I'm right!

"Bullshit!" As Parker reached out to shove Sean again, he was suddenly in the air, hauled back against Adam's familiar body.

"*Stop*," Adam commanded in his ear, carrying Parker backward.

"Handle your ord!" Sean barked.

"Put me down!" Parker wriggled in Adam's grasp, elbowing him.

Sean vibrated with fury, fangs bared. "If he ever talks to me like that again, I'll shut him up for good."

Adam's powerful growl reverberated against Parker's back. "Stay away from him."

"I'm right here!" Parker struggled to free himself from the iron bands of Adam's arms. His feet were still off the ground, and as Adam turned and strode down the pier still carrying him against his chest like a misbehaving toddler, Parker found dozens of people watching from the shore.

Humiliation slammed through him, and he begged, "Put me down. Please!"

Adam did immediately, his arm going around Parker's shoulders and keeping him upright as he stumbled on a loose board.

"It's okay," Adam murmured. Louder, he called out, "Everything's fine!"

Connie and Theresa waited at the foot of the pier, and too many people lingered, werewolves and humans alike whispering and watching Parker humiliate himself. Gemma and the rest of Sean's pack thundered up, fangs bared.

Connie assessed Parker coolly. "We'll discuss this in the morning."

"What? I'm not allowed to have a fight? I didn't pull a gun on him or anything." He needed to stop talking, but his mouth didn't cooperate. "You're the one who let that—"

"*Parker!*" Adam gripped him. "Please."

"I'll see you in the morning," Connie said. She shared a glance with Adam, then nodded.

Parker wanted to protest that he wasn't a child, but he knew he was acting like one. He wanted to run again, but he wouldn't give Sean the satisfaction. He strode the path to their cabin with Adam shadowing his steps.

The front door handle stuck sometimes, and as Parker jiggled it, Adam murmured, "Here, let me—"

"No!" Parker went rigid. "I've got it." He could tell Adam wanted to comfort him, his hand still hovering in midair. "Don't touch me right now. Please." With a final jiggle and shove, he opened the door. It thunked back into the wall.

Everything had been good until Sean and his pack had shown up. This was exactly why Parker didn't want any more newcomers. This was why he wanted the rest of the world to stay the fuck away.

Chapter Six

PARKER USUALLY LOVED the sound of rain on the roof of the wooden cabin, but this morning, he cursed. Not out loud—he didn't want to wake Adam as he crept out of the bedroom in the predawn murk, even though Adam had surely clocked the movement. He still let Parker tiptoe around and pretend he was stealthy.

All the things he'd said and done the night before played on an endless loop. He'd barely slept an hour, curled away from Adam, keeping as much room between them as possible. Cursing himself for getting in over his head. For humiliating himself in front of everyone.

Whatever the truth was about Sean, Parker hadn't handled it the right way. He'd flown off the handle instead of acting like the adult he was supposed to be. His whole body was jagged edges. This was what happened when he didn't take care of himself and do all that mindful shit.

A little rain wasn't stopping him—even if he was already wet when he reached his spot. He tucked his damp towel under a thick palm grove, stripped off his shorts, and strode into the water, pausing to let a wave break and wash past him. The swells weren't huge, but they were big enough to dump him if he didn't time it right.

Diving under the waves, he quickly acclimated, swimming lengths up and down the beach just past the break where he could quickly find a sandbar to stand on if need be. He always started with his fastest freestyle stroke, swimming north until he was level with one particular palm tree with a leaning trunk, then back down the way he'd come to a rocky outcropping.

Next was breaststroke and sidestroke. No backstroke since it made him feel vulnerable not being able to see where he was going. As a kid, he'd loved backstroke, gazing up at the Cape summer sun and blue sky, Eric yelling at him to straighten out when he inevitably veered off course.

Now, Parker needed to see exactly where he was and who—or what—was around him.

The routine soothed him, counting laps and cycling through his strokes. He couldn't completely shut out the mess he'd made, but at least he could breathe. If he was wrong about Sean, he'd make it right.

He knew Adam was lurking as he hustled out of the water to his damp towel. Hard to believe it had been sweltering so recently. The rain had stopped for the moment, but the wind whipped, and Parker shivered, rubbing his naked body dry. Or drier, at least. Sand stuck to his skin, and he wished their cabin was closer to his beach.

"I'm fine," he said.

Adam stepped out of the leaves, again paying the sharp acacias no mind even as a trail of blood appeared on his arm below his faded blue T-shirt. "I know," he said, toying with the camera in his hand and switching it off.

Parker rubbed the cut on Adam's arm until it disappeared under his palm. Adam watched him closely, whispering, "Thank you."

"I know it doesn't really help." Parker dropped his hand.

"It does." Adam's soulful hazel eyes searched Parker's face. "You're cold."

He tried to hide a shiver. "I'm fine."

"Can I?" Adam lifted his hands, and Parker knew what he

meant.

"I'm going to get you all wet and sandy." Still, he didn't fight as Adam pulled him close, running his big, warm hands over Parker's back and ass.

"I don't care."

It had sucked not waking up spooned in Adam's arms, and Parker melted against him now with relief. They had to talk about it, but not right this second.

"How'd I look out there?" he asked after a few minutes of soothing caresses. "Your movie's going to have a lot of swimming footage. The critics will complain about the pacing."

"Good thing Rotten Tomatoes is no more. And you looked gorgeous."

He had to smile. "Thanks. I just needed to get in my swim and meditation." He was grateful Adam wasn't bringing up the elephant in the room just yet.

Adam said, "It's chilly this morning. Come back to the cabin to meditate. You'll be alone—I'm going to a meeting."

Tension returning, Parker pulled away and tugged on worn shorts and a T-shirt. "A meeting, huh? Okay. Is it about handling your 'ord'?"

"*No.* Come on. You know I'd never think of you like that."

Parker exhaled, crossing and uncrossing his arms. "I know, but *Sean* sure does."

"I don't care what Sean thinks."

Remembering what Sean had said about Adam wanting his help in shifting, Parker said, "I hope not." It wasn't the time to get into that. He had to find control and calm. Sitting on his rock, he took a few breaths and crossed his legs at the ankles.

He let his mind hop around and the words flow. "One year, it was so cold on Memorial Day weekend that Dad had to bribe me to jump off the boat so he could take our annual pictures."

"How much did he pay you?"

"A buck. Cheap bastard." Parker laughed softly. "You know how they say rich people are the stingiest? So true with my dad. Not that my parents didn't give me a lot."

"Materially," Adam said, standing behind Parker and running his warm hand over Parker's wet hair.

"Mm." Parker picked at a loose thread on the towel. "I miss them so much even though they could be jerks sometimes. Like all parents can be."

He should have been dealing with the mess he'd made with Jacob, but his brain wanted to think about anything else. Naturally, it couldn't focus on something nice like tasting sweet oranges or kissing Adam.

"Of course you miss them," Adam murmured.

"Eric wouldn't go in for a dollar. He negotiated Dad up to ten bucks while I treaded water like an asshole." He grinned. "Eric was always a good negotiator. If he hadn't become a broker, I'm sure he would have gone to law school."

After a few moments, Adam quietly said, "You could still ask Connie to broadcast a message to Eric again. You had her stop after only a few weeks when we got here. She'd say yes."

Parker's chest tightened, and he struggled to breathe through it. "I know," he managed.

From what they'd learned from fellow survivors and the odd radio conversation, the majority of people on Earth were dead or infected. If Connie put out a message to Eric again and there was no reply, that would somehow be worse than not knowing. This way, Parker could fantasize that Eric was alive and okay—maybe even well.

Maybe Eric had found love like Parker had. Maybe he was living in some UK commune, growing strawberries and churning milk into cream, having chubby babies and being happy. For all Parker knew, his parents had somehow survived the fiery hellscape of Boston and would show up at Salvation Island and rip him a new one for not waiting for them at the Cape house in Chatham. Maybe one day. Maybe the virus would die out and the creepers would go extinct and—

He sucked in a ragged breath. He couldn't let himself dream that the world would go back to normal even for a second. It was impossible, and that was one fantasy he absolutely could not allow.

Adam pressed his lips against the top of Parker's head in a tender kiss, running his hands over Parker's shoulders until the high-wire tension seeped away. Parker counted to four as he inhaled for the first side of his box breathing. He completed the square, imagining drawing it on his mental chalkboard until he was in the zone.

"See you later," Adam murmured. "It's okay."

Parker's gut clenched as he remembered saying that to Abby. Telling her that lie.

"Parker?"

"I'm fine. Just…thinking. I need to stop for a while."

Adam's lips brushed over Parker's head, and then he was gone. Eyes still closed, Parker meditated, inhaling through his nose and blowing it out gently. He had to halt the vicious cycle. He thought too damn much and not enough at the same time.

The air was rich with earth and ocean brine, and he tried to focus on the scents…

Connie had said they'd talk, but she'd find him when she wanted to, right? He had a shift in the kitchen after breakfast. They'd probably ask him to do the dishes or maybe peel potatoes since he was a terrible cook—

No. Stop.

Focusing his wandering brain back on the chalkboard, he drew another box. The chalk scraped the blackboard lightly…

"Parker?"

He jolted at Lilly's voice, opening his eyes and jumping to his feet. She stood just beyond the tree line, still wearing her polka-dot PJs and a satin night cap. Her bare feet sunk into the sand.

"You haven't seen him?" she asked in a hushed tone.

"Who? Your dad? Did you have a bad dream, sweetie?"

Her eyes narrowed as she huffed. "*No.* I'm not a baby. And Dad's still asleep."

"Then who—" His stomach dropped. "What's Jacob gotten himself into this time?" Guilt slithered through him.

"He ran away." She bit her lip and pulled a piece of paper from her pocket, holding it out for Parker. His hand trembled as he took it.

> *Lil, please don't be mad. I'm so, so sorry I missed your party, and I'm sorry I didn't say goodbye. It's time for me to man up. I need to see what's out there. Wear this for me until I see you again.*
>
> *Love,*
> *Jacob*

Parker's heart thudded dully as Lilly solemnly pulled the silver dove on its delicate chain from her pocket.

Fuck. Fuck, fuck, fuck!

Seeing his own angry words in Jacob's compact scrawl made him queasy. *Man up.*

It was fine. Parker could roll this back. It wasn't out of his grasp. "Okay, well, we're on an island, so his options are limited."

"*Diana's* gone."

"Who?"

The second the question was out of his mouth, Parker realized with a powerful wave of dread that she was a *what*, and that Sean was a fucking liar.

Chapter Seven

"THEY'RE GONE?" PARKER demanded as he slammed through Connie's office door. "Sean and his pack? You let them go?"

"Parker!" Adam's face burned as he jumped up from his chair and blocked Parker's path.

What had changed in twenty minutes? Parker had been calm at the beach, but now Adam could hear his heart banging like a drum. The scent of his fury and—yes, that was *fear*—clawed at Adam.

Parker's wild eyes flicked over the small room's occupants, a group of eight werewolves including Adam, Connie, Theresa, and Barry, the solar engineer, with his wife Amanda.

Parker's jaw clenched. "Only wolves allowed, huh? No *ords*?"

"Stop," Adam hissed. He turned to Connie, who still sat behind her desk, her expression unreadable. "I'm sorry."

"Don't apologize for me!" Parker tugged his arm, and Adam let go.

Adam gritted his teeth, fangs driving at his gums. "Sean and his pack are gone. I thought that's what you wanted!" He lifted his hands and let them drop to his sides. "I don't know what to do. You're letting your anxiety control you!" He regretted it as soon as the words escaped.

Parker jerked as though Adam had slapped him. Before Adam could try to make it better, Parker shouted, "I didn't want Sean to take Jacob with him!"

A heavy, thick silence descended. As Adam tried to make sense of it, Connie stood from behind her desk and quietly asked, "What do you mean?"

"It's pretty self-explanatory," Parker snapped. His face creased, and for an awful, heartrending moment, Adam thought Parker would burst into tears. He reached for him, but Parker squirmed away, voice hoarse. "I shouldn't have confronted him about whatever the fuck is going on with him and Sean."

Theresa stood stock-still, staring at Parker. Her voice was low and urgent. "The accusations you made about Sean last night—those were baseless." She looked to her mother. "You said they were Parker's imagination getting the better of him."

"They were. They are," Connie declared confidently, though for the very first time since Adam had met her, he spotted a sliver of doubt in her eyes. He tasted bile. She ordered, "Find Jacob now. I was going to speak with him this morning, but—"

"You're too late," Parker insisted. "He left Lilly a note."

"He's probably just blowing off steam," Theresa said. "I'll ask Devon—"

"He left his mother's necklace," Parker said.

Adam inhaled sharply. Before he could respond, footsteps thundered toward Connie's office, and Craig appeared in the open doorway, panting and sweaty. He held up a piece of paper, almost crumpled in his hand, as he shouted about Jacob.

Adam moved to Parker, but Parker crossed his arms tightly, shaking his head. As much as Adam wanted to haul him into his arms, kiss and hold him and tell him he was sorry and wrong, he stayed put.

Connie sent two of the werewolves who'd crowded into her office for the meeting out to search for Jacob, and another to radio the *Diana* immediately.

"Why did you call us here this morning?" Adam asked Connie.

Still standing behind her desk, she picked up her "World's Best Grandma" mug. "I wanted to discuss the expedition with a small, trusted group before telling everyone."

Despite everything, Adam's heart soared. He'd proved himself trustworthy enough to be included? There were many other wolves on the island, yet *he* had been granted this privilege? Where was Damian?

Connie held the mug but didn't drink. She put it down. Adam's warm elation dissipated. He'd never seen her so uncertain.

Finally, she said, "The goal is to establish a sister community on the mainland. This island is finite. There's a limit to how many people it can sustain. While there's nothing to worry about now, we must plan for the future."

"You think we're going to run out of food?" Parker had paled, some of his angry, nervous energy visibly draining from his body. Adam ached to touch him.

"There's nothing to worry about now," Connie repeated. "We're being proactive. Theresa and I have been discussing ideas for some time. When Sean and his pack arrived, I decided it was an opportunity to explore the possibilities without putting too many of our numbers at risk."

"You trust him?" Barry asked. He was an older white man with a shock of snowy hair, yet he was still wiry and fit.

"I do," Connie said. Her gaze flicked to Parker. "If Jacob really has left the island with them, I'm sure there's a reasonable explanation."

"There'd better be," Craig bit out. "If he hurts my boy—"

Connie lifted a hand. "I understand. We're all on the same page. I truly believe there's been a misunderstanding of some kind."

"Do you seriously trust him?" Parker demanded. "You've only known him, what? A month? Is this alphas sticking together or something?"

Connie laughed. "Alphas aren't historically known for 'sticking together.' But Sean and I are in complete agreement about working together for all of our sakes."

"What about the rest of his pack in England?" Amanda asked, fiddling with a thread on the sleeve of her tie-dyed dress.

"He performed a rite of separation," Connie answered.

Barry and Amanda shared a significant look, while Parker and Craig looked to Adam. He glanced at Connie, who nodded before he said, "It's what it sounds like. When an alpha leaves their pack, there's a ceremony severing their connection and responsibility." He looked to Connie again. "You told me it was rare?"

"Very."

Over the past few years, Connie had filled in the gaps in Adam's knowledge. Werewolf hierarchy and pack structure wasn't complicated and could vary, but she had told him everything she knew. Which was, of course, much more than the nothing he'd been told by his parents.

"Why would he do that?" Craig asked.

"He has his reasons," Connie said. "Gemma and the others who came here with him chose to make a new start."

Parker muttered, "Maybe he got kicked out because—"

"That will be enough." Connie hadn't raised her voice, and she gazed at Parker evenly. Not glaring or threatening.

Yet everyone in the room stilled, and Adam stepped closer to Parker, the bare skin of their arms brushing. Parker didn't move away this time.

Connie said, "All right, folks. You have questions, and rightfully so. Here it is in a nutshell: You know my daddy had more money than anyone should. He bought this island to be our sanctuary. Our haven, where we could be wolves without fear. He valued privacy."

Theresa snorted. "Mom, that's the understatement of the century."

"Indeed." Connie smiled again, as if lost in a memory. Adam waited, transfixed. He could listen to her talk for hours. Beside him, Parker fidgeted, and Adam wished he could soothe and smooth those sharp edges.

"As Theresa and a few others know, the upshot is that Dad had a compound on the mainland south of Orlando. He made his fortune in plastics, but he loved the land. He funded local agriculture and had his own fields he worked when he retired."

Adam allowed himself a moment of hurt that he hadn't been trusted with this information before.

"Isn't that the Everglades down there?" Craig asked. He still held Jacob's note, but he'd folded it carefully.

"Everglades are farther south," Connie answered. "There's incredibly fertile soil on the shore of Lake Heewoolee, where Dad built the compound. The main crop in the area was sugarcane, but Dad grew squash, tomatoes, beans, peppers, potatoes, and the like. The lake is full of speckled perch and wide-mouthed bass."

"Don't we have enough fish out here?" Amanda asked.

"We have plenty, sure. But for those at the compound, there'd be a local supply. The idea is to create redundancies for the long term. We don't know what the future will bring. We don't know how many new community members might join us here."

"Isn't everyone else pretty much dead by now?" Parker asked. "And we can stop taking newcomers. Stop broadcasting your message. Close the gates." He waved a jittery hand. "You know what I mean."

Connie calmly said, "We still have plenty of room. We aren't overcrowded. But a hurricane could destroy this island next week. Could pollute our groundwater filtration system with saltwater. We've been lucky with the weather, but we can't predict the future. Establishing a base on the mainland makes sense."

"Why didn't you tell all of us about it before?" Adam asked. Had that sounded plaintive? He cleared his throat. "Why wait to establish the redundancies?"

Connie gave him a reassuring smile, and Adam was able to breathe easier. She said, "I kept it under my hat because it's much safer for all of us here on the island. We have far more control. We can prevent infection not only from the creeper virus, but other diseases. I thought patience was prudent. Wait to see how our new world developed. We've had more than enough food and medicine, and we still do. But with Sean's pack arriving, it felt like an opportunity at the right time."

"Do you know the status of the compound now?" Adam asked. "What if it's overrun?"

"I don't know the status, no. We've radioed messages periodically with no reply. Of course, that could just be the wonky signals, though the compound has a more sophisticated radio setup than here. But if the creepers got in, we can clear it out if need be."

Adam flashed back to the desert motel—creepers swarming, teeth tearing his flesh, saying goodbye to Parker. He blindly reached for Parker's hand, sweet relief flowing when Parker threaded their fingers together.

Adam had to ask, "Are we sure werewolves are immune to the virus?"

"As sure as we can be," Connie said. "Anecdotally, from your experience and that of other newcomers in our pack the last few years—and from what Sean's pack reports—there's every reason to believe it's true. The best course of action is always avoidance. We have significant advantages over humans and infected on several levels."

"We should consider going north as well," Amanda said. "What happens to the infected over a subzero winter?"

Connie nodded. "We've heard rumors that the cold does affect them but that they're remarkably resilient. The trade-off is sustainability. How do we feed our people over a long winter? Do we have the skills necessary? Certainly, it can be done, but we're a long way from the snow. If we meant to move our whole community, how would we travel?"

"Mm." Barry stroked his bearded chin. "There are complex logistics to examine. Better to start closer to home."

Connie nodded again. "As I said, this is an exploratory expedition. Very early stages."

"How are they going to get there?" Parker asked. "To this lake? We have no idea what the roads are like, and they don't have a vehicle anyway. What's the transportation plan?"

"Horses are the long-term plan," Connie said. "They're fast, trainable, and they eat grass. We should have plenty of that. And to answer your other question, there's a river flowing from the lake to the ocean." She raised a hand as Parker opened his mouth. "Yes, I know the current will be flowing to the sea. They'll use their boat's engine to travel to the compound. We've hoarded our diesel for important expeditions like this."

With a quiet knock on the door, Kenny squeezed inside the office. "I was told there's a possible problem with the *Diana*? I've tried to raise her on the radio but no luck."

"See?" Parker still held Adam's hand, but he shifted from foot to foot, nervous energy rippling through him. "If Sean wasn't hiding anything, why isn't he answering?"

Kenny frowned. "It's not unusual. The radios have been spotty. I'm sure it's not his fault."

"And why did he run away in the middle of the night?" Parker demanded.

"They were always planning on leaving today," Theresa said. "After your outburst, we decided it was best for everyone if they set sail without fanfare. Unfortunate for Damian and Bethany, who didn't have the chance to say goodbye to their friends."

Adam ran his thumb over Parker's knuckles. If he were anyone else, Parker's grip might break his hand. "They're your representatives?" Adam asked.

"Yes," Connie said. "It will be some time before we hear from them. Again, this is exploration."

"That's all well and good, but can we get back to my son?" Craig demanded. "If he's on that ship, I want him back here *now*."

"Understood." Connie came around her desk to take Craig's hands. He slipped the note into his pocket first. "If Jacob's gone, we'll get him back ASAP."

"I'll find him," Adam said. "I'll leave today."

With an iron grip on Adam's hand, Parker said, "*We'll* find him."

Adam couldn't hide his surprise. "You can't go to the mainland."

Parker's eyes flashed. If he were a wolf, he'd be all golden laser gaze and fangs. "Why the hell not? I've done it before."

"Yes, but—" Adam's skin prickled with the awareness of so many eyes on them. *But your post-traumatic stress is a game changer.* "It's not safe. Let's talk about this privately. We don't even know for sure that Jacob's really gone."

Parker tugged his hand free. "He left Abby's necklace. They're not going to find him holed up on the island."

"I'm going too," Craig said. "Jacob's my responsibility." He swallowed thickly, his voice cracking. "I need to get him back home."

Parker shook his head. "You have to stay with Lilly. This is my fault. I'm going."

Craig nodded reluctantly. Adam said, "Let's talk about it." To Connie, he added, "Excuse us."

"We'll update you when we know more," she said, reaching out to squeeze Adam's shoulder warmly. She stepped toward Parker, but he was already striding from the cabin.

Adam followed, letting Parker march ahead. When they reached the sanctuary of their own cabin, Adam closed the door behind them. Parker paced in front of the saggy blue couch, the old floor creaking under his rapid steps. Adam waited for the barrage of words.

Finally, Parker croaked, "I'm sorry." He still paced.

"I'm sorry too."

"No, you don't get it. It's my fault. I yelled at him. I told him to 'man up.' What does that even mean? It's bullshit. I was mad about Lilly's party and worried that Sean was taking advantage of him. I just wanted him to be safe. I promised Abby, and now I've fucked it all up."

Tears suddenly spilled from Parker's beautiful eyes, and Adam embraced him, wishing he could draw out every ounce of pain and take it for himself. Parker shook his head, his hair tickling Adam's nose.

"I don't deserve this. It's my fault."

"Shh. You do."

"I don't!" He pushed against Adam's chest, and Adam released him. "I was so pissed and worried, and now he's out there alone."

"Damian and Bethany are aboard too." Though that would be cold comfort.

"You'll excuse me if that doesn't fill me with confidence." Parker ran a hand through his hair, which had dried in ragged spikes. "I'm going to get him back. And before you launch into your spiel about how it's not safe for a human, I agree. It's not safe. But I'll lose my fucking mind staying here waiting for you to get back. I'm going with you."

"It's too risky. After what it took for us to get here, you—" He tried to find the right words.

Parker laughed darkly. "Lost it? Trust me, I know. I never, ever want to leave this island again, even if it means starving eventually. I can't even think about what it might be like on the mainland these days. And that's exactly why I have to go."

Adam's head spun. "*No.* That's why you need to stay right

here."

Parker took a shuddering breath, swallowing thickly. "I need to face it. I'm so goddamned scared, Adam. I hate it. Jacob's out there because I pushed him. He's a kid, and I was such an asshole. I can't climb under the covers and let you fix this."

"You can. You *will*. I'm going by myself."

Parker clenched his jaw. "Yeah? Cool, cool. You're going to sail *Bella* on your own? How are you going to get across the Gulf Stream?"

"Uh…" He'd witnessed Parker do it—and it hadn't been easy. As much as he'd learned about sailing on their journey down the coast from Cape Cod, it had been three years. There was no way he could captain a sailboat solo. "I'll take a motorboat."

"You know we're conserving fuel for necessities and emergencies. There's no infinite supply. We're still working on converting more boat engines to solar batteries. Which *Bella* has."

They'd belatedly discovered the solar battery mechanism packed away in a crawlspace in the galley. It had likely been intended as a backup system that had never needed to be used when fuel was abundant.

Adam said, "I'll go with another wolf who can sail. Richard. Or…Dawn! She can sail."

"I'm *going*." The momentary anger seemed to vanish, and fresh tears shone in Parker's eyes.

Adam wanted to lift Parker off his feet, take him to bed, and kiss him until Parker's heart slowed and he could breathe without the little hitching half-sobs that scraped Adam's soul raw.

"Parker, I don't want you to get hurt."

"I have to clean up my mess. I promised Abby—" He sucked in a ragged breath. "I can't fail her. I have to face this. I can't hide forever."

"Hiding from the zombie apocalypse is a sound, logical plan."

Parker swiped at his red eyes. "I mean, yeah. But I need to face reality. You said it yourself: I'm letting my anxiety control me."

Adam shuddered with shame and regret. "I should never have said that. You're traumatized. It isn't your fault. You have PTSD. Of course you're anxious. I'm so sorry." Eyes burning, his throat thickened with emotion. "Please forgive me."

Parker instantly took Adam's hands, threading their fingers together, his generous heart guiding him. Adam loved him so much he could barely breathe.

"I do, I do, I do." Parker's words tumbled out. "Yeah, I'm traumatized. So are you. So is *everyone*. I'm not special."

"Of course you are!"

A ghost of a smile lifted Parker's lips for a moment. "Thank you, baby. But you know what I mean. I have to get over it. I have to…" His fingers twitched, his palms damp.

Adam kept holding on. "'Man up'?"

Parker grimaced. "Well, yeah."

"You just said that's bullshit. And it *is*. That's not how trauma works. And it doesn't matter if we've all been through hell. That doesn't lessen the effect it has on you."

"Yeah, okay. But why am I a basketcase and you can just…move on?"

"Years of experience?" Adam half joked. "And you're not a basketcase." He squeezed Parker's hands gently.

Parker took a deep breath and blew it out loudly through his mouth. "If I stay hiding with my head in the sand, I'm going to snap one day and pull a gun on someone again. I need to prove to myself that I can face the fear. The thought of leaving the island makes me fucking sick. What's left out there terrifies me. And I have to deal with it. If I stay here and wait for you to come back with Jacob, I'll have a nervous breakdown."

Adam knew the truth in what Parker was saying. He could understand the soul-deep need to stand up and fight rather than wait and hide, even if he ached to keep Parker safe and happy and peaceful forever.

Adam said, "I wouldn't be here if it wasn't for you. You're brave and smart and so much stronger than you know. You don't need to prove anything to anyone."

"Except to myself. I love you, but I'm going." Parker smiled crookedly. "My big, bad wolf will protect me, right?"

Adam had to kiss him. Parker moaned—*sobbed*—into his mouth as they kissed deeply until gasping for air.

"Always," Adam whispered, pressing kisses to Parker's flushed cheeks and tasting his salty tears. "Always."

Chapter Eight

"**I**S SHE OKAY down there?" Parker called from the deck of the *Bella Luna*. As they'd crested a small wave in the moonlight, a *thud* had sounded from below.

"Yep!" Adam responded. "The flashlight fell. Mariah's fine."

They'd wrestled Mariah back below deck and wedged her into the second cabin, where she'd stayed during their journey south. A few werewolves hanging around the pier had offered to help, but Parker had stubbornly refused even though he had to admit Adam was doing most of the lifting.

Adam hadn't complained because he was the best boyfriend ever. They might not even be able to use Mariah, depending on road conditions and whatnot—creeper conditions, for example—but they wanted to have her on hand just in case.

Even though they were supposed to share everything on the island, *Bella* was Parker and Adam's space. Sure, Craig, Jacob, and Lilly had shared it with them after Abby was gone, but that was different. Once they'd reached the island, Parker and Adam had gone sailing every so often to get away, never going too far.

That was about to change.

Where he stood at the wheel, Parker gulped from his water bottle and almost lost the cap overboard with his shaky fingers. Adam lunged for the black plastic, catching it just before it disappeared in the depths.

"Thanks." Parker managed to screw on the cap. The skies had cleared, and they'd had fair winds navigating the outer reef as the sun set. When he glanced behind, the lights of Salvation Island were gone.

As they sailed on, they fell easily into their old routine with Parker at the helm and Adam following his instructions when need be. Parker zipped on a hoodie and closed his eyes for a few moments, breathing in the fresh sea air, the smooth deck cold under his bare feet.

When music flowed up from below through the stereo, Parker's heart swelled. They watched movies on the island, and music wasn't uncommon, but he and Adam didn't often put on CDs.

"Is that okay?" Adam called up.

"Yeah. What is it?" Parker didn't recognize it from the collection that had been on *Bella* when they'd found her.

"Old stuff. Dolly Parton and Kenny Rogers." Adam joined him. "This one's called 'Islands in the Stream.' I was cataloging Yolanda's collection, and I remembered this song. Made me think of you."

Parker watched the waves and listened to the lyrics. He grinned. "We *do* got something going on."

Arm around Parker's shoulders, Adam sang along softly about sailing together, relying on each other, and no one coming between them.

"It's kinda perfect," Parker said, tapping the wheel.

"My parents loved Dolly. I used to sing along in the back seat."

For a moment, Parker was in the car on the way to school with his mom and Eric, only able to see the back of their heads as they talked about something boring and grown-up, and the radio played the top forty on repeat.

"Can we hear it again?" Parker asked as the song ended. "I want to learn the words."

They listened three times before turning it off. Then there was only the sound of water slapping the hull and the *shush* of light wind in the sails.

"Probably should keep quiet just in case," Adam said.

"Yeah. It was fun, though." The song looped through his head. "Dolly was quite a prophet. Sailing away to another world. Boy, do I relate to that."

"Mm. Another world," Adam said quietly. Gazing out at the horizon, he leaned against the rail, his feet bare. He still only wore his jeans and tee though the evening was getting chilly. "And now we'll see what's become of the old one."

God, Parker wanted to go back. Steer *Bella* toward home and never, ever risk this unknown. But he had to face it. Yeah, it was bullshit, but he still had to man up.

Why did I have to say that to Jacob?

He cringed, wishing uselessly again that he could take it back. His old friend Jessica would have called it "toxic masculinity."

Parker realized with a dull ache that he hadn't thought of Jess in a long, long time. Had she survived New York City? He remembered her excitement when she'd received her admission letter from NYU. It felt so long ago that her face was weirdly blurry in his mind.

He wiped a spray of saltwater from his cheek, relieved that he was apparently out of tears for the moment. The metal wheel was cool beneath his hands. He gripped it, spreading his toes on the polished deck.

I can do this. I will *do this.*

Adam asked, "The winds are looking good for crossing?"

"So far. We can't wait, so I'll figure it out. Use the motor if we have to, but I'd really rather conserve our battery power for when we need it." For example, trying to outrun whatever assholes would probably be chasing them sooner rather than later.

They'd filled the fuel tank too, just in case. But if the conditions in the Gulf Stream weren't favorable, even motoring across was a huge risk. If the wind blew from the wrong direction, the swells could get enormous without warning.

"If we drown, that's not going to help Jacob," Adam said quietly.

"We're not going to drown. I've got this."

"I know you do, but you can't control the weather."

Parker squeezed the wheel as they dipped over a wave. "Dude, I said I've got this."

"Okay. You should get some sleep. I can keep us steady for a few hours until dawn."

"*Sleep?* As if. My anxiety is raging a little too strongly for that, as you mentioned earlier in front of everyone." He hadn't intended to bite the words out so sharply. He winced.

"I'm sorry." Adam spoke calmly and evenly. Honestly.

"Do you have to be so perfect?" Parker put on a scowl, relaxing his grip on the wheel.

Coming up behind him, Adam wrapped his arms around Parker's waist and kissed the nape of his neck. "You know better than anyone that I'm not perfect."

"Pretty freaking close, buddy. Anyway, you should sleep."

"I'm too worked up."

Parker had to laugh. "Funny way of showing it, Zen werewolf. You know, I could help you with that. Being worked up, I mean." He glanced over his shoulder. "We are on the boat, after all."

Adam's eyes flashed gold in the darkness. "This isn't really the time."

"We live in the zombie apocalypse. Carpe diem and all that." Despite Adam's clear show of interest, Parker faltered. "Unless you're not into it these days? If you don't think I can..." Maybe it was another thing he was failing at these days.

"Oh, I'm into it." Adam's gaze flicked down over Parker's body.

Parker stretched out the fingers on his right hand before clenching into a fist, desire building quickly. He needed this just as much as Adam. "Yeah? I know most of the time you're good with just fucking me."

Adam's brows met. "That doesn't mean I don't want this sometimes." He swallowed audibly.

"I'll shorten sail."

Adam glanced around. "You're sure it's okay?"

"We don't have to worry about shipping lanes anymore. Scan the horizon with your wolfy vision."

With the binoculars, Adam did, moving as necessary to see in all directions. "Clear."

Parker lifted his chin. "Get ready."

Licking his lips, Adam disappeared below, surely going into the head. Parker knew he could be bossy, but Adam didn't argue when it came to this. Parker never fisted him on the island. Adam had refused, only willing when they were alone on the waves, miles away.

It wasn't that he'd make too much noise—Adam could control himself far better than Parker could. Besides, Theresa surely would have been happy to craft another gag if they asked. Parker had asked once if it was because he was ashamed, but Adam had fiercely denied it.

Parker hadn't pushed him, but now, it suddenly occurred to him that Adam could be doing this just to make *Parker* feel better. To help him feel in control.

When Adam finally emerged naked and ready from the head, Parker put down his charts and asked, "Why only here?" He backed into the cabin and stripped off his clothes, kicking them into the corner as he waited for an answer.

Adam seemed to ponder it, not needing to ask what Parker meant. In the silence, water lapped the hull. Finally, he said, "It's safe here."

"Huh? It's way safer on the island. Out here, anything could happen." He quickly added, "Angry mermaids. Coordinated attack by dolphins. They've been waiting to take over." He kept his tone light, especially since he'd just assured Adam everything was okay.

But he couldn't quite hold back his uncertainty and the niggling feelings of inadequacy. The question bubbled out. "Are you sure a werewolf couldn't do this better for you?" He motioned toward Adam's butt. "Give you more?"

Adam's eyebrows shot up. "Haven't we had this discussion in the past? You think I'd let just anyone stick their hand up my ass? Besides which, I *don't want anyone else.* Werewolf, human, merman, or yet to be determined."

"No, I know. I'm not—maybe I am. Sorry. I just hate to think of you giving up anything you really want for me."

"Of course I'm giving up things I want for you."

Parker's stomach dropped. *Fuck.* He shouldn't have brought it up. Why did he always have to open his stupid mouth?

"I want the coffee pot to be scrubbed out every morning. I want all wet towels to be hung up *immediately* and not five hours later. I want—"

"Come on, not stupid shit like that." Still, Parker had to laugh, relief warm and heady in his veins. "The towels get dry eventually. And hold on, let's talk about your penchant for leaving hair in the sink when you trim your beard."

Adam's lips quirked. "Guilty." He grew serious. "And I love fucking you. I love what we do together. The fact that you let me fuck you when I'm transformed—no, that's the wrong word. You don't 'let' me—you crave it. Demand it. Don't you know how powerful that is?"

Parker swallowed with a *gulp*, his eyes locked with Adam's.

"And when you fist me, it's…everything I want. And I like it on the boat because you're in charge here. You're the captain. It's the safest place we could be."

Adam answered so seriously, so damn sweetly, that Parker had to kiss him and kiss him and kiss him some more, tasting a hint of coffee as they rubbed together. After the shit show of a day and all his failures, he let himself revel in taking charge. This? This, he could control. This, he wasn't going to screw up.

He pushed Adam onto the bed, and Adam toppled willingly despite being a million times stronger. And *fuck*, that made Parker hard as hell.

On his back, Adam scooted to the very edge and held his meaty thighs open. He moaned as Parker dropped to his knees on the worn wood and lapped at his ass. The clean, textured flesh still tasted earthy, and Parker loved the way Adam's hole puckered as he flicked it with his tongue. Hair tickled his cheeks.

"God, Parker," Adam gritted out. "You're so good at that."

He ran his hands over Adam's spread thighs and grinned. "You know I have a talented tongue." He lapped at Adam's heavy, hairy balls, then pushed his tongue into Adam's hole.

"Fuck!"

Parker ate his ass, Adam's moans and shaking legs turning him on even more. Adam was totally at his mercy, and Parker was tempted to make him come quickly like this to give the release Adam was begging for…

No. They both needed more.

Adam's back arched, and he cried out as Parker thrust his lubed fist inside without warning. He'd have been way too afraid to do that when they'd first started experimenting, but after a few years, he knew what to do. He trusted that Adam's werewolf physiology meant he truly didn't need prep. Didn't *want* it.

Adam craved the fullness, and his healing ability meant his body would quickly accommodate. Parker didn't hesitate, pumping his arm as he fist fucked Adam mercilessly, watching with satisfaction as Adam's hard cock strained. He'd only used a bit of lube, and Adam's passage was tight around him as he pushed deeper.

Adam's mouth was open and his eyes were closed, his big body bent in half as he groaned in time with Parker's thrusts. Parker hadn't put down a cushion for his knees, but he couldn't stop now. Wouldn't stop, enjoying the bite of discomfort.

He was elbow-deep now, and even though he knew that some regular humans did things like this, he always marveled at seeing his arm disappear inside Adam. Never wanting to hurt him but trying to provide the friction and pressure he craved.

Sweat dripped down Parker's spine, and he tasted salt on his upper lip. "Feel full?"

"*Yes*," Adam gasped. "So good."

Parker carefully flexed his fingers inside Adam. "You ready to come for me, baby?" he rasped.

Adam *whined*, and god, Parker lived for that sound. He was already shuddering through waves of what Parker called his ass orgasms, which Adam described as not as forceful as a traditional orgasm, but just as intense. When they'd first started fisting, Adam wouldn't be hard despite the pleasure. Now, he strained for release, his cock flushed.

Parker burned to jerk his own rock-hard dick with his free hand, but this wasn't about him. He kissed Adam's trembling thighs. He wished he could get Adam's cock in his mouth, but he couldn't quite reach with his arm inside.

He didn't need to though, Adam practically levitating off the mattress as he came with a shout. His ass relaxed so much that Parker was able to ease out smoothly, reaching for the bowl of soapy water Adam had put out.

He barely had a chance to dry his hand before he was being hoisted in the air straight up from the floor, Adam's hands powerful around his waist. Adam stretched back on the bed, lifting Parker right over his face. Towel clutched in his fingers, Parker planted his hands on the mattress and fucked Adam's willing, slick, incredible mouth.

Adam's fingers dug into Parker's waist, urging him on as his hips snapped into the wet heat, Adam taking him amazingly deep. Parker was desperate to come, his balls tight, words spilling out.

"Oh, fuck. So good. Love you, baby. Don't stop. I don't want to stop. Don't want it to end. But I need this. Need you, please... *Please*."

Parker wasn't sure what he was saying as he shot down Adam's throat. He shook and babbled, Adam sucking out every drop until Parker had to tell him to stop.

Gently, Adam lifted him up and laid him on his side, rolling over to nuzzle and stroke him. They panted, little gusts of warm air between their mouths.

"We don't have to go," Adam whispered.

For a wonderful, terrible moment, Parker yearned to take the out. He wanted to leap up, trim the sails, and point *Bella* back to Salvation Island as fast as the sea would take them. They could go home, and someone else could chase down Jacob.

Exhaling, Parker pressed their lips together. "We do. *I* do."

"I'll protect you."

"Big bad wolf mode activated?"

Taking Parker's face in his rough hands, Adam held his gaze, his eyes glowing gold. He kissed Parker slowly, deeply, and they drifted on the current for just a little longer.

Chapter Nine

"OKAY. OKAY," PARKER muttered to himself as he trimmed the sail.

Adam stood nearby, bracing as they rolled in a swell, staying close if Parker needed help but out of his way at the same time. Parker had talked to himself almost constantly during the endless hours of navigating the Gulf Stream.

Which had taken three endless days after they'd had to turn back repeatedly.

The wind had started blowing from the northeast at twenty knots according to Parker as they'd neared the stream, waves crashing higher and higher. The sea had changed so quickly—swells transforming to steep-sided breaking waves that seemed to Adam to come from every direction.

They both wore sunglasses and baseball caps now against the late-afternoon glare, and Adam could see the back of Parker's neck was turning pink. He squeezed a dollop of sunscreen from the tube in the storage console by the wheel and beckoned him.

Parker winced as Adam smoothed the cream over his hot skin. "You can't see anything yet?" Parker asked, turning his head side to side, on high alert.

"Not yet. Stop moving."

"Sorry." Parker lowered his head, taking a few breaths while Adam gently rubbed in the cream. "I think we're through, so we should see land soon unless I royally fucked up."

"You didn't." Adam rubbed his shoulders, dipping his hands

under the cotton of Parker's T-shirt. After two attempts and retreats, they'd managed on the third try when the wind had shifted, although it had been tense work to stay vigilant in the choppy waves.

It was only a few minutes before Adam did spot land in the distance. He peered through the binoculars. "Lots of buildings. Condos on the beach. Daytona?"

"No, our course took us north. It might be St. Augustine." He had a turn with the binoculars. "I can't see it yet. We're just lucky as hell the wind changed today. But Jacob could be anywhere by now." His voice went hoarse. "We're so far behind."

"We'll find him. We know where they're headed." Adam scanned around them as they sailed closer. No other ships in sight. No smoke or signs of chaos from land. It was only the two of them and the faithful, merciless sun. They'd tried to reach *Diana* by radio, but there was only static.

"Too bad your wolfy sense of smell can't track them."

"Miles and miles over the ocean? Afraid not. I wouldn't be able to track you over open water, let alone anyone else."

"It's weird," Parker said after a minute. "Last time, shit was on fire. When you came on that supply run, was it still the same as it had been?"

The boat rolled over a swell, and Adam inhaled the briny air deeply, trying to banish the flare of guilt at how he'd found Parker when he'd returned from that trip. It had been years now, but he had to reach out and run his hands over Parker's back. Had to touch to remind himself that Parker was okay and that they were together, and Adam wouldn't let anything happen to him.

Finally, he answered, "Yeah, it was the same on that run." He inhaled deeply again now, but only smelled the sea, fresh and alive all around them. "There were dead everywhere on the beach then."

Parker swallowed hard. "Yeah. I remember."

Adam took the binoculars back and scanned as they slowly approached, Parker handling the sails and making sure they didn't get too close.

"It looks…deserted," Adam said.

"Not sure if that's good news or bad."

"Me either. I guess it's true that they've become largely nocturnal."

"Wait, what?" Parker took off his hat, running a hand through his sweaty hair. "Since when? They go toward the light."

Parker had never wanted to hear the snatches of information they learned after arriving on the island, and it frustrated Adam even though he'd envied the coping mechanism.

"Dude." Parker held out his hands briefly before taking the wheel again.

"Yes, they've always been drawn to the light, but in the darkness. Bright or flashing lights in the dark attract them in a way that sunlight doesn't."

"Like bugs? You know, moths or whatever. They come out at night and go for the lights. That's why my parents had those ugly bug zapper thingies in the backyard. Mom insisted on the ones that looked like old-fashioned lanterns, but they were still ugly if you ask me."

"Right." He thought of the creepers with their bulging eyes and chattering teeth, that horrible hum coming from within them, the rictus claws their outstretched hands had locked into. "There's an…insect quality to the creepers."

Parker shuddered. "Definitely."

"Sean said they've taken to staying inside much of the daytime in his experience, although they *can* come out. And will, if we're not careful."

"Huh. When did Sean say that?"

"I'm not sure," Adam answered carefully. "Pretty soon after he arrived."

Parker was quiet for so long that Adam had relaxed into the rhythm of the waves again when Parker blurted, "Did you ask him to help you fully shift?"

Adam blinked. "No, though I was tempted to ask him more questions. When I first saw him, on the deck of the *Diana*... He made me think about transforming fully."

"Okay," Parker said. "Why?"

He pondered it. "Something about his...aura."

"Big wolf energy?"

"I suppose so. I know you're going to make a joke about his dick now."

Hand to his chest, Parker drawled, "*Moi?* I would never."

Adam waited with eyebrows raised.

"Okay, but seriously, the guy is *hung*. Is that an alpha thing? No, it can't be—you're not an alpha and you're huge."

Adam shook his head, smiling.

"By the way, incredible restraint in not asking me how your dicks compare."

Yanking Parker against him, Adam ground against his ass. "I haven't heard any complaints yet."

Parker laughed. "Are you kidding? If you were bigger, I'd never walk straight again." He wriggled as Adam slid his hand under Parker's T-shirt and across his belly. "That tickles!"

They wrestled playfully, Adam of course not using even a fraction of his strength. Then a thought occurred, and he asked, "Why?"

Parker knew what he meant. "Just something he said about shifting. I don't trust him."

"I'm not sure I do either."

Parker exhaled noisily. "You're not *sure*? I mean, we're here because he took Jacob with him. It's fucked up. He's sixteen years old, and he has no idea what he's doing."

"I agree. I just can't imagine Sean voluntarily taking Jacob with him. Why would he invite such a huge complication?"

"Because he gets off on power dynamics?" Parker adjusted the wheel, peering up at the sails and muttering about wind direction.

"It's possible."

"It's not like Jacob could sneak aboard without a boat full of werewolves knowing, right?"

"Unlikely," Adam had to admit. Even if Parker's suspicions were true, the risk seemed far too big. If the idea was Sean and his pack establishing a sister community, why begin on that note? Unless Sean had no intention of following through on the commitment he'd made to Connie.

"Aren't they, like, starving?" Parker asked contemplatively.

It took a moment for Adam to shift gears and realize he meant the creepers. "You'd think so." There was so much Adam hadn't considered or thought to ask. Maybe he'd been sticking his head in the sand too.

"Tacking—get on the winch!" Parker had snapped into action, all business.

As Parker focused completely on captaining their boat, Adam followed orders. Once they could relax again, he pulled out his camera and zoomed in on Parker, loving the easy confidence that flowed through him.

Barry had helped him rig a solar charger for the battery so he could keep filming long term. He should have left the camera on the island, but he hadn't been able to resist. Watching Parker barefoot at the wheel, the wind in his hair and—*yes, there it was*—an undeniable smile, Adam was grateful he could capture the moment.

"I missed this," Adam said after turning off his camera. "Sailing, I mean. *Really* sailing."

Parker inhaled and exhaled deeply, his eyes on the water. "Me too. I wish it could just be like this."

Adam watched the tension return to Parker's body like a wave crashing over him. Back to business, he ordered, "Keep an eye out." He put his cap back on and bustled about, tying a knot with nimble fingers. After a few minutes, his brow creased. "What? You're staring."

"I like watching you."

Parker laughed, but his heart skipped, his face flushing. "I still need to concentrate. Don't give me any ideas."

"But you have such wonderful ideas."

A smile tugged on Parker's lips. "Maybe we can take an overnight sail sometime? Head down near the Bahamas for a few days. Once we're back home and this is over, I mean." His smile faded.

"I'd like that."

First, they'd have to handle *this*, whatever it might entail. Adam turned his gaze back to the ghostly condo towers, searching for signs of life and not sure what he hoped to find.

"IS THAT A 'Z'?" Parker asked, peering through the binoculars in the fading light. "Painted on that house."

Adam followed Parker's finger as he pointed. "Yeah. It is."

They stared at the jagged slashes of red paint on gray clapboard. The house was surrounded by overgrown grass and plants, a concrete walkway already cracking.

"Like…for Zechariahs?" Parker asked quietly.

"Maybe."

They shared a glance. Gulls cried distantly, and the mainsail fluttered. Parker adjusted it, and they continued on in silence until Parker asked, "Do you think we'll ever really know who or what caused this?"

Adam kept his voice low. It seemed right to be…solemn somehow. "No. Whether it was terrorism or just nature going haywire. I don't think we'll ever know definitively. If this were a movie, someone with all the answers would show up and fill in the blanks."

"Right. What's that called? A 'deus ex machina'?"

Adam smiled. "You *were* paying attention in film class."

Parker chuckled. "Sorry, I think I picked that up in English lit in high school." He ran his fingertips over the wheel, his gaze distant. "But yeah, I think you're right. I guess that's why I don't like thinking about it. What's the point? It is what it is."

Where the river met the sea, the water turned brackish. Under motor now with the sails down, Parker steered them through the wide, flat estuary after examining the map. There was still no sign of life—human, that was. Or werewolf. Herons and storks peeked out from the tall grasses near the shore as they sailed inland.

It was a substantial river. Wider than Adam expected. "Are there alligators here?" he asked as they slowly passed seemingly abandoned houses with docks. Trees and foliage grew thicker as they traveled away from the ocean, though not particularly tall. The motor only operated on low using the battery power. Slow and steady.

At the wheel, Parker fiddled with his sunglasses where he'd hung them on the collar of his shirt as night deepened. "Definitely." His gaze darted around even as he yawned.

"You're smudging the lenses." Adam held out his hand, and Parker passed over the sunglasses. Polishing them on his shirt, Adam suggested, "We should stop for the night," knowing what Parker would say.

"We need to make up time. If it hadn't taken me so long to get through the Gulf Stream—"

"It didn't 'take you so long.' You can't control the direction of the wind. Didn't you tell me that before, people would wait a week or more sometimes before crossing? That they'd examine the weather reports, which don't exist anymore?"

"Yeah, but..." Parker gripped the wheel. Clouds scattered the sky, moving in front of the moon. Adam could still see the tendons in Parker's neck. "Sean made it."

"So we assume. In a much bigger, more powerful boat. Even if we'd motored across, the waves were too big for *Bella*. We can't do anything for Jacob from the bottom of the ocean."

"We probably wouldn't make it to the bottom. We'd get eaten and ripped apart way before that."

Adam had to roll his eyes. "You know what I mean. Is it safe to drop anchor here?"

Parker shrugged. "We need to keep going. According to Connie and the map, the river's about fifty miles long. We're only going four-point-five knots under power with the sails down, but it's too hard to sail against the current, even if the wind was on our side."

"But is it safe to drop anchor? We're no good to Jacob exhausted."

Parker seemed like he was going to argue, but sighed. "Yeah. I'll find a place. I guess sleep makes sense."

Adam hugged him from behind, kissing the back of his neck, the skin still sun-warm.

IT WAS HOURS later when the howl tore through Adam's consciousness.

The sound was miles away, yet it pulsated inside Adam's head. He leapt out of bed in a single movement, grateful that Parker slept on. Curled on his side with lips parted, he breathed deeply, his heart beating steadily. Adam hoped he wasn't even dreaming and was lost in the sweet abyss of truly restful, overdue sleep.

Naked, he waited, but Parker didn't so much as murmur or shift an inch.

Up on deck, the boat bobbing in the river's current, anchored a hundred feet from the western shore, Adam peered intently. He held his breath.

The howl echoed again through the thick foliage.

As a fist squeezed his heart, Adam squinted into the mix of palm trees and laurel oak. It required every ounce of his strength not to dive straight into the water and swim desperately for shore to answer the child's call.

Every instinct in him ached—*burned*—to help, to ease the suffering of this fellow werewolf. Not just a werewolf, but a pup. This was a child suffering. He wasn't sure how he knew. The thin, hoarse quality of the howl could have come from an adult, but he *knew*. That this was a child in need resonated deep in the marrow of his bones.

In the years on Salvation Island, he'd never, ever heard a howl like this one. He wanted to weep with agony—yet slash with his claws and bare his fangs all at once.

Over his pounding heart, he listened. Parker still slept below, out cold after the days of sleep deprivation and stress on the water. If Adam woke him, Parker would either talk him out of going or insist on coming along.

In the forest in the dead of night, even if he could get her to shore, Mariah would be cumbersome and too loud. In the chaos before the island, there had been noise all around. Now, it truly was a new world. They hadn't even spotted a creeper yet.

Another howl brought him to his knees, his vision turning gold, compulsion overpowering him. Parker was asleep and safe, and Adam would be back before he woke. He had to go, and Parker was far safer on *Bella.*

He *had* to go.

This pull was a thousand times stronger than Connie's voice on the radio beckoning them to Salvation Island. That had been like a song he didn't quite know the words to, yet couldn't get out of his head, the refrain repeating on a loop.

This was a chainsaw splintering his spine.

His dive off *Bella*'s bow took him halfway to shore, arcing through the air with a burst of supernatural power. He reached the reeds by the shore with only a few strokes and was already running, running, running, naked and wet.

A dirt road slithered through the trees. Perhaps he could have ridden Mariah after all, but it didn't matter. Parker was safe, and Adam had to keep going, the compulsion throbbing through every muscle and tendon.

He'd shifted, his claws and fangs extended, hair thicker on his body, his senses deeper. He strained. He was so, so close to the final form. If he could only tap into whatever instinct was responding to this howl, he could push harder and lunge across the finish line.

Almost there…

The howl was a plea—yet his instincts responded as if it were a command. If only Adam could be worthy to answer. Shame made him stumble in the dry scrub, his muscles growing heavy, nausea rising. *No!* He had to focus. He had to shift completely. This was the moment. If not now, when?

He fought with every ounce of will and energy, so close, so close, so close…

In full wolf form, he could race past the abandoned cabins and trailers at double time. He'd never known the joy of running on four legs. The *completion*.

A sob choked him. What was wrong with him? Why was he like this?

It was torture to be on the precipice of true transformation. Heartbreakingly close yet still out of grasp. His jaw was about to snap, and—

He stumbled again and focused on his surroundings through the golden filter of his werewolf eyes. The chattering hum of creepers filled his ears for the first time in years, their rancid smell burning his nose.

But the movement in his peripheral vision was too low. It didn't make any sense. It surged like a river, and Adam realized too late what the creepers were eating.

In the faint moonlight, thousands of eyes reflected, the ground a writhing carpet of rats.

Adam swiped at his bare legs with his claws, slowing his frantic pace as rats climbed his shins. His nose stung and eyes watered from a strange odor like ammonia.

Creepers swarmed closer. They wore only remnants of clothes, their cadaverous bodies those of ghouls. Adam fought against the current of rats and creepers as another distant howl echoed, an invisible chain yanking him farther and farther—

Farther from Parker.

How did I get here?

Now it was Adam howling, tasting metal as he sliced his tongue, clenching every fiber of muscle to stop running and overpower the vicious undertow wrenching him away from Parker. Rats streamed up his legs, and he slashed at them.

Go back!

Rail-thin creepers surrounded him, their huge eyes bulging, clawed fingers tearing. With a roar, Adam cleared a path, escaping the horde of rats and creepers by leaping high into the branches of a tree. The world that had seemed eerily empty in the daylight now teemed with life—with violence and death and a primal fight for survival.

Another howl.

Screaming, bark scraping his bare flesh, Adam clung to the tree trunk, fighting the command to keep running until he found the wolf. The gold-tinged world spun around him, and he dug his claws into the tree.

No! Stay with Parker. Go back, go back, go back!

He had to help the child, but he couldn't leave Parker. He

wouldn't. Squeezing his eyes shut, he clung to the tree while the tidal wave of creepers and rats surged below. Adam prayed to the godless night that this was a terrible dream and he'd wake with Parker sleeping safe in his arms.

Chapter Ten

"YOU LET ME sleep too long," Parker mumbled as he rolled over and stretched his arms above his head.

He'd known before blinking awake that the other side of the bed was empty. Through the open cabin door near his feet, the galley was still. Adam had to be on deck, tiptoeing around in the dawn, being the most considerate and sweet boyfriend ever.

"Morning," Parker said, knowing Adam would hear him. He waited for Adam to call down a greeting.

Silence.

Frowning, Parker pushed himself up. They had to get moving to find Jacob. He rubbed his face, yawning as he padded to the head and pissed. Scratching his ass, he yawned again and tugged on his briefs and cargo shorts. Adam's jeans and tee were still folded on the port-side shelf where he'd left them, his boots in the corner.

"Baby, you want coffee?"

Silence.

Unease slithered around Parker's spine. Abandoning the cold coffee pot, he climbed up top. It only took a glance to see that the deck was empty.

Still, Parker called out, "Adam!"

He has to be swimming.

Lunging to the railing, Parker called Adam's name again as he scanned the flat surface of the river. Mist hung low over the water and would soon burn away in the glare of the rising sun. Parker circled the deck, eyes roving desperately for any sign.

"Adam!"

The dinghy was secure in its rack at the stern. He raced back below deck, practically jumping down the stairs. He wrenched open the pocket door on the second cabin, at first relieved to see Mariah's shiny red chrome before dread slammed through him.

If Adam hadn't taken Mariah—not that he could jump her to shore—and he hadn't taken the dinghy...

Where was he?

"Where the fuck, where the fuck?" Parker muttered, his pulse galloping and palms clammy as he searched every possible hiding place, knowing full well that Adam would never hide. This wasn't some cruel game.

Still, he searched. It was better than standing still and screaming.

On deck, he paced *Bella*'s length, willing Adam to appear from the forest. How could he have disappeared? Where? Why?

What if he's gone forever?

Racing to starboard, Parker puked into the river, the metal railing digging into his stomach. He heaved and coughed, fighting down a sob. He couldn't break down. He had to be strong. There had to be an explanation.

Adam would never leave me.

Bare feet slapping the wood, Parker paced. How long had he been gone? The mattress had been cold, and there'd been no note waiting in the galley in Adam's neat, tight handwriting. Though Parker had slept wonderfully deep and long, he'd have heard a struggle.

Even if an intruder had somehow crept aboard and shot Adam with a tranquilizer like at the Pines, Adam would have had at least ten seconds to wake up and fight. He wasn't a baby that could be snatched from its cradle and whisked off into the night. He was *heavy*. There was zero chance Parker could have slept through a scenario where Adam was kidnapped.

Could I?

Fuck, why had he been so tired? If it hadn't taken so damn long to make the crossing—

Something splashed near shore, and Parker squinted in the soft light. All he could see were trees and tall weeds, lily pads growing in clusters. There was no breeze, and sweat dampened his brow.

Could werewolves fight off an alligator?

"Of course. He's fine. Alligators would be no match. He's fine. He went... He went somewhere, and I'm sure he had a good reason even though I'm going to murder him when he gets back."

An egret on long, spindly legs watched Parker from the marshy shoreline. Alligators weren't really interested in humans, right? Crocodiles, yes, but alligators didn't usually attack people.

"Fuck, I miss Google."

He stared intently. Had something moved? Was it Adam? Was he hurt? What was he doing? Why did he go? Where? How? *Why?* Parker grabbed the radio communicator and put out another message to Sean or *anyone*.

Static.

He turned the dial, listening for any chatter.

Static.

"Come back, come back, come back." He chanted the words like a prayer.

Parker whirled and checked the river behind him, suddenly remembering how Shorty and his crew—*Bethany holding a shotgun, having the nerve to fucking* smile *at him*—had snuck up when he'd been distracted.

The river was empty under the pale blue sky but for birds and whatever lurked below the placid surface.

"He must have had a good reason to go ashore and not leave a note. It's fine. Everything's fine."

Breathing deeply, Parker closed his eyes and tried to draw the box in his mind. Everything was fine.

He was sitting on his rock after his morning swim. Soon, he'd eat breakfast with Lilly, Craig, Jacob, and Adam. Scrambled eggs and grilled fish and a juicy orange. Adam would kiss him goodbye before they went to do gardening or laundry or teaching, and Parker would see him again at lunch…

With the bitter acid of vomit still in his throat, he checked the forest. Still empty. Parker would have given almost anything to will them back to Salvation Island and its familiarity and routine. Why had he fucked up with Jacob so badly? Why was Sean a fucking liar?

"Where the fuck is Adam?" he shouted, sending a few birds flapping from a tree.

He examined the options.

One: Row the dinghy to shore and search on foot, not knowing on which side of the river Adam might have gone. They were closer to the western side, so he'd start there.

Two: Drag Mariah up from below somehow, get her into the dinghy without Adam's super-strength, row her to shore—again not knowing for certain which side to go to—and search for Adam without draining the solar battery too much.

Three: Take *Bella* up and down the river searching.

Four: Stay put and wait for Adam to get back.

Option four made the most sense by far. The odds that Parker would even be able to get Mariah up the stairs without Adam were slim to none. If he moved *Bella*, Adam might return and not be able to find him.

Parker had learned at Camp Weepecket all those years ago that if you got lost in the woods to sit down and stay put and let the searchers come to you. With all Adam's wolfy senses, he could find Parker much more easily.

"Four. Four is the most logical. There's no question."

The problem with option four was that it meant doing nothing but waiting. It was torture to just stay there and scan the water and trees endlessly, waiting and hoping. Praying.

"Come back, come back, come back," he muttered.

Every minute lasted an eternity as Parker waited powerlessly. The sun rose higher, and he desperately wanted to rewind and fix whatever had gone wrong. He'd gone to sleep with the familiar weight of Adam spooned behind him, and if he could only go return there somehow, it would be okay. This had to be a nightmare. It couldn't be real.

When Adam finally appeared from the trees a hundred feet up the shore, Parker's knees wobbled, sweet, pure relief flooding him even as he blinked in confusion. Was Adam...naked? In the woods? "What the fuck?"

Before Parker could even call out, Adam was swimming back to *Bella*. Parker met him at the stern ladder, offering a hand, joy coursing through him as he felt Adam's warm, still-alive grasp.

"Where did you go?" Parker rasped, his throat thick as he yanked Adam into a hug.

"I'm getting you wet."

"Jesus, I don't give a shit!" Parker rubbed his cheek against Adam's furry chest, pressing kisses to his collarbones. Adam's arms were iron around him.

"Are you okay?" Parker peered at him. Adam's eyes seemed slightly glazed. "Where the hell were you?"

"I'm fine."

The cocktail of endorphins, anxiety, terror, and relief had Parker vibrating. He stepped back, hands on his hips. "Well?" he demanded.

"I'm sorry." Adam didn't meet Parker's gaze. "I thought I'd be back before you woke up."

"Back from *where*?" Parker punctuated the last word with a slash of his hands through the air.

"I..." Adam's brow furrowed. "I don't know."

"What? You took off butt naked in the middle of the night and you don't know where?" His heart stuttered. "What's going on?"

Adam immediately pulled him into a hug, rubbing his back slowly. "Don't worry. I'm okay."

Parker let himself cling to Adam and inhale his familiar scent even though they were both wet with river water. Parker didn't care. He had half a mind to lift Adam's arm and shove his face in his armpit the way Adam did to him.

"You scared me," he whispered. "Why did you do that?"

"I'm so sorry, sweetheart. I don't know." Adam pressed little kisses to Parker's ear and head.

Parker drew back. "Why do you keep saying you don't know? Were you sleepwalking? Sleep-swimming?"

"I don't know." Adam looked back to shore. He shuddered.

"You're officially freaking me out, dude. And I was already plenty fucking freaked out from waking up to find you gone without a trace. Just *gone*. You couldn't have left a note?"

Adam's face creased with pain, and he cupped Parker's cheeks with his rough hands. "I'm so sorry." He pressed their lips together softly.

Parker's eyes burned. "I don't understand," he whispered, roaming his hands over Adam's damp skin, needing to touch, touch, touch.

"There was a howl. Another wolf. A child. Honestly, it did feel like sleepwalking." His voice went hoarse. "I've never felt compelled like that."

Parker took a deep, long breath. "Okay, let's sit down. You need water. *Sit*. No arguments."

He ducked below to fill a bottle from their water supply and was relieved to find Adam sitting on the bench when he got back. "Here." He'd also brought a towel, which he rubbed over Adam's damp skin.

Adam drained the bottle, and Parker went to refill it with shaking hands. When he returned, Adam had wrapped the towel around his waist. It was an orange beach towel with bright pink daisies that contrasted the dark hair on Adam's legs.

This time, Adam sipped from the bottle, and Parker perched beside him. "That's it, baby. It's okay." His own mouth was dry, worry gnawing his gut. He could still faintly taste vomit. If he didn't know better, he'd think Adam was hungover, but there wasn't any of Salvation Island's moonshine aboard, and his tolerance was extremely high.

Parker asked, "You said there was a howl? It was a kid? Are you sure?" He listened carefully as Adam explained the overpowering need to find the wolf. "Sounds like the perfect trap to me."

"We don't know that. Don't be—" Adam broke off.

Jaw clenching, Parker inhaled deeply through his nose. "Are you seriously about to call me paranoid? Because I think anything that lures you into running through the woods naked in the middle of the night is suspicious!"

Adam covered Parker's fisted hand, his palm warm and heavy. "You're right. I'm sorry."

Parker exhaled and turned his hand, threading their fingers together. "It's okay. It was just, like, my worst nightmare to wake up and you were gone. Vanished without a trace. What if I never saw you again?"

"If I'd woken and it was you missing…" Adam shuddered. "I'm sorry." He lifted Parker's hand and pressed a dry kiss to his skin, his beard scratching. "I've never encountered anything like this. A biological pull, like I *had* to respond to help this pup in need."

He continued relaying what he'd experienced, and Parker was unable to keep in his, "Ugh!" when Adam got to the part about the rats. "I guess rats and creepers will inherit the night if not the Earth, huh?"

Adam said, "Seems that way."

"And you couldn't find the kid? You couldn't tell where it was coming from? You're usually really good with direction."

"They might have been moving. But I stopped following. I knew I'd gone too far, and I had to get back to you. I climbed a tree and closed my eyes. Hung on and fought the urge. I thought of you and tried to block it out."

The image of Adam naked in a tree, fighting an overpowering biological instinct so he could return made Parker's breath catch. He caressed Adam's damp hair. "Thank you, baby. Thank you for coming back as soon as you could."

Adam squeezed Parker's fingers. "It took me long enough to figure out how to get back to you."

"But you're so good with directions and smelling stuff."

"The rats complicated the trail. Their odor is…pungent."

Parker grimaced. "Makes sense. This howl—do you think it had something to do with Sean's pack?"

"I'm not sure. There could be another pack here. Or an orphaned child. Anything's possible. Whoever it was, they were in trouble. Or it was a trap."

"Yeah." The pit in Parker's stomach grew deeper. "Did the creepers look the same?"

"Thinner." Adam shook his head. "Still fast though. Strong. Their bulging eyes seem about to pop out of their skulls. Hair matted and long."

"So, just as terrifying. Great to hear. Did any of them get close to you?"

He nodded. "The swarm was powerful. I might have been bitten when I was climbing the tree. I'm not sure."

Parker automatically slid onto his knees on the polished deck and ran his hands over Adam's legs even though he healed so quickly any bite marks would be long gone. He examined Adam's shins, the hair scattered there tickling his palms. Pushing higher, he slipped his hands under the towel to stroke Adam's thick thighs.

"If I was bitten…" Adam shook his head. "We should keep our distance from each other. Just in case. I shouldn't have kissed you."

"Abso-fucking-lutely not." Parker dug his fingers into Adam's legs. "We did that before, and it was the worst. It would break me now."

Adam still frowned. "I worry."

Parker tried to joke. "That's my job, remember?" He dropped the lighter tone. "Look, if they bit you and you're somehow not immune anymore, you'd be eating my face by now. And yeah, the virus could have mutated or whatever—who the hell knows how any of it works. Baby, I can't worry about that. There's too much else going on. I need you." He motioned between them. "I need this. Or I'll break."

Adam caressed Parker's hair. "I know."

"You were immune before. You're not even positive you were bitten last night. We seriously have enough to worry about, okay?" At Adam's nod, Parker exhaled slowly. "Okay. No more howling? I haven't heard anything, but it might be too far for my ears. Though I guess you'd be freaking out if you could hear it?"

"Yes. It stopped before dawn."

Parker sat on his heels, still rubbing circles on Adam's thighs. "How long were you out there?"

"I'm honestly not sure." Adam turned to peer into the trees as if they'd give him an answer.

"You sure you're okay?" Though the rising sun was warm already, he wanted to hustle Adam below and wrap him in blankets.

Memories of the Pines invaded Parker's mind—Adam unconscious and helpless, chunks of his flesh being harvested, cut after cut after cut. He actually wasn't sure how many cuts there had been, but in his memory, they were endless.

"I'm sure." Adam smoothed a hand over Parker's bed head. "I'm sorry I put you through that." His nostrils flared. "If anything had happened to you—"

"I'm okay. You know, except for having a nervous breakdown when I realized you were gone." He tried to laugh.

Face creasing, Adam bent and pressed their foreheads together, his whisper warm on Parker's lips. "I should never have left you."

"You came back. You fought it. You fought for me." He spread his fingers on Adam's hips. "That's what matters."

They kissed, and Parker worried Adam would taste the puke residue, but if he did, he didn't seem to care. They had to get moving and find Jacob, but Parker needed this first. He needed to stroke Adam's tongue with his own and sigh into his kisses.

Adam's here with me. He came back. He's real.

He climbed onto Adam's lap, the towel soft between them. Adam's strong arms locked around Parker's back. Parker sighed into their kiss before they faced the world again.

An hour later, he was profoundly grateful for those stolen minutes when *Bella*'s motor sputtered and died.

Chapter Eleven

"THE PROBLEM WITH the zombie apocalypse is that you can't look on Mechanic Tube for how-to videos." Parker ran his palm over the smooth top of the stern. "It's not your fault, hon."

Adam had to smile at the tender tone Parker used. He had such a good heart. A wave of fierce love gripped him, and he lifted Parker off his feet in an embrace.

"Whoa! Easy there, big guy." Parker laughed, squeezing Adam back.

He *loathed* that he'd left Parker alone in the night. That he'd abandoned him to wake to a terrifying, baffling nightmare. Adam nuzzled Parker's hair now and inhaled his scent deeply. It grounded him. He needed Parker by his side more than ever.

"Um, you should probably put me down so we can come up with plan B."

Adam wanted nothing more than to carry Parker close to his heart to keep him safe, but it wasn't practical. He lowered Parker's bare feet to the deck and said, "She must need a part. The battery's still working. We tried the diesel. We double-checked the fuses. I've learned a lot about engines on the island, but not enough, apparently."

Parker licked his finger and lifted it into the air. "Even if I wanted to try and fight the current with the sails, Mother Nature is giving us nothing. We could tack back and forth upstream—in a zigzag—but we need wind."

"Good thing we brought Mariah. We can use that dock we passed downriver. The current will take us, right? Can you steer us over without the motor?"

"I've got this." Parker nodded determinedly. "We're finding Jacob and bringing him home if it's—" He broke off.

Neither of them wanted to finish that sentence.

Once they'd crammed supplies into a day pack, Parker ripped a piece of paper free from a lined legal pad that had belonged to the original owners. He scrawled:

Back in an hour! If you try to steal our boat, we will hunt you down to the ends of the Earth.

xoxo

Adam chuckled, pressing a kiss to Parker's scruffy cheek.

At the end of the dock, they looked back to *Bella*. They'd dropped her anchor and tied her off, Parker looping extra intricate knots with his nimble fingers.

"I hate leaving her."

"I know." Adam swallowed hard over a surge of guilt. He still couldn't explain the compulsion that had driven him to run into the night. Maybe if he'd been able to fully shift, he could have rescued the child and returned to Parker before morning. If the child even existed. Not that that would solve the broken motor, but they'd lost time because of Adam.

"Ready?" Parker slipped his hand under Adam's open leather jacket, stroking his ribs.

"I've got this," he said, echoing Parker.

Mariah's motor would be loud in the stillness, but walking wasn't an option once they reached the road. At least not as their first choice. It was likely fifty miles to the compound, and that was assuming they could easily find it. Adam had memorized the map that was folded into the day pack Parker had slung over his shoulders, but he didn't want to take anything for granted.

"You've got it ready?" Adam asked.

"Yep." Parker smiled tightly, patting the back waistband of his jeans. "Feels weird to be carrying a gun again."

"You don't have to. I can take it."

Parker hesitated before shaking his head. "I can do it. But thank you." He glanced back at *Bella*, inhaling deeply and closing his eyes for a few moments. He blew out a long breath. "Okay. Let's go."

In daylight, the forest didn't seem as forbidding. Adam easily pushed Mariah, weaving around trees as he scanned their surroundings. The land was alive with sounds—birds calling, small animals rustling leaves and scurrying through the undergrowth. He prayed the rats were sleeping—along with the creepers.

"I thought you said the road wasn't far?" Parker tied his jacket around his waist and fanned himself with the collar of his tee. Despite the humidity, they both wore their jeans, boots, and jackets. It was best to be prepared for any weather.

"It hadn't seemed so last night. We were farther downstream." Adam glanced around. "Do you want to ride?"

Parker shook his head. "Stupid to waste the battery."

Before long, a cluster of seemingly abandoned trailers appeared, the road curving beyond. Parker whispered, "Do you think the creepers sleep in old houses during the day? Or, like, in caves?"

"Wherever they can, I imagine. We should wait until we're down the road to make any noise."

Parker nodded, though every broken twig under their boots was like a gunshot in Adam's ears. They passed one trailer, then another. Walking quickly, not speaking, eyes darting left and right.

Another trailer loomed on the left. A wooden sign hanging crookedly from one nail read:

The porch light's on, but nobody's home!

Two moldy lawn chairs sat by the door, their frames rusted. Yellowed curtains hung over a window and—

Had the curtain flickered? Adam's gums ached with pressure from his fangs as he jerked to a halt.

"See something?" Parker hissed so softly only a werewolf could have heard him.

The sheer curtain didn't move. No eyes peered through it. Adam concentrated, and the only heartbeats he heard were his, Parker's, and some woodland animals in the vicinity. He shook his head, and they walked on, faster now.

The dirt road snaked through the trees; likely it had been a driveway. They followed it, breathing a little easier once they'd passed the homestead. Again, Adam listened intently. They were alone.

After checking the map, Adam turned on Mariah's familiar engine. She purred, and Parker climbed on behind, looping his arms around Adam's waist, thighs snug around his hips.

"It's been a while," Parker murmured.

"Okay?" Adam placed his hand over one of Parker's.

"Yeah. I didn't think I missed it." He laughed with a puff of warm air on Adam's ear that sent a shiver down his spine. "Is it weird to be nostalgic for the beginning of the zombie apocalypse?"

"Everything seemed so simple then," Adam deadpanned. "Life was easy."

"The music was so much better. Although I did hear a great song the other day."

As Parker hummed Dolly and Kenny, Adam twisted the throttle.

ADAM *HAD* MISSED this. The wind in his face, sunglasses on,

Parker wrapped around him, and faithful Mariah their chariot.

He snorted a laugh. Chariot? He was being dramatic verging on maudlin.

"What?" Parker asked, not having to shout with Adam's hearing.

"Nothing. More early apocalypse nostalgia." He veered into the left lane on the two-lane road to avoid a pothole.

It was amazing how much nature had encroached in only a few years. Tree branches extended over the narrow road. Grass and vines sprouted through cracks in the blacktop.

"What do you think the Pines is like now?" Parker asked.

"Nature-wise, I bet the grounds aren't as fastidiously manicured," Adam shouted. "For anything else, it depends on whether Angela Yamaguchi is still in charge." If she was still alive. "If they have order. It might have all gone south after we left."

Parker seemed to ponder this before saying, "If it's up and running, I wonder if Angela's asshole brother is still working on a cure." His arms tightened around Adam's waist. "Cutting up other werewolves for his experiments."

"Maybe one day we'll find out. Seems unlikely, though."

"That we'll find out or that he'll crack the code?"

"Both. With the radios unreliable, it's going to be a long, long time before communication is even at ancient levels. And I hope he can find a cure, but realistically…"

"Yeah." Parker was quiet again before whispering, "I wonder if Evie and Jaden are still alive."

"Me too. And those people we met in the desert. They were going to…Northern California, I think?"

"Oh yeah! They were really nice. They gave us sandwiches. Shit, I can't remember their names."

"Me either."

They drove on, Adam letting himself feel a mild, melancholy sort of grief for the people they'd met along the way and what their fates might have been. His mind drifted to Abby, and the grief turned sharp and specific, stealing his breath.

"Okay?" Parker asked.

Adam nodded, his throat too thick to respond as he remembered Parker on his hands and knees trying to scrub Abby's blood from the deck of the boat she, Craig, and the kids had been using.

"Do you think Jacob would really try to find his father in California?" Adam shouted.

"Jesus Christ, I hope not. But…no, not really. I think he'll get a huge reality check if he hasn't already. I'm more worried about what Sean's doing to him."

"I really hope you're wrong about that."

Parker barked out a laugh. "Same, believe me."

Adam tensed at the flash of movement a few seconds before Parker exclaimed, "Oh, shit! Be careful."

The black lab barked from the side of the road as they approached. It was scrawny, its coat matted. Adam pulled back on the throttle.

"We can't stop!" Parker shouted. "It might have distemper. Or rabies. Distemper won't affect me, but both of us would be fucked by rabies, that's for sure."

Still, guilt washed through Adam as the dog's tongue lolled, a happy expression on its face as they neared. "Doesn't seem sick."

Parker groaned. "I know, but we have to be vigilant. Man, he looks like a good boy."

Adam kept a wide berth as they passed the dog, who ran after them for a minute before disappearing from sight as the road curved.

"Ugh," Parker muttered. "That sucked so hard. I feel like the world's biggest asshole."

"Me too." Even though Adam had been raised to stay clear of dogs for safety, he wasn't immune to their sweet, friendly appeal. "I wish—"

He broke off, hearing and smelling the humans at the same time—distant talking, heartbeats, and the scents of many people mixed with detergent and other household smells. He stopped Mariah in the middle of the road and checked the map.

"I think we're close to the compound." He dragged his finger across the map, showing Parker, who looked over his shoulder. "There are people nearby. Dozens at least."

"Could be creepers? I know you said they're nocturnal now, but there's no guarantee."

"Not creepers. I'm positive."

Parker blew out a long breath, the gust warm on Adam's neck. In the silence without the engine, cicadas hummed and birds trilled. Parker said, "The compound's not empty, then."

"Seems not."

"If it *is* the compound. Feels like we found it too easily."

"I wouldn't call last night easy." Adam shuddered at the memory of creepers and rats streaming around him. He wanted to scrub his skin raw.

Parker squeezed his arms around Adam, the embrace simple and comforting. "Good point. Okay, we need to find out the situation. Jacob might be there. Can you sniff him out?"

"I can try. The only person I can reliably detect from a distance is you."

"Is it weird to be flattered by how much I stink?"

Adam had to laugh. "You don't stink."

"I dunno, dude." Parker lifted his arm and sniffed dramatically. "I'm sweating like a mofo in this jacket. I bet you're into it."

Adam stroked Parker's thigh. "I'm not *not* into it."

They shared a laugh before returning to business, agreeing on escape plans depending on what they found up ahead.

"Maybe we should wait for dark," Adam said.

"Then we have the added risk of creeper swarms," Parker said. "Plus, night is hours away. I'm going to go nuts waiting when

Jacob could be close."

Adam would have insisted on patience if not for the terrible thought of Parker facing creepers like the ones he'd encountered. There was likely no good time to approach. The risks were high day or night. It all came down to who exactly was waiting down the road.

"If we're going to do this, let's go," Parker said hoarsely.

"We don't have to. We can go back to *Bella* right now. Take the river's current to the ocean."

Parker reached his arms around Adam again, pressing his lips to the nape of Adam's neck. "You have no idea how tempting that is," Parker mumbled. "But no. For all the reasons we talked about on the island, I need to do this. It'll be fine. We have your wolfy abilities and my charm. Plus a gun."

Moving again, they were on high alert, Adam ready to wheel around and retreat. The blacktop curved, and he spotted the wall Connie had described through the trees. The metal barrier was dark and blended into the vegetation. A human likely couldn't see far enough, and indeed, Parker asked if Adam was sure when he turned onto the overgrown, unmarked driveway.

A high gate blocked the road after half a mile. On the right, a dark-glassed command booth sat atop a tall platform. Several people stood guard on the platform with shotguns, one woman carrying what looked to be an assault rifle.

"Whoa," Parker muttered. "That's a hell of a wall. That thing must be two stories."

"I guess that's why it's a compound and not an estate."

"This has serious Pines vibes. I'm not digging it."

With the guns trained on them, Adam stopped a good distance away. Mariah still purred quietly, and he was glad of the sun overhead recharging the battery. Adam lifted both his hands and called, "Howdy," as if he was in a Western.

"*Howdy?*" Parker whispered. "Seriously?"

The Asian woman with the assault rifle aimed at them raised a dubious eyebrow. She wore her dark hair pulled back into a severe bun. "Well, hiya, partner," she drawled, and the three men also guarding the gate sniggered. In a blink, all humor and mocking vanished. "Are you one of them?" she demanded.

Parker called back, "Dude, if we were creepers, we'd be trying to eat your face."

The woman scowled. "Not *them*."

Parker fidgeted, stress rippling through his body. He kept an admirably polite tone as he replied, "Sorry, we don't understand what you're trying to say."

It hit Adam, dread coiling around his spine. They didn't mean...

He steeled himself at the last second and managed to keep from flinching as the woman barked, "Fucking *werewolves*."

Adam couldn't see Parker's expression, but he could sense his tension and imagine the tornado of emotion inside him. Pride swelled in Adam when Parker only laughed, his heart banging like a drum as he lied more convincingly than Adam had ever witnessed.

He was typically so honest and open, his face and his mouth betraying any attempts at deception. He was bad at even the most innocent lies. When he'd arranged a surprise party for Adam's birthday, Adam had guessed long before, though of course he'd pretended to be shocked.

"Is that supposed to be funny or something?" Parker asked. "Like we don't have enough on our hands with zombies? Are vampires next? No, wait—abominable snowmen. Of course, this is Florida. Swamp creatures? Did the Loch Ness Monster swim across the Atlantic? What's her name? Jessie? No, that's not—"

A white man holding a shotgun and wearing flannel and a red baseball cap snarled, "Y'all mean to tell me you haven't come across one of them in the past three years? The fuckers are going to outnumber us soon."

The idea that werewolves were actually close to outnumbering humans seemed far-fetched, even with the virus. Adam scanned the area, listening for heartbeats, trying to control his own and finalize a plan-A escape path.

"We've been on a boat," Parker said. "We have no idea what you're talking about." He huffed. "You're joking, right? Is this a hazing ritual? We're just looking for a friend. Sorry to bother you. We'll be on our way."

The cocking of weapons might as well have been gunfire. With Parker still behind him on the bike, Adam raised his hands again. "We don't want any trouble."

One of the other guards scowled. "Why are you *asking* them?" He spoke in a posh British accent similar to Sean's and pulled what looked like a whistle from a chain around his neck.

Parker's heart rabbited, sour sweat emanating from him. "Seriously, we're cool. Everything's cool."

Then another voice rang out. "Parkster?"

Chapter Twelve

IN THE THREE years since Parker had heard his brother's voice, he'd imagined it in his head a thousand times.

Eric had been a tenor in the school choir and captain of the debate team, his voice warm and reassuring. Now, it was ragged, breaking on that one word that Parker hadn't expected to ever, ever be called again.

He only knew he was moving when Adam blocked his path, keeping Parker behind his broad back. Peering around Adam's leather-clad arm, Parker stared up at his brother. He was going to wake up any second. This couldn't be real.

But a man who wore his brother's face—blue eyes, high cheekbones, clean-shaven skin, everything symmetrical in a way that had driven Parker nuts as a gawky kid—stared back at him from the doorway of the command booth.

Eric's golden hair was trimmed short and neat, and if he'd been wearing a suit or a polo and khakis, Parker would expect to see his parents step out next, his father holding a Manhattan and his mother wearing her favorite pearls.

This Eric wore sneakers, shorts, and an orange tee with the Florida Gators football logo. He opened and closed his mouth, shaking his head. When he spoke again, his voice was high and reedy, about to snap.

"Is it really you?"

Parker was aware of eyes on him, but he couldn't look away from Eric as one of the guards with a huge gun asked, "You know these guys, Mr. Osborne?"

"It's my brother," Parker mumbled to Adam, taking a step forward. As he moved, Eric disappeared out of sight, and Parker wanted to tell Adam it was okay and not to growl or wolf out, that he was safe because his brother was actually *here* and *real* and *alive*.

Eric burst out of the door at the foot of the gate. Parker was laughing and gasping as he hugged him, and Adam apparently had gotten the memo because no one was shooting.

Parker squeezed his brother, inhaling the familiar scent that was just *Eric*. He'd known it since he was a kid being piggybacked, or wrestling in the basement, or borrowing Eric's too-big jacket to wear to the eighth-grade graduation dance.

"Parkster," Eric whispered. "It's really you. Thank you, God. Thank you."

Memories whirled through Parker's mind like he was scrolling photos when he'd had a phone:

In front of the Christmas tree smiling in their new dress shirts and slacks when all Parker wanted to do was build the Death Star Lego set, Eric promising to help.

On the Cape house porch in Chatham peeling fresh corn on the cob from the farmer's wooden stand on the side of the road, making a mess of silk strands on the white wood while Eric told him about the girl he'd kissed.

Diving off the boat and racing to the buoy, trying to keep up with Eric's long strokes, tasting salt water and kicking as hard as he could. Just the two of them racing back and forth, Parker determined to catch Eric one day...

"Mom and Dad?" Eric whispered.

Parker shook his head. "They never made it to the Cape house. Boston was..." He shuddered.

Eric squeezed him even tighter.

"How?" Parker asked, his voice thick with the tears that spilled down his face. "What the fuck are you doing in Florida?"

At Connie's compound? When did you find out werewolves exist? What does that mean for me and Adam?

With a shuddering breath, Parker stepped back. Blinking, he forced himself into the present with the armed guards around them. Adam, a few feet away with one hand on Mariah. The bullets wouldn't affect Adam, but what if they had tranqs as well? And the bullets would sure as hell affect Parker.

"Mr. Osborne," the woman with the semi-automatic said. "I'm sorry to interrupt, but we haven't cleared these guests yet." There was something about the way she said "guests" that was anything but welcoming.

"What?" Eric swiped at his eyes. "Didn't you hear me? This is my *brother*." He laughed, grinning and messing up Parker's hair the way he always had. "My brother's here." He seemed to give himself a mental shake, clearing his throat. "I guarantee he's not a *werewolf*."

The disdain—no, the *hate* with which Eric spat the word stole Parker's breath.

Eric's gaze slid to Adam, and shit, could Adam look any more like a stereotypical hairy werewolf?

The pieces clicked into place in Parker's brain. The whistle the other guard wore around his neck would surely emit a piercing frequency only Adam could hear and would be biologically forced to react to. The man fingered the gold chain, and Parker's heart went *boom*.

"This is Adam, my boyfriend," Parker heard himself say, reaching for Adam's hand and holding on tight.

"I'm sure you wouldn't be dating a *werewolf*," Eric—it was really *Eric*—said with a laugh.

A corner of Parker's soul withered and died.

Time slowed like it was trapped in a thick, viscous gel.

"Of course not," he lied to his brother, who was *alive*. "What the hell are you guys even talking about?" He forced a high, strangled laugh. "Werewolves? We sailed down from the Cape and we've stayed on the boat as much as possible. Apparently we're out of the loop." He didn't dare glance at Adam, clutching his fingers and feeling like a traitor.

Eric said, "I'll get you caught up." He extended his hand to Adam.

Adam let go of Parker and took it, because of course he did—that's what he was supposed to do. Parker still wanted to grab it back.

"Great to meet you, man," Eric said. "Come in, come in."

The gate creaked open enough for them to wheel Mariah inside, Adam guiding her, shadowing Parker and Eric. They continued down the drive, and Parker was very aware of the guards watching them—and the gun still tucked safely against his lower back.

"What are you doing here?" Parker asked.

At the same time, Eric said, "Why did you come here of all places?"

They laughed, and Eric added, "I mean, how did you know about us?"

What a great fucking question.

Parker wasn't sure he'd ever lied to Eric before aside from fibbing about taking the last donut or swiping his ID to try to get into a bar in Provincetown one summer.

Until he'd lied to him thirty seconds ago.

"Who's 'us'?" Parker asked. He glanced back at Adam, who watched warily.

Eric laughed. "Why don't we start at the beginning instead of exchanging twenty questions. Are you hungry? Thirsty? You can park your bike in the garage. We have a solar hookup."

"Oh, is it cool if we keep her with us?" Parker's heart thudded. It was fine. This was Eric! They had to be safe here. Everything had to be okay. "We're really attached. Her name's Mariah, and this girl saved our lives way more than once. Like, a hundred times at least, right, Adam?"

Adam nodded silently.

"Sure," Eric said. "I mean, Mr. Burton won't want mud tracked into his place, but let me take you to our spare guesthouse."

As they came over a rise, Parker blinked at an enormous stucco mansion with orange Spanish-style tiled roof and vines creeping up the walls. A dozen smaller versions that had to be guesthouses sat among the trees, along with plainer cabins that looked newly constructed due to the lack of vines and simpler utilitarian design. Beyond, the sun glistened on a lake. He could barely make out the distant shore.

Fields of produce spread out for what had to be acres near the water. Parker was very aware of more eyes on them, and Eric nodded and spoke to people they passed, who stared curiously. Parker tried to focus on what was being said over the buzzing in his brain with no success.

He reached out and touched Eric's elbow, and Eric slung his arm around Parker's shoulders with a grin.

Eric was *alive.*

And Eric hated werewolves.

No, Parker didn't know that. It had to be a misunderstanding. He'd figure it out. Everything would be okay. It had to be.

Pinballing between joy and despair, Parker couldn't focus on anything else. Adam watched him, brow furrowed and lips tight. Parker tried to smile.

"*I'm sure you wouldn't be dating a werewolf.*"

Eric was saying, "We're having water issues at the moment, so don't drink anything from the tap."

"Okay," Parker heard himself respond as he followed Eric inside the stucco guesthouse. It was small yet elegant and high-ceilinged, one main room with a bed and kitchenette and door to a bathroom. Everything was decorated in tasteful neutrals, the walls a warm white. Several windows had been boarded up, leaving the interior dim with only one window that offered a view of the lake in the distance.

Eric flipped on a huge ceiling fan. "Sorry it's stuffy. A/C takes too much power even with our solar grid. We limit windows to keep out the sun during the day and prevent unnecessary light at night. There's no hot water in the guesthouses, but the ground never gets cold-cold, so it's fine." After a pause where Parker only stared at him, Eric asked, "You okay, baby brother?" He ruffled Parker's hair and pulled him into a tight hug. "Holy shit, I never thought I'd see you again."

I don't think I'm okay.

"You were in England," Parker stupidly said.

"Yeah, luckily for me, Mr. Burton had a stocked bomb shelter. A bunch of us stayed down there for months. Safe from the buggers as we called them over there." He huffed a laugh. "Because of the bug eyes. It started as a joke in the bunker. British people love that word, so it stuck."

"How did you get here? When?" Parker glanced at Adam, who stood in the open doorway. Beyond him, Mariah's red chrome shone where she was parked outside in a patch of sunlight.

"We sailed over about a year and a half ago on a freighter while the engines were still running." Eric motioned toward the main house. "This place belonged to an old business friend of Mr. Burton's. We took the chance it was empty, or that we'd be welcome."

"Which was it?" Adam asked quietly.

Eric looked to him. "Empty. Had to clean up the woods— buggers and rats and rabid dogs roaming around. But it's remote, and we haven't had many problems. Not like London."

"What happened in London?" Parker asked. He asked *Eric,*

who was standing in front of him in a Gators T-shirt.

Eric grimaced. "It was a real shit show. As if we didn't have enough problems with a catastrophic global pandemic. Then the werewolves decided they were taking over."

"Because the vampires were too busy sucking blood?" Parker laughed weakly. *Ha-ha.*

Eric asked, "You really haven't come across any werewolves?"

"We've been keeping to ourselves for the most part," Adam answered.

Eric nodded. "How did you find us here?"

Right, *great fucking question.* If Eric's boss had known the owner—was that Connie's father? Connie herself? If they weren't supposed to know about werewolves, they had to pretend not to know her. Right? Did that make sense?

Parker's stomach churned. All he wanted was to tell Eric about the last three years—let the words and memories spill out. It was an absolute gut punch that he couldn't.

"Dumb luck," Adam said, crossing the threshold and coming to rest his warm, solid hand on Parker's shoulder. "The engine on our boat broke down in the river nearby, so we decided to explore on land."

"We were playing the right or left game," Parker blurted. "Remember when we were kids on our bikes? One of us would call a direction, and we'd ride down that random street. Sometimes, we'd go for miles and it would take forever to find our way home. Then you got too old for bike riding, and that one time, I played the game by myself, and Mom and Dad had called the police by the time I got home."

Eric swallowed hard, his eyes gleaming and voice thick. "You were in so much trouble. They bought you a phone after that."

"Yeah. That ugly flip thing." Parker sniffed, tasting snotty tears as he stumbled forward into his brother's arms again. "I missed you so much. I never thought... I never thought."

Parker was crying all over the Gators T-shirt, and there was so much he needed to think about and figure out and make Eric understand, because werewolves weren't bad, and it was all a big mistake. The joy and despair made it so hard to breathe or *think.*

"We have so much to catch up on," Eric said, releasing Parker with a watery smile. "Do you guys want to get cleaned up? Are you hungry? There's filtered water, although it's room temp. We have a team purifying water day and night." He motioned to a water cooler in the white kitchenette with a big plastic jug like the kind used in offices. "Do you need clothes?"

"Only if they're as stylish as yours," Parker said.

Eric laughed—*really* laughed, and Parker loved him so fucking much. "My Brooks Brothers suits didn't make the cross-Atlantic journey. You little shit."

Parker took off his pack. "We're good anyway for clothes, but thanks."

"Your boat's on the river, you said? The Keehassee? This is Lake Heewoolee, and the Keehassee River leads to the ocean." At their nods, Eric added, "We can tow it."

"That would be amazing, thank you." Parker exhaled in relief. He hated leaving *Bella* unprotected, and now Eric was fixing it. Everything was going to be okay. Eric always fixed things. "Remember that time I shoplifted a bottle of wine from the 7-Eleven? And I gave the police your number and you pretended to be Dad? The cop was dubious until you went off on a tangent about kids today, and he let me go because he figured I'd be in enough shit at home."

Eric grinned. "I remember. Jessica dared you, and of course having no self-preservation instincts, you did it. Also, I think 'wine' is a strong word." He made a gagging sound. "It was that pink zinfandel that was practically juice. Your self-preservation skills have certainly improved."

"Yeah," Parker said as their smiles faded. "Yeah," he repeated.

Wordlessly, they hugged. "Never thought I'd see you again," Eric murmured.

"I know. I know."

Parker clung to his brother, and from the corner of his eye, he spotted Adam filming them before slipping his camera back into his pocket.

Taking a deep breath, Eric stepped back and smiled. "Look at you. Growing facial hair and everything. Showing up with a boyfriend. Not just any boyfriend—a tattooed biker type. You're really all grown up."

"Adam doesn't have tattoos, actually. But he is a stone-cold fox, as you can see."

A smile ghosted over Adam's lips, and he stiffly said, "Thank you."

The knot in Parker's stomach tightened. This was no time for joking. It was the time for... He truly didn't know what.

Eric said, "Get settled while I log your arrival. Normally, Mr. Burton vets everyone, but obviously I know you're safe. I'll organize some food. Don't worry about anything. You're here now."

He shook Adam's hand again. "So glad to meet you. I said that, right? Sorry, my head is spinning. I can't believe it. But you're here now. That's all that matters." He turned back in the doorway. "And don't worry about werewolves. I know it must sound freaky, but we have it all under control."

Parker's throat went dry. "Great," he croaked.

Eric still stood in the entryway. "I don't want to stop looking at you. I keep thinking you're going to disappear." He half laughed. "Promise you won't, okay?"

Parker could feel the weight of Adam's gaze on him. "I promise."

With a grin, Eric hurried away, and Parker tried to make sense of promises and the two words that ricocheted through his brain.

Under control.

Chapter Thirteen

IN THE SILENCE after Eric left, Adam remained frozen in place. He could hear Parker's heart pounding and smell the salt of his sweat, knowing that if he cupped the back of Parker's neck, it would be damp. Adam had to reach out and assure him, yet his boots had been fused to the hardwood floor.

What he would have given to keep driving, just the two of them forever.

"Are you okay?" Parker asked hoarsely, even though he couldn't be okay himself, and Adam loved him so much in that moment it *hurt.*

They moved into each other's arms, breathing together. Adam could imagine how incredible it was for Parker to see his brother again. He was so, so happy for Parker amid the dread and horror and anger bubbling in his gut. There was so much he wanted to say, but he couldn't find the words.

Parker did, because of course he did.

"Eric's not a bad person," Parker mumbled into Adam's neck as they clung together. "It has to be a misunderstanding. Were-wolves seem scary at first, but I'll explain it to him, and he'll understand."

Adam pulled back. "You can't tell him anything."

"Right, I know. Not yet. We have to figure out what's going on first. But I know it'll be okay."

"Who are you trying to convince?" Adam asked gently, running his hands up and down Parker's arms, the worn material of his jacket soft.

Parker wiped his eyes. "Both of us, I guess. But I *know* my brother's a good person."

"I believe you. But this is a new world. We can't trust...the things we used to."

"Yeah, but—" He looked over Adam's shoulder and called, "Oh, hi!"

A young woman with a British accent brought them a large Tupperware container of what she called "fish salad" sandwiches and two apples, chattering excitedly about meeting Eric's brother. Adam smiled as much as he could.

He thought she'd never leave.

Parker closed the door behind her, flipping the lock. He peered around the guesthouse. "This really is all very Pines two-point-oh."

"It is. Connie once called her father a 'billionaire hippie.' Made his fortune in plastics but was into sustainability." At Parker's dubious expression, Adam added, "People don't always make sense. It *does* make sense that the eco-friendly places are thriving now. Solar power, et cetera."

"And her dad knew Eric's boss, I guess?" Parker took an apple, then screwed up his face and washed his hands in the kitchen sink with a bar of homemade soap.

"I think her husband is more likely."

"Connie's married? Huh. I never thought about it somehow."

"Ex-husband, I should say. He was human. He ran her father's company for a time, but the marriage didn't last."

"Was he a dipshit?"

Adam found himself smiling. "I believe so."

"Okay, so if this Mr. Burton—Eric's billionaire boss, I guess?—knew Connie's husband, then does he know Connie's a werewolf? That this is a werewolf compound?"

"I don't know. Would he have come here if he'd known?"

Parker tossed the apple from hand to hand, pacing the kitchenette. "Probably not? Obviously we have to pretend we don't know Connie and this is all a coincidence. In case they do know about her."

"Yes."

"So, let's say they didn't know about Connie and her dad. There weren't any werewolfy things around this place?"

"Like what?"

"I don't know! A lot of hair? Lint brushes?"

Adam had to laugh. "Thinking back to my house growing up, I don't imagine anyone would have known by looking around."

"Right. Not like a family of vampires with their coffins instead of beds. You know, it really has to be a mistake," Parker said, still tossing the apple. "I get being afraid if they don't know better. But it's stupid to be fighting werewolves *and* creepers. And for all we know, those Zechariahs are out there. We can't fight each other. We have to band together."

Adam nodded, resisting mentioning all the historical examples of people not banding together when they should have.

"It's going to be okay. Eric's here. We'll figure it out." Taking a deep breath, Parker gazed around. "This is nice." He fidgeted, a grin breaking out on his face. "Dude, my brother's *here.*"

Adam could only imagine how he'd feel if one of his sisters reappeared, miraculously alive. The joy would be soul deep—more powerful than he could contemplate. He wanted to be thrilled for Parker.

He didn't want to allow the dark, desperate fear to sink into him.

Parker removed his jacket and carefully folded it around the gun before sliding it under the bed. Then he stood and took a bite of the apple, moaning. "Oh, this is good. Try it." He held it out even though there was another in the container.

Adam steadied Parker's wrist, meeting his gaze and biting the apple.

Parker's eyes widened. "That was weirdly biblical and hot at the same time."

Their lips met with crisp, sweet apple juice on their tongues. Parker laughed into the kiss, and there was something so innocent and beautiful in it. Adam's breath caught with a surge of love and gratitude and a swift, shocking lust. He circled his arms around Parker, lifting him.

Legs wrapping around Adam, Parker still gripped the apple. "Whoa," he murmured. "You really want to fuck me right now, don't you?"

Adam realized he was hard, and he deposited Parker onto the white counter, claiming his mouth. One of Adam's favorite memories filled his mind: Parker climbing onto the narrow bunk in the pitch black after Adam had first revealed his secret. Parker comforting him and trusting him. Still wanting him in the light of day, taking him in his beautiful mouth...

Moaning into the kiss, Parker rubbed their dicks together through too many layers as Adam urged him closer.

"Wanna come inside me with your huge cock? Baby, you know I love it when you fuck me hard. Make me scream. Gag me because I'm being so loud..."

Growling, Adam tugged at Parker's fly.

Parker groaned and pulled back, his lips shiny with their shared spit. "Whoa, okay. As much as I want you to bend me over this counter and plow me until I can't walk, we have shit to do." He laughed as Adam rocked his hips. "I know I'm irresistible, but we need to get our heads together. The ones on top of our necks, for the record. I think we're both freaking out." He searched Adam's face. "Are you okay?"

No.

Parker was right that this wasn't the time, but Adam wanted to roar. "You're *mine*." The words were little more than a growl, but Parker understood.

He took Adam's face in his hands, thumbs caressing. "I'm yours, baby."

He kissed Adam deeply. Adam let his fangs out, and Parker circled them with his tongue the way he had years ago when it was new. Adam moaned, his balls tightening already, his claws eager to extend. He almost came right there when Parker spoke against his lips.

"I'm yours, and you're mine. All of you."

The flood of relief and love was almost as powerful as an orgasm. Adam shook with it, catching his breath as Parker pressed kisses to his face.

"We're going to figure it out," Parker promised.

When Adam could speak again, he echoed, "We'll figure it out." He lowered Parker to his feet.

They were both on edge, Parker antsy and pacing again as they ate. Adam couldn't sit either, leaning against the counter as he forced down the sandwich. It was delicious—tangy and creamy like a good tuna salad with crunch from carrots. The sourdough bread was fresh. This was clearly an established community.

A community that hated him.

It was ridiculous that it *hurt*, but it did. He was thrilled for Parker that he'd been reunited with his brother. He wanted so much to believe that Eric was a good, trustworthy person.

How could he?

Adam wanted to throw Parker over his shoulder and run. Why had they ever left Salvation Island? Parker had been right all along. They should have stayed safe in their bubble and left the rest of the world to its own devices.

A flood of guilt heated his face as he thought of Jacob. He was being unbearably selfish.

"You don't sense any wolves here?" Parker asked before filling a glass with water from the cooler.

"No. I'm not as skilled as other wolves though. My instincts aren't as honed."

"Sure they are. You're selling yourself short."

Adam hesitated. "I don't sense anyone. Sean and the others should have been here days ago."

"Unless they lied. I mean, I *know* Sean lied about Jacob." Parker gnawed his apple to the core. "What if they never had any intention of coming here to start some sister community? They could be anywhere."

"They were coming to see if it was viable. Why lie?"

"Because he enjoys fucking with people? Because Connie gave them fuel and food and other resources?"

"It's possible."

Parker narrowed his gaze. "You're humoring me. Stop it."

"I'm agreeing it's possible. It *is* possible. Incredibly shortsighted, but possible. Sean's an alpha. The pack's wellbeing should be his priority."

"A-ha!" Parker jabbed his finger in the air. "'Should' isn't a guarantee."

"True."

"What did he say about humans and werewolves in England? There was something, right?" Parker rubbed his face. "My brain is overloaded."

"He said there'd been conflict."

"That tracks. What does he call us? 'Ords'? Not as bad as Ramon from the Pines, but still." Parker lifted the neck of his T-shirt and sniffed. "I stink. We should shower and change before we meet other people." He stripped on his way into the small bathroom.

Adam picked up Parker's discarded clothes and resisted sniffing them for reassurance. He did fold them, however.

After squeezing together in the glass shower stall, Adam washed Parker's hair, enjoying the satisfied hums he made.

Shampoo and conditioner filled plastic dispensers on the white tile wall, and he smoothed the conditioner through the ends of Parker's hair.

Parker did the same for him. "Anthropologists would say this is a grooming ritual. Which I guess it is."

They kissed, the burning, desperate fire from the kitchen cooled. Adam felt more rational and calm, which was a good thing considering he was facing anti-werewolf...what? Enemies? Opponents? He hated to think of Eric as an enemy.

"I didn't want to let myself dream I'd see him again," Parker whispered in the steady, soothing rush of the lukewarm water.

Adam kissed his head. He wanted to beg him to be careful, to tap into his paranoia and suspicion. But Parker deserved this joy. He wanted Parker to have every ounce of happiness out there in the new world they'd inherited. He didn't want Parker to have to lie to his brother about Adam, even though he had without hesitation.

Sighing, Parker turned off the shower. "I know something fucked-up's going on. But like I said, Eric's a good person. We'll figure this out. Right?"

"Of course." Adam pressed their lips together.

"I'm really feeling that 'it was the best of times and worst of times' vibe. We still have to find Jacob. I can't get sidetracked." Parker inhaled, his breath catching and heartbeat spiking. Adam could almost hear Parker's mind whirring anxiously.

"One step at a time." Adam smoothed his palms down Parker's damp skin. "First step: You get to be happy to see your brother again."

"Right. Yeah." He smiled crookedly, looking younger than he had in a long time. "Actually, first step is to put clothes on and not show up naked."

"If you insist."

In T-shirts, jeans, and work boots, they approached the main house as the sun moved lower in the sky, casting a golden caramel light. The mansion was enormous, and honestly, far too extravagant for Adam's taste.

"Should we knock?" Parker hesitated.

"Can't hurt?"

Before they could, Eric opened the door, beckoning them inside. Despite his comment earlier about his wardrobe, he'd changed into business casual slacks, a striped button-up shirt, and leather loafers. Adam and Parker were decidedly underdressed.

Adam reached out with his senses, straining, trying to pick up some whiff of Sean or Jacob or any wolves. Ceiling fans stirred the air, and the biggest scent that filled his nose was spicy men's cologne.

The wearer appeared at the top of a grand staircase. His hair was white, face florid, veneered smile engineered. A gold watch flashed on his wrist as he opened his arms wide and boomed, "Welcome!"

"This is Mr. Burton," Eric said before introducing them. Curious that he still referred to him by his surname after the collapse of society.

Burton took the stairs with an enthusiastic bounce. He was likely in his sixties, fit and over tanned. The redness in his face could have been the sun, but it looked more like the effects of alcohol. He wore linen trousers and a button-up shirt rolled to the elbows. His leather sandals slapped on the wooden stairs.

"Atticus Burton at your service!"

The name and Cockney accent rang a bell in Adam's memory. He recalled news stories and CNN appearances about grandiose, ludicrous plans to fund a colony in space. Adam shook his hand reluctantly.

"And I understand you stumbled upon us here by chance?" Burton asked.

Parker laughed sharply. "Yep! What are the odds?"

Burton opened his arms wide again. "Must be fate."

"The universe works in mysterious ways," Parker said.

Burton barked a hoarse laugh. He didn't smell of cigarettes, but Adam suspected he'd been a smoker in the past. Burton shook his head. "I've always said our time on Earth is limited. Now here we are at the end times. If more people had listened to me, we could be safe in the stars."

Parker frowned. "Like, in Heaven?"

Burton's laugh boomed. "No, my dear boy. Let's hope that still awaits." He put his arm around Parker's shoulders and walked him past a sitting area of beige leather couches. "Outer space. We could have made it if only others had shared my vision."

Following, Adam wondered how much pressure he'd have to apply to rip Burton's arm from his body.

"Oh, before I forget, you mentioned at the gate that you're looking for a friend," Eric said.

"Huh?" Parker laughed. "Did I? I was just freaking out at the guns. My mouth got away from me. No clue what I was saying."

Eric shook his head fondly. "That tracks."

"How about a tour?" Burton asked, already leading them to the massive, pure white kitchen with a double island. Its windows, which faced the forest, were boarded. The young woman who'd brought the sandwiches waved cheerily from where she peeled carrots alongside a few other young people who bustled about preparing food.

Eric leaned in to mutter to Adam, "He's...a lot, but he's kept us alive."

Adam nodded, peering around as Burton expounded on the use of solar power. The house design and decor were all smooth, sleek lines. There were lights recessed in the walls that glowed red as the sun disappeared.

It was almost futuristic and about as far from the homey, wooden cabins on Salvation Island as you could get. Connie had mentioned that the island was about getting back to nature, so her father had clearly gone for a different style on his mainland compound.

"What's with the light?" Parker asked.

"The walls should be tall enough to keep the infected from spotting any lamps, but we transformed all bulbs to emit red."

"Huh. I thought night vision was green?" Parker asked.

"Ah yes, it can be." Burton chuckled. "I'm sure you've seen that in movies. And it certainly does exist, or at least it did. There's some debate about whether the photoreceptor cells in the eye perceive red or green better in the dark. The rhodopsin in human rods is—"

He broke off and waved a hand. "Apologies. I fancy myself a bit of a scientist, and I'm sure I'm boring you already. In summation, we find the red light effective for our needs. We have noise limits in effect twenty-four hours a day. The buggers are drawn to light, but of course they can hear as well. Better safe than sorry."

Burton, who *still* had one arm on Parker's shoulders, pointed up, expounding about the master bedroom's jacuzzi. Apparently, there was plenty of hot water in the main house.

Adam unclenched his jaw to ask, "How did you discover this place?"

Burton grinned, flashing his veneers. "I'd love to say fate. I visited once with an old friend. This was one of his father-in-law's hideaways. I thought it would be safer and more fortified than my Palm Beach estate."

"Cool," Parker said. "Is your friend here too?"

"No, he turned up brown bread years ago. Luckily for us, his bitch of an ex-wife wasn't here so we could make ourselves at home."

Maybe if Adam just ripped Burton's head clean off his body...

Parker scrunched up his nose. "What does bread have to do with it?"

Burton laughed, slapping Parker's back. "It's my old slang, sorry. You'll pick it up soon enough. Now how about a tumble down the sink?"

"A drink," Eric clarified.

Considering the man had likely not lived in the east end of London for decades, the rhyming slang was a ridiculous affectation as far as Adam was concerned. To be fair, if it was anyone else, it might have seemed charming.

There was an elevated wooden deck at the rear of the house with a view of the lake. They settled onto cushioned patio chairs while Burton insisted on playing bartender. Adam asked for a scotch on the rocks after Burton refused to accept that he only wanted water. Not that Adam had any desire for it, but he figured it would be a manly enough drink to satisfy Burton.

"Ah, a man after my own heart! A pimple and blotch we used to call it." Burton slapped Adam's back.

Adam's fangs ached to be free.

Apparently, red wine was also acceptable, and Parker and Eric received very full glasses. Burton's tumbler of scotch neat was almost full, and Adam was glad of the ice in his. Also glad of his werewolf metabolism.

"In a way, it does feel like fate that I'm here," Burton mused as the splash of red on the horizon faded into black. "I made an offer on this place after the old man finally died, but the bitch said no. I was going to copy the design on my own version. Bought the land for it outside Miami. Now, here we are."

"Why here?" Adam asked, sipping the scotch and not minding the burn down his throat that distracted him from thoughts of murder. He couldn't remember the last time he'd disliked someone so viscerally. "Why not stay in your London bunker?"

"Oh, if this had been a nuclear event, we'd still be down there, happy as clams. Safe for decades. But there's no sunlight." Burton waved his arm, the rising moon glinting off his watch. "No fresh air. After six months, we'd had enough. Isn't that right, Eric?"

"Definitely." Eric swatted the air. "On the bright side, there were no mozzies down there."

On cue, a young man appeared with a smoldering mosquito coil and a citronella candle. Adam wondered who the staff were. Had they been employees in London? If so, Eric seemed to possess a higher rank, though he addressed Burton formally.

Burton went on as if performing a monologue. "It was fate as well that I happened to be in the London office of my financial companies when the virus took hold."

"Lucky for us," Eric said. "Without you, we'd be dead."

"My helter-skelter saved the day. People used to mock me for my contingencies." Burton grinned, feral and too starkly white. "Who's laughing now?" He gulped from his glass. "So, after six months, we decided to explore our options. Limited given the buggers and fucking werewolves running rampant."

It was Adam's turn to gulp the scotch.

"Yeah, um, what's the deal? Is this some offshoot of the creeper virus?" Parker asked.

"No, apparently, the bastards have been around forever." Burton barked a laugh. "I tell you, they kept that under their bloody hats. I never heard so much as a rumor, and I dined with presidents and prime ministers."

"Wow!" Parker exclaimed, playing his role perfectly. "That must have been incredible."

"Yes, yes." Burton winked at Parker. "Oh, the stories I could tell."

And undoubtedly will, Adam thought with an internal sigh.

"They've taken over the UK. I wanted to stay and fight the beasts for my home, but I had to think of my people." Burton motioned to Eric. "Your brother, for example. I had to put them first over my own desire to stand my ground."

How noble. Adam resisted rolling his eyes.

"How would you fight werewolves?" Parker asked casually. Too casually? No one else seemed to notice.

"We have a number of strategies and tools," Burton answered. "A few tricks up our sleeves."

Adam's uneasiness intensified. "How many people are here with you?" he asked. He'd spotted some around the grounds and near the guesthouses and other cabins, but even listening for heartbeats, it wasn't clear. He guessed dozens. A hundred, perhaps.

"What's the current count, my boy?" Burton asked, and before Eric could answer, kept talking. "Parker, your brother has been invaluable. He'd never come to my attention in the office, but he's been my right-hand man since we voyaged to the new world."

"You sound like Christopher Columbus," Parker said with a fake smile.

"Thank you!" Burton boomed. "A hero of humanity."

"Uh-huh." Parker swigged a mouthful of wine.

Adam smiled into his glass, imagining Parker's indignant mental commentary about colonizers and genocide perpetrators.

"Eric mentioned you're having an issue with your water?" Adam asked.

Burton sighed heavily. "The old setup wasn't designed for this many people. We're digging a new well and filtration system. Right now, we're having to boil all our drinking water. It's laborious, as you can imagine."

Adam could very well imagine that Burton was doing exactly none of the labor. "Mm." He wondered how they were keeping the rats out, but perhaps the rats stayed clear of people and creepers.

"We have a whole new system in the works," Burton added. "It's going to be better than ever."

"Cool," Parker said. "You have the equipment to dig a big enough well? Why don't you just drink the lake water?"

"Far too many contaminants," Burton said. "We're drinking it at the moment, but only after a strict boiling regimen. And I assure you, all our food is safe to eat. Not to mention delicious, as you'll soon discover." He beamed as if he had anything to do with preparing it.

They dined on grilled bass and roasted potatoes around a long table with a few other British survivors. The dining room was eerie in the red glow, putting Adam even more on edge even though he could see just fine. Better than the humans, undoubtedly.

Burton, who had popped the cork on a bottle of champagne with delight, raised his flute. "To new friends. No, family! Our Eric reunited with his brother at long last. We're so glad fate brought you here. As a great man once said…"

Adam lowered his glass from his lips, where he'd been about to sip, tuning out the rest of the toast, which went on and on. Finally, they clinked glasses, and he forced a smile.

A Scottish woman whose name he'd missed asked, "Where's our other new friend tonight?"

Someone answered, "She wasn't up for it. Poor thing. You can imagine how traumatized she is."

Beside Adam, Parker said, "Sorry to hear that. Hope she'll be okay. If there's anything we can do to help, please let us know."

Eric beamed at Parker. "Thank you."

Parker put a small roasted potato into his mouth. "Mmm. This is amazing."

It really did all have strong Pines vibes, and Adam tried to smile and eat and not hang Burton by his ankles to shake him until he confessed what was really going on. Eric seemed to trust him, though he likely had little choice given the circumstances. Sticking close to the billionaire with a bomb shelter in apocalyptic chaos made sense.

Adam didn't know what to make of Eric. He'd heard so much about him, and he wanted to like him. Trust him. He wanted to let Parker enjoy their reunion for at least one night.

Parker brought up werewolves again, which was a smart plan of action given they needed as much information as possible. But Adam's skin felt too tight. Hot needles of anger and shame and hurt pricked him endlessly.

If he could remember having his flesh cut away at the Pines piece after piece after piece, he imagined it would have felt similar.

"The scorn they have for us," said a middle-aged Scottish woman. "Like we're something stuck to the bottom of their shoes."

The blond man beside her, whose hair looked pink in the lighting, nodded and looked to Adam and Parker. In a brogue, he said, "Be glad you've avoided the beasts this long. Wouldn't surprise me if they were in league with the Zechariahs to plan this whole thing."

Burton nodded. "A hostile takeover."

Beneath the table, Parker slid his hand over Adam's thigh. Adam focused on that warm, steady pressure grounding him.

Parker cleared his throat. Toying with his fork, he asked, "What if they aren't bad? Like, maybe they're just tired of living in the shadows. Now, they're free to be themselves."

Eric paused in cutting his potato into quarters. "It's not the same as gay people. You haven't done anything wrong. You haven't hurt anyone."

"Not everyone would agree with that," Parker replied. "Plenty of people thought we were dangerous for loving each other. I'm sure some still do. Maybe with werewolves—"

"They're *evil*," the Scottish woman said forcefully. "Worse than the buggers." She glanced at Eric, who stared at his half-empty plate. "Eric can certainly attest to that."

On Adam's thigh, Parker's hand jerked. He peered at his brother, but Eric didn't look up. "What do you mean?" Parker asked.

Eric raised his head and smiled tightly. "Come on, this is supposed to be a celebration. Let's not talk about werewolves."

"It's distasteful," Burton agreed. "Those creatures aren't appropriate dinner conversation. If the prime minister was here, she'd scold us all. Did I ever mention that she asked me to dine one-on-one when she wanted my guidance on the technological freedom bill?"

As Burton droned on, Adam could barely chew his food. It tasted like ashes, and he choked it down with wine.

After dinner, all he wanted was to hide away with Parker and pull the covers over their heads. They had to find Jacob, but tonight, he just wanted to sleep with Parker in his arms, skin on skin.

"Wanna hang out in my room?" Eric asked Parker. "I've got another bottle of wine."

"Yeah." Parker's face was already flushed, and he grinned at his brother, his smile faltering as he turned to Adam. "Is that cool, or...?"

"Of course. I'm ready to turn in." How could he say no? Even though he again fought the urge to carry Parker far away. If Parker had too much wine, would he say something he shouldn't? No. Adam trusted him completely.

Eric extended his hand high for a bro shake. "Can't wait to get to know you, man."

"Same." Adam grasped his palm and then kissed Parker before turning.

Parker grabbed his wrist and pulled him back into a hug. On his tiptoes, he whispered in Adam's ear.

"*All of you.*"

Those words echoed through Adam's heart, and he vowed to remember them as they faced whatever came next.

Chapter Fourteen

"I**S HE ALWAYS** so quiet?" Eric asked as he passed Parker a half-full glass of red in the eerie crimson light.

"Who?" Parker's mouth was fuzzy and dry from the tannins, and he reminded himself to sip slowly. His skin was warm and his head buzzed lightly.

"Who do you think?" Eric ruffled Parker's hair before flopping down beside him on the love seat by the window in his room. It was in the main house down a ground-level corridor, decorated in earth tones and much more like the homey, folksy color and pattern of the cabins on Salvation Island. Maybe this had been Connie's room. "The king of England."

"What do you think happened to the royals? Weird to think of them eating each other's faces like us shlubs."

Eric said solemnly, "Celebrities really are just like us."

"The royals probably couldn't wait to eat some faces after having to smile for the cameras their whole lives."

Eric laughed. "I bet." He switched off the lamp shining red light beside him and motioned to the dark window facing the lake in the distance. "Check it out."

As Parker's eyes adjusted to the dark, he noticed yellow flickers. He blinked. "Fireflies?"

"Cool, huh? Remember we caught one in a jar that summer at the Cape house? You started crying right away, watching it flap against the glass trying to get out."

Parker could imagine his fingers sticky with ice cream, the part of his hair stinging from a sunburn. Being so determined to catch the firefly, then almost immediately freeing it. "Dad called me a 'bleeding heart liberal.' Little did he know I was queer too. Or maybe he did know already."

"Maybe." Eric sipped his wine. "He loved you, though. I know he didn't always show it."

"Yeah." Parker let himself feel the ache of missing his parents. No matter what, they'd been his only mom and dad.

"So?"

"Hmm? Do you know why fireflies light up? I can't remember. God, I miss Google."

Eric laughed. "Why do you keep trying to change the subject?"

Shit, he'd noticed. Of course he had—this was *Eric*. Sitting beside Parker, their bare elbows brushing occasionally, bodies slouched. "I still can't believe it's really you."

"I know." Eric leaned his shoulder into Parker's. "And I want to hear all about your hot boyfriend, so spill."

"You keep mentioning he's hot. Should I be jealous?"

Eric laughed. "No, I'm still straight. But I have *eyes*. I mean, Jesus, that's a lot of muscles."

"He's extremely hot, it's true."

"Who is he? What's his story?"

"I don't know. He doesn't have a *story*." Parker's heart pounded. He was being weird.

Stop being weird!

Eric's brows met. "Why are you being weird?" He hesitated. "Come on, you know I don't care that you're gay."

"I know." Parker tried to laugh it off.

"And actually, that's not true. That I don't *care*. That doesn't sound right. I care a ton. I love you just the way you are."

"I know you're not a homophobe. It's cool. I guess it's just nerve-racking. Introducing my boyfriend to my big brother and all that." That was the truth, at least. He didn't need to be specific about precisely why it made him so nervous. "We actually met on the last day. Of the normal world, I mean. He was my TA, and I went to his office to bitch about my grade."

"Did you not do the work but still expected a good mark?"

Parker sputtered. "No! Well, *maybe*." He slugged Eric's arm. "Shut up. Anyway, I ran into him again on the quad that night, and..." Images flashed: students running, screaming, blood spraying, bulging eyes and open mouths. "I'd be dead or a creeper if it wasn't for Adam and Mariah. His motorcycle. We were stuck together from that night. After a while, it was a choice."

"Fate," Eric murmured.

"Maybe. If that world hadn't ended, I'd have dropped his film noir class and probably would never have seen him again. Maybe I'd have passed him on campus one day and thought, 'There's that hot asshole TA,' and he would have flitted out of my mind. That would be it. And now, he's..." Parker had to swallow the lump in his throat. "Everything."

"I'm so glad you found each other." Eric held out his glass, and Parker clinked it.

"What about you? No hotties in the bomb shelter?" Even in the darkness, Parker could make out the shadow that passed over his brother's face. "Shit. I'm sorry. Was there someone?"

"Yeah." Clearing his hoarse throat, Eric swallowed a mouthful of wine. "Pippa." He chuckled. "I know, I know—could there be a more British name?"

"Aside from Mary Poppins? Not really." Parker's smile slipped. Part of him didn't want to know. Didn't want to hear whatever this awful, terrible pain would be. Because he could tell it was going to be bad. But he had to hear it. If his brother hurt, he had to know. "What happened?"

"She was older one of the VPs. In her late thirties. Divorced, no kids. Honestly, I'd had a crush on her since I started at the London office. I never thought she'd give me a second look."

"Zombie apocalypse is a great equalizer," Parker joked half-heartedly, dread growing. "Although, come on—girls were always chasing after you."

Eric shrugged, his gaze on the fireflies. "Pippa was different. Maybe that's part of why I wanted her. The challenge or whatever. But she was *smart*. The numbers she could calculate in her head— it was amazing. And she was funny and beautiful, and she'd take the piss, as the Brits would say."

Parker smiled. "She sounds great." *Sounded.*

"The shelter was pretty luxurious as far as these things go. Typical Mr. Burton."

After a few beats of silence, Parker said, "Yeah, he's..." His brain spun trying to think of an appropriate word.

"A blowhard? Trust me, I know."

"Oh, thank God. I mean, I'm glad the guy's kept you alive and safe all this time, don't get me wrong, but..."

"He's insufferable, but as you said, we're alive and safe." Eric's gaze went distant again. "Alive and safe," he repeated, almost to himself. "What was I saying? Right, the shelter. It was comfortable, but it was still a tight squeeze. I didn't have my own bunk, and one night, Pippa told me she was tired of me sleeping on the floor like a kicked puppy. Told me to get my 'skinny arse' up there. No funny business."

"How long did that last?"

A smile ghosted over Eric's lips. "A week. Then she kissed me. Said she was tired of waiting for me." He watched the golden trails of firefly light dancing in the darkness. "She had the most beautiful hair. Long and curly. So soft."

Parker watched the fireflies, thinking of Adam's hazel eyes turning to the purest gold as he shifted.

"It happened a month after we crawled out of the bunker. We'd realized we couldn't stay in the UK. Too many werewolves. We'd stocked the freighter with supplies to leave the next day.

Pippa thought we needed more medicine. We were almost back to the dock. The werewolves blocked our path. They were *disgusting*. Some half human, some completely turned into *animals*," he spat. "Soulless."

Parker's heart hurt so much he was sure it had to be splintering.

"I begged like a coward. To just let us by. There were infected coming. We could hear them—" He turned to Parker with haunted, wide eyes. "You know that horrible sound they make?"

Parker could only nod.

"Pippa said the only way to deal with bullies was to stand up to them. They're not bullies, though. They're *monsters*. Inhuman. Worse than the infected."

If he spoke, if he defended Adam and the wolves who'd become his community—his family—Parker would only be able to scream.

"They tore out her throat." Tears spilled over Eric's smooth cheeks. He squeezed his eyes shut. "I couldn't stop them. I couldn't do anything. I knew I was next, but they didn't kill me. They said, 'Let that be a lesson to you.' A *lesson*." He shuddered. "All I could do was watch her die. Listen to her choke while I tried to stop the bleeding with my hands. Feel her disappear."

Visions of Abby's warm, caring eyes turning vacant swelled in Parker's head. "I'm sorry," he whispered. "I'm so sorry."

Parker couldn't remember the last time he'd seen his brother cry. *Really* cry. Had he ever? It had never been this desolate weeping, Eric curling into Parker's arms for the first time in their lives. No slapping his back and ruffling Parker's hair.

Eric collapsed against him, and Parker could only hold him, wishing uselessly that he could fix it.

PARKER KNEW ADAM was waiting up for him—of course he was.

Parker closed the door and flipped the lock. Adam had shut the blind on the one unblocked window, and Parker could barely see to stumble his way to the bed. A red nightlight glowed from the kitchenette socket.

"Turn on the big light," Adam said softly, the bed creaking as he sat up.

"No." Parker's voice sounded rough to his own ears. He yanked off his sneakers and clothes, his foot connecting with their pack on the floor beside the bed.

"What happened?"

He shook his head, knowing Adam could see him in the gloom. After rooting around in the pack, he shoved aside the sheets and crawled over Adam's naked body, straddling his lap and kissing him with deep strokes of his tongue, their bare chests pressed together. Parker breathed harshly as he reached back to fuck himself open with slick fingers.

In the darkness, Adam's eyes glowed perfect, breathtaking gold as he hardened.

Adam let Parker push him back on the mattress. Parker impaled himself, groaning as he took every inch.

Almost every inch.

"All of you."

Adam sucked in a breath, his eyes flaring brighter. His cock inside Parker thickened, the fullness almost unbearable. The hair on his chest under Parker's hands grew denser, and Parker leaned forward, squeezing with his ass, rubbing himself over Adam's hairy body.

The cool breeze from the ceiling fan danced across Parker's skin, his nerve endings lit up like a Christmas tree. So many sensations washed over him and through him and bloomed deep inside.

They kissed again, Adam's fangs pushing against Parker's lips, his claws skimming Parker's spine. This was all Adam, and he was good and kind and brave, and Parker loved him with every piece of his broken heart.

Sitting tall, he rode Adam's cock, moaning and impossibly full, his own shaft already leaking. Adam circled his claws gently on Parker's hips, knowing exactly how much pressure to apply without breaking the skin.

He was the furthest thing from an animal.

"Fuck," Parker muttered. "God, Adam."

"It's okay," Adam murmured. "We're okay."

Adam was here and alive and inside Parker, stretching him, filling him completely. "Need you." He rocked his hips faster, jerking his aching cock now. "Need to come."

He was so full—not only with Adam but a messed-up mix of emotions that threatened to explode from his brain and mouth and veins. Straining, Parker whined and grunted. He was the animal now.

Circling his hips, he found just the right pressure, Adam huge and hot inside him. With desperate strokes of his hand, he spilled over Adam's chest, the white jizz visible on his thick pelt of hair.

"Oh, baby," Parker moaned. "*Please.*"

Adam was thrusting up into him, coming and filling him, whispering little nothing words of love and comfort. They stayed locked together, Parker slumped over him, kissing and nuzzling as Adam returned to his human form.

After cleaning up, they huddled under the covers. Parker couldn't sleep, but he also couldn't talk about what Eric had told him yet. Not tonight. Tonight, he couldn't worry about Eric or Jacob or any of it, as selfish as it was. It was late, and he just needed to be with Adam. He had to catch his breath and deal with it in the morning.

"You really do look like a guy who would have tats. You never wanted any?" Parker traced a finger over Adam's biceps.

After a few moments, Adam went with the new topic and said, "I thought about it a lot. Never could quite decide on a design."

"Yeah? What were you pondering?"

Adam was silent too long.

Parker hesitated, wishing he could see Adam's face clearly in the darkness. "Sorry. Is that too…" *Personal? He just shot his werewolf load up my ass.* "You don't have to tell me."

Adam's warm huff of laughter brushed Parker's cheek. "There's nothing I wouldn't tell you. It's just embarrassing."

"Ohhh. Can I guess?" He propped up his head on his hand, spreading his other palm over Adam's chest and playing with the rough hair there.

"If you must."

"A motorcycle. A red one like Mariah."

"Nope."

"A roll of film? Like a movie reel."

"No, but I like that idea."

"Hmm." He circled one of Adam's nipples idly. "Is it something to do with your family? Because that's not really something I want to make light of."

"Partly, I suppose, but not directly." Adam nuzzled Parker's chin. "It's okay."

"Not directly…" Parker snapped his fingers. "It's something wolfy, right? I'd say a full moon, but as you love reminding me, that's a myth. But it's wolfy, isn't it?"

Adam sighed. "Yes."

"Okay, so it's a little basic, but what the hell? No shame. The only tattoo I ever almost got was a baseball bat that looked more like a dildo. It was a dare in senior year, and lucky for me, the tattoo artist had a conscience."

Adam ran his hand over Parker's hip, settling his palm there, heavy and reassuring. "I'm glad. If you get a tattoo, it should be beautiful."

Parker scoffed even as his heart soared. "Too bad the parlors went belly up with most of humanity."

"Damian does tattoos. Bethany has a few."

"Oh, right. With the needle by hand. I guess if we ever see him again, we can ask." Skirting right over *that* issue, he added, "What would you get? What's your most wolfy tattoo desire? No answer is too basic, I promise."

Adam stroked Parker's hipbone with his thumb, sweeping back and forth, back and forth. "I used to doodle a design. Simple black curving lines almost in a circle. Kind of a Norse vibe? A wolf with fur and his tail curving up."

"Like the snake eating its own tail? I can't remember what that's called. Have I mentioned I miss Google?"

"Once or twice. And yes, similar. More the *idea* of a wolf rather than a realistic drawing."

"Right, totally. Stylized. That sounds amazing. Unbroken."

Adam kissed him. Their tongues met, and they kissed until they couldn't breathe.

"Maybe I should get one too," Parker whispered. "I mean, I know I'm not a wolf, but…matching tattoos. Since I'm yours."

Adam rolled on top of him, and Parker squeaked in surprise at the hardness against his hip. "I dare say you like the idea of marking me."

Scratching the tips of his fangs lightly over Parker's collarbone, Adam murmured, "Unless you'd rather go with the dildo baseball bat."

Parker's laugh hitched on a ragged moan as Adam took him in his mouth, the fangs receded. He wouldn't have thought he could come again so soon, but sometimes he loved it when Adam proved him wrong.

PARKER WISHED HE'D grabbed his sunglasses the next morning when he followed Eric along a lakeside path to the harbor, which was just out of sight beyond the curving shoreline. Eric was back in sneakers, shorts, and a T-shirt—this one plain blue that matched his eyes.

Was it weird that Parker was noticing his brother's eyes? It was just so incredible to actually be *looking* at him. He purposefully moved closer as they walked so their arms would briefly brush.

Parker had tiptoed around while getting ready, at first touched that Adam was still pretending to sleep so Parker had some independence. Then he realized Adam actually was sleeping, which made sense given his naked escapades in the woods. That had somehow only been the night before even though it seemed like ages. Adam had to be drained, more from the emotional toll of hearing a kid in distress than the physical.

Had that call come from the compound? Was it one of Burton's "tools"? Some kind of trap?

A man walked toward them, and Parker realized it was Red Hat from the gate. He forced a friendly smile.

Before Parker could greet him with a banality about the weather, Red Hat bit out, "Thought you said you were from Cape Cod."

"Morning! That's right."

Hands on hips, Red Hat sneered. "Fuckin' lie. This boat's from Rhode Island."

Parker scoffed. "*Provincetown.* Not Providence. Also, the boat could be from anywhere. That wouldn't mean we didn't sail down the coast from the Cape." He forced a smile. "But thanks for the tow."

"Everything's fine, Mike. We're all good here," Eric said, a hand on Parker's shoulder as they walked on, leaving a grumbling Mike in their wake as they came around the bend. "Sorry about that."

The sight of *Bella* safe and sound flooded Parker with warm relief that calcified into ice as he realized she was moored in the shadow of *Diana* on the calm waters of the harbor.

Chapter Fifteen

PARKER COUGHED TO cover his sharp intake of breath. He tried to smile at Eric. "Swallowed a bug!"

"Ugh, that's the worst. Remember that one time at Camp Weepecket when you ate a cricket on a dare and almost choked to death?"

Humiliation flashed through him. "Actually, two boys held me down and forced it into my mouth but said it was a dare."

Eric jolted. "Wait, what? I don't remember that."

Parker tried to keep his tone light. "That's because you were too cool to spend any time with your little brother at camp, even when I told you those assholes were bullying me."

Eric peered at him with wide, concerned eyes. "Parkster, I'm sorry." His hand on Parker's shoulder was warm and comforting.

"It was a million years ago. You were a kid too. It's no big deal!" Parker wasn't sure why he was dredging up old hurts from another life when he had far more pressing issues. Such as, where the fuck were Sean and his pack?

"Wow. That's quite a ship." He motioned to *Diana*. "Who modified it?"

"Not sure. It's a new arrival. Impressive, huh?"

God, Parker hated this. He was dying to blurt out the truth to Eric. Lying to him was like death by a thousand kicks to his balls. But he had to play it smart. Eric had been traumatized by werewolves. He'd witnessed someone he loved murdered. It made sense that he saw them as the enemy.

"Totally," Parker managed. "Do you get a lot of newbies showing up to the compound?"

"No." Eric walked on, leading Parker to a long pier. *Diana* was moored at the end where it was deepest, *Bella* closer, along with other various boats. Eric added, "We encountered some people like Mike once we reached Florida. He's an idiot, but Mr. Burton insisted we don't need him as an enemy."

Parker's boots thudded on the dock. He couldn't wait to change into his sneakers and grab a few other things from his boat.

As they stopped in front of *Bella*, Eric said, "She's a beauty. I can see why you and Adam preferred to stay on the water."

Parker hopped onto her and ran his hand over the sun-warmed metal railing before yanking off his boots. "She's the best. There's also the whole zombie apocalypse thing on land. Water and islands are easier."

"Islands? Which ones?"

"Oh, just one. Small private island near Hilton Head," he lied, hating it more and more with each falsehood.

Eric climbed onto *Bella*'s deck and took off his purple-soled tennis shoes. Their father had drilled into them to only wear white soles or bare feet on deck. "As long as you didn't get sucked into going to that Salvation place."

Parker's heart *banged*. "Huh?"

"You must have heard the messages those weirdos put out? We caught a few when we were on this side of the Atlantic. 'Come to our island, where we promise not to eat you even though we sound exactly like a cannibal doomsday cult.'"

Parker laughed too loudly. "Oh yeah. I forgot about that. The radio doesn't work as well as it used to. Do you guys find that?"

"We do. It's strange. Mr. Burton can't figure it out."

"Must be environmental?" Parker asked, relieved that changing the subject worked. "Unless the Zechariahs had some way of borking radio signals. Phase two of their attack or something."

"I don't think they really exist. It's the werewolves, if it's anyone, trying to take over the world."

"Although... Dunno. I can't imagine them wiping out most of humanity. Pretty big gamble unless they were extremely sure they're immune to the creeper virus."

Eric frowned. "How do you know that?"

Shit.

"You must have mentioned it. Or Mr. Burton did? Someone said something at dinner? I'm not sure." As he spoke, Parker automatically began checking *Bella*'s ropes and regular upkeep. "It's all been a whirlwind, and I barely even know what my own name is today. Never mind what day it is. Do you guys still keep track of the days and months? We do, but sometimes I'm not sure we haven't messed it up and skipped days. I guess it doesn't really matter, right? The calendar is just a societal construct."

Eric blinked. "Yeah, I guess so." He laughed. "I missed your tangents. Your brain's still going a million miles an hour, I see."

"Yep." Parker shrugged. "Guess I'm never growing out of it."

"You're only twenty-one. Still a baby."

Parker tested the bilge pump. "Jesus, I feel about forty-seven these days. Nothing like a zombie apocalypse for premature aging."

"Ain't that the truth. But hey, you're doing great. You have Adam. He clearly adores you, so I approve."

"Does he? I mean, duh, he has great taste and definitely adores me. But is it 'clear' that he does?" Parker couldn't resist asking.

"Absolutely. The way he looks at you like you hung the moon. It's the same when you look at him. You two are obviously meant to be. I'd be jealous if I didn't love you so much."

Parker's face heated. "I'm incredibly lucky. Not many people could put up with me in such close quarters."

"True. He must have the patience of a saint." Eric winked, joining in with a rag as Parker polished the deck.

After a few minutes of silence as Parker tried to figure out where the hell Sean and the pack could be, Eric spoke again.

"I wish I could have taken Pip sailing."

The longing in Eric's eyes *hurt*. Parker hated it so fucking much. "She sounded awesome."

"Yeah." On his knees, Eric rubbed hard at a spot on the deck. "She was funny. Even after everything, she loved to laugh. She'd say we had nothing to gain by being miserable all the time."

"She was right."

Eric swallowed hard. "We were almost back to the ship. A minute away. A *minute*. I begged them to let us pass." He shook his head. "Sorry, I told you this already."

"It's okay. You can talk about it. You can tell me anything."

Eric's jaw tightened. "They're evil. Merciless. They killed her without a second thought. I couldn't stop them. Why didn't they kill me too?" His breath hitched. "Why did they make me watch?"

Images of Abby's last moments unspooled, and Parker closed his eyes. That had been horrendous, and it would haunt him for the rest of his life. But if it had been Adam…

Just imagining it made Parker sick. In that desert motel room when he'd seen the creepers tear into Adam's flesh, he'd thought that was the end. Driving away alone that night *would* have been the end of it if Adam wasn't a wolf.

A shiver of dread rippled through Parker. To have lost Adam that night would have been…impossible. Soul destroying. Unsurvivable.

"I'm sorry," he murmured, placing a hand on Eric's tense back. Eric only nodded and scrubbed at the deck, not so much polishing the wood but scouring it with the harmless rag.

Parker wanted to tell him that not all werewolves were killers. That if he could open his mind and heart, he'd see the world wasn't black and white. As Eric fought tears, now didn't seem like the right time—uh, *understatement*—but when would Parker be able to make him understand?

What if he couldn't?

He must have made some low sound of despair because he suddenly had Eric's full attention. "I'm sorry. I'm being a huge downer." He ran his hand over Parker's hair affectionately, the way he had a million times. When Parker was a teenager, he'd usually squirmed away and rolled his eyes. Now, he drew Eric into a hug.

"Don't be sorry. It's good to talk about it."

Eric exhaled, giving Parker a squeeze before drawing back. "Yeah. I guess I haven't talked much to anyone. It's different with you. I don't have to pretend."

An iron band circled Parker's lungs. How could he keep lying? It wasn't right—but he couldn't betray Adam. And shit, where was fucking Sean and his pack? The thought of them killed only made him queasier.

"Eric, we have to talk." His throat was too dry. The words were like sand. "I need to—please understand. The thing is—"

As a quizzical expression passed Eric's face, someone called his name and he jumped up. Blood rushed in Parker's ears, and he couldn't follow what Eric was calling to the woman at the end of the dock. His heart thumped too hard, and he really was going to throw up the muffin he'd grabbed from a tray in the main kitchen that morning.

Shit, Eric was talking to him. "Sorry. I traded my gate shift to hang with you, but we've been having issues with that all week." His brows met. "You okay?"

"Yep!" Parker had no clue what issues Eric had to handle, but it didn't matter. All that mattered was that he didn't vomit and pass out. He wiped his sweaty brow. "This Florida heat's getting to me. So humid."

"Tell me about it. You want to come with?"

"Nah, I'll just have a look at the motor. Maybe I can…"

What? Suddenly fix it?

"Don't worry about it. Mike's great with that stuff." Eric glanced around before adding, "His saving grace."

"Cool, cool. Hey, can I have a look at that new boat? Curious how they rigged the mainsail."

"Sure. It's on the schedule to give it a thorough scrub today."

"I'll help. Happy to pitch in."

Eric looked pleased. "I'll tell Roberta."

Parker had no idea who Roberta was, but it didn't matter. He nodded and smiled and waved bye before forcing a casual stroll to *Diana's* mooring. He had no idea what he hoped to find. A helpful note?

If Burton had Sean's boat, and Sean and his pack were nowhere to be found, it didn't bode well, to say the freaking least. But how would Burton's people have overpowered them?

A sickening memory of Adam collapsing with a tranquilizer dart in his neck slithered through his mind.

It was probably useless, but Parker couldn't just stand around with his thumbs up his ass. Maybe there would be something on board that he could bring to Adam or something werewolfy that could help.

After a glance around the deck, Parker ducked down into the hold. It was a large ship that was designed to hold fish in pallets of ice. The forward was divided up with curtains made of hilariously floral material and woven hammocks, while the aft likely held supplies judging by the shadows of crates and barrels in the distance.

The air was still and stale and what his grandmother would have called "close," and what he called humid as hell.

"What the hell am I looking for?" he muttered. As much as he didn't like Sean, it felt like trespassing to be poking around his pack's boat. "Great, now I'm talking to myself. Have I always talked to myself? I honestly have no idea."

A dull *thunk* from the stern made him jump. Then a voice hissed his name.

"Parker? Is that you?"

Parker rushed forward, tripping and righting himself by grabbing a daisy-strewn curtain that impressively held. "Jacob?"

Jacob emerged from behind a shadowy stack of crates, hurling himself into Parker's arms. "I'm sorry. I'm sorry!"

"You'd better be!" Parker grumbled before getting control of himself. "It's okay. I've got you. I've got you."

Jacob shook in his arms, gasping. "It was dumb. I know it was dumb." He felt so thin and young.

"It's okay." Parker rubbed a hand up and down Jacob's back, crinkling his nose at the oily residue on his palm. It was all over Jacob's hoodie and tee and skin. Parker squinted in the gloom, the only light coming from the forward hatch. "What the hell is all over you?" He shook his hand, crystals sticking to his skin. "Is that salt?" He sniffed. "Why do you stink like fish?"

"I rubbed a salt and fish oil paste all over so they wouldn't smell me."

"What?" Parker's brain tried to process and move past the incredible relief that Jacob was alive and, if not well, then at least alive. "Oh my god, you're a stowaway? Sean didn't lure you on board?"

In the gloom, Jacob screwed up his pimply face. "Lure me? What the fuck are you talking about? I snuck on. Devon told me how to hide my scent."

"Devon helped you with this plan?" Parker's voice rose. "*Devon?* Boy, is he in trouble."

With a full-body pang, Parker missed Salvation Island and kids getting in trouble with their parents. He missed *home.*

"He didn't know what he was telling me or why I was asking. It's easy to get Devon to do what I want."

"Yeah, because he has a huge crush on you. That's not cool,

taking advantage of him." Parker wanted to shake Jacob. "Don't take friends for granted. We can't take anyone for granted in this world."

Jacob groaned. "I know. I know, okay? Just get me back there, and I swear I'll be good. I'll listen to Craig. I know Craig's always right. I know my mom would—" He broke off on a sob. "I know."

"It's okay. We'll figure it out. First things first. What happened to Sean? And did he ever touch you inappropriately?"

"Dude, *no*. I told you. He hasn't done anything. My bathing suit places are completely untouched, believe me."

"Why were you at his cabin that night?"

He groaned. "It's humiliating, okay? Yeah, I tried to get him to kiss me. He was like, no fucking way. Trust me. He was *not* interested."

"Why didn't he tell me that?"

"Because I begged him not to." Jacob crossed his skinny arms. "It's so embarrassing. I already kissed you and had a stupid crush—which I was over a long time ago, for the record—and then I did it again. I guess I have a thing for older, unattainable men."

Parker sighed. "It's okay. You're a teenager. You're confused. The world sucks on top of normal teenage shit."

"Yeah," he mumbled, eyes down.

"We need to focus here. What the hell happened?"

"I have no clue. I was hiding in a barrel with my water bottles and dried fish strips. It was so hot, but I figured when they came down to sleep eventually, someone would figure it out and I'd be busted. I thought if we were at the mainland, they wouldn't want to go all the way back to the island through the Gulf Stream."

"I guess that makes sense," Parker grudgingly admitted. "To a teenager, at least."

"Anyway, I could tell from the motion of the boat that we'd

made it to the river. I thought maybe we'd get to the compound before I got caught. They were using the big engines, so we got through the Stream overnight way quicker than on a sailboat."

"Yeah, it took us three days." Parker gritted his teeth, still annoyed with himself even though logically he knew he couldn't control the wind.

"What are you even doing here?" Jacob shook his head. "I just realized. You shouldn't be here."

"Adam and I came after you."

For a moment, Jacob looked like he'd burst into tears. His voice was high and reedy. "Seriously? You're here for *me*?"

Parker took his face in his hands. "Yes, we're here for you. Because we love you. You're family. I'm sorry for the things I said. I shouldn't have—"

"Yes, you should! You're right. I need to man up."

Cringing, Parker shook his head. "You're still a kid. It's okay to be a kid. We're here to bring you home, but now every-thing's...complicated." He threw up his hands. "Understatement of the century."

"You really came for me?" Jacob whispered.

"Of course. The only reason Craig's not here is because he couldn't leave Lilly."

"I'm so sorry I missed her party. Do you think she'll forgive me?"

Parker hugged him. "Yes. You're her brother. She loves you. And she has your necklace, okay? Safe and sound."

He shuddered. "Okay."

Inhaling deeply, Parker winced. "Jesus, you really do stink." They laughed, and for a few seconds, Parker let himself be in the moment. But there was shit to do. "Okay, tell me."

"It was dark again. I couldn't see any light coming in any-more. Suddenly, there was a huge racket. It went from quiet with people talking on deck to a total clusterfuck. I couldn't hear what anyone was saying, and then it was quiet again for a long time. Like everyone was gone, except at least one person was here. I could still hear footsteps. Pacing."

"And you have no idea what anyone said?"

"No. Like, when it was calm before and people were talking, I couldn't make out the words. Then it was too confusing. After a couple of hours, Bethany screamed, and there were more voices and footsteps like thunder."

"Bethany? How do you know?"

"Gemma and Michelle wouldn't scream like that. It was Bethany for sure."

Parker's mind whirred. If the wolves had left—lured by the same trap as Adam?—and Bethany stayed behind, she would have been alone. And wait, hadn't they said something at dinner about another new guest who was traumatized?

Fuck. Bethany was at the compound.

He breathed through the mixed emotions slamming through him. Of all people…

"Then the boat was moving, and I just stayed hidden."

"That's good." Parker nodded rhythmically.

What was he supposed to do now?

"Parker?" Eric's voice echoed faintly from above.

"Shit!" Parker hissed. "You have to pretend you don't know me or Adam."

Jacob gaped. "Huh?"

"Just trust me. You don't know us. Can you pull that off?"

"Um, I guess so? Why?"

Parker's head spun, his neck so tense it felt like it would snap in half. The lies were piling up so fast. Could he change course and confess everything to Eric? In flashes, he played through the different scenarios.

They all ended with Adam in danger.

Footsteps thudded overhead, and Eric called his name again.

Time was up.

Parker whispered, "That's my brother. He thinks all were-wolves are bad. That they're killers. I know I can make him understand, but I need more time. I need to figure out what happened to Sean's pack. If they're here, Adam can't sense them. But they could be alive somewhere. Held prisoner, I don't know."

Jacob's eyes widened. "We have to help them!"

"Shh! I know."

"How is your brother here?"

"He came over from England with these people. Their leader is a pompous billionaire dickhead, and they hate werewolves and think they're the enemy."

"But—"

"Just go with it. Say as little as possible. You don't know me." Footsteps thudded overhead from the bow. "They don't know Adam's a wolf," he whispered. "We're pretending we had no idea werewolves existed and that we've been alone on our boat. If we say we know you and you're on Sean's boat, they'll know we know."

What was he even saying? Parker's chest was going to explode.

"Hey, Parker?" Eric's voice was closer. At the top of the steps.

Parker called out, "Eric! There's a kid down here!" He glared as Jacob opened his mouth, surely to protest that he wasn't a kid. Jacob snapped his jaw shut and made a zipping motion before grabbing his pack.

Jacob shielded his eyes with his hand, blinking and ducking his head as Parker brought him up and said, "This poor kid was hiding. A stowaway."

Eric stared in shock. "What on Earth? Where did you come from?" When Jacob didn't answer, Eric added, "Don't worry. You're—" His nostrils flared as he jerked back. "Are you one of them?"

"He's not," Parker quickly said.

Eric still inched away. "You don't understand. They can look totally normal until they show their true animal selves." He dug in his pocket, pulling out a whistle and almost dropping it before blowing so hard his cheeks puffed out.

"It's okay." Parker raised his hands slowly. "You're safe. He's not dangerous." He ached to see Eric so afraid.

Eyes still glued to Jacob, Eric nodded with a shaky breath. "Can't be too careful." He looked more closely at Jacob. "What's all over you?"

"I'll explain later," Parker said. "At dinner, that Scottish woman said there was someone else new here. Was she from this boat too?"

Eric nodded. "Do you know her?" he asked Jacob. "What's your name?"

Jacob peeled off his T-shirt and scratched his arms. "Can I get in the water?" He tugged off his sneakers and jumped in at Eric's nod. Surfacing, he sighed. "That feels so good."

"I don't understand why he'd be stowing away with a ship of werewolves," Eric murmured.

"Who knows why teenagers do what they do?" Parker answered. That was sure as hell the truth, at least.

When they came face to face with Bethany not long after in one of the guesthouses, she stared at Jacob and Parker like she was seeing ghosts. She wore yoga pants and a T-shirt, her red hair hanging lank. No lip gloss today. Before she could say anything, Parker jumped in.

"Hey! I'm new here too. I'm Eric's brother. It was totally fate that my boyfriend and I stumbled on this place and my brother's here. And he came all the way from England! I guess miracles still exist."

He held his breath, waiting. Was Bethany going to play along? For all he knew, she'd told Burton everything. That would be just like her. Appease whoever was the most powerful, never mind about right and wrong.

Eyebrows almost disappearing into her hair, Bethany said, "Well, shit, I guess they do." She extended her hand. "Pleasure to meet you."

Parker made himself step forward and pump her hand. It was small and warm and a normal hand, and it was the first time he'd ever touched her.

Bethany's gaze flicked to Jacob, who rubbed his hair with a towel Eric had apparently asked someone for. She didn't say anything.

Parker barreled on. "This is Jacob. He was a stowaway. He must have sneaked aboard, uh...somewhere."

"Daytona," Bethany said smoothly. "Had to be Daytona. My goodness, are you alright, sugar? Those beasts didn't hurt you, did they? Come here." She opened her arms.

Jacob obediently hugged her. "I'm fine," he mumbled, stepping back.

"Thank God you found him," she said. "Thank God you found *me*." To Parker, she said, "Eric and his people rescued me from those monsters."

"Bethany was being held captive by a band of werewolves," Eric said.

Pack, Parker almost corrected. He reminded himself that Bethany had to be playing a part, but it still set his teeth on edge. "Wow," he gritted out. "Where are they now?"

"Don't worry," Eric said. "They've been neutralized."

Bethany's eyes widened. For a moment, her mouth opened and closed, all color draining from her already pale face. "Dead?" she asked hoarsely.

Did she *really* care? Sure, she'd been dating Damian for... Well, for quite a while, Parker conceded.

"No," Eric answered. "Neutralized."

When Eric didn't say more, Parker nodded. "That's, uh,

good."

What the fuck did "neutralized" mean?

"Sugar, you come stay with me." Bethany motioned to Jacob, and he came to her side. To Eric, she said, "I could use someone to take care of." Her gaze flicked to Parker's, and she nodded at him solemnly.

Before long, Parker raced back to the guesthouse where he'd left Adam early that morning—approximately a thousand lifetimes ago. He burst through the door to find Adam at the water cooler, naked. He clutched a plastic cup.

"You're not going to believe this," Parker announced. "First off—" He jerked to a stop by the cooler. "Why are you so sweaty?"

"Get away," Adam growled.

Parker stared. "Huh?"

"Stay back!" Adam's hoarse voice rose sharply.

Parker's brain spun. Jacob was alive and at the compound, and Bethany was at the compound too, and Sean's pack was missing, and Parker had lied to Eric *again*, and he had to fix it all but he didn't know how. And now, Adam was being all weird.

Now, Adam looked sick.

Chapter Sixteen

"HOW ARE YOU sick?" Parker's voice rose on a note of panic. Instead of backing up as he should have, he shot forward like a rocket, fingers digging into Adam's arms.

Normally, that wouldn't hurt at all, but Adam's whole body ached, his skin oversensitive. "What happened?" Parker demanded. "Who did this to you? You can't be sick!"

Adam wished desperately that he knew the answer. He shook his head. "I've never felt like this." He stumbled back, wrenching free from Parker's grasp, the cup crashing to the floor and bouncing. "It's not safe. Get away from me."

Ignoring him, Parker shepherded Adam to the bed and urged him onto his back. Adam had to admit it was a relief to lie down again.

Parker muttered, "I've only seen you this gray at the Pines when you were unconscious in that psycho's lab. Who did this?" He whirled around as if expecting to find an assailant.

"Please. You have to go." Adam gritted his teeth. "*Go.*"

"Don't you growl at me." Parker pulled the sheets over Adam, but Adam pushed them down, his legs tangled.

"Too hot."

"Sorry." Parker sucked in a breath, his heart racing. He glanced up at the ceiling fan, which whirred quietly. "Are you...?" He pressed the back of his hand to Adam's forehead. "Fever. Okay. Okay. I've got this. It's fine."

"You have to get out of here. Don't touch me. I could be

contagious."

Parker huffed. "If you're contagious that ship has sailed. Besides, we've played this song before, remember? It sucked." His chest rose and fell rapidly. "You're fine. This is nothing."

"Make your box," Adam whispered. Even talking felt like it took so much energy.

Parker shot him an impatient look. "Dude, there's no way I'm making calm breathing boxes in my head right now." He blew out forcefully. "But I'm breathing. See? We're fine. Jacob's here. Did I say that? That's huge, right? Huge. He's safe."

Though his stomach still churned, some relief flowed through Adam. "How?"

He listened as Parker relayed the story of finding Jacob and "meeting" Bethany. Of all the people for him to have to trust and collaborate with. At least it sounded as though that aspect had gone smoothly thus far.

"So, we need to find out where Sean and his pack are." Parker breathed shallowly, his fingers clutching Adam's. "And figure out why you're sick." He pressed his free hand to Adam's forehead again, his beautiful face pinched.

"Don't worry." Adam's throat was dry, so why was his mouth flooding with saliva? His gut roiled, heavy and strangely light at once. "I'm—" He coughed and choked, his stomach rebelling. He gagged.

"Shit!" Arm under Adam's shoulders, Parker hauled him up, rolling him to the side of the bed.

Lurching to his feet as his stomach heaved, Adam doubled over. Dropping to his knees on the smooth wooden floor, he coughed and sputtered. With a horrible pressure deep inside, he vomited.

Kneeling, Parker rubbed Adam's back, murmuring that it was okay and to get it all out. He'd already had the strangest bowel movement of his life earlier, and now his stomach cramped painfully as he retched, emptying every drop of fluid from his body, the awful taste overwhelming his senses.

He moaned. "I hate this."

"Oh, baby. I know." Parker stroked him in a slow, steady rhythm. He kissed Adam's sweaty shoulder. "Is this actually the first time you've puked?"

Adam nodded, though his heavy head throbbed. "Felt queasy a few times, but it always went away."

He hated for Parker to see the disgusting mess he'd made, but Parker only stepped around it and returned with a fresh glass of water. Adam was eager to wash away the acid taste, but he didn't think he could keep anything down.

"Little sips. You can do it. That's it. Come on, let's get you cleaned up and back into bed." With a cool washcloth, Parker wiped off any splashes of vomit from Adam's body before helping him stand.

"I could give this to you." Adam was *so* tired, but he had to try again. If he made Parker sick, he'd never forgive himself.

Parker only clucked his tongue impatiently. "If it's transmissible to me, I already have it. We've fucked, we've kissed—we spend a lot of time in each other's mouths, in case you haven't noticed. It's one of our favorite activities." He pulled the sheet up to Adam's waist, then lifted the bottom edge to his knees so his feet were free. "This way it's here if you feel cold, okay?"

Drained completely, Adam could only watch as Parker cleaned his disgusting vomit from the floor with sure, even movements. His heart beat normally as he bustled around. He brought Adam his toothbrush with a line of paste on it, giving him sips of water and holding up a bowl for him to spit into.

When Parker was finished his tasks, he sat on the side of the bed and stroked Adam's chest soothingly. "Did you eat anything different? Could it be food poisoning? Do you get food poisoning?"

"We ate the same things. I don't know. I've never had it. I guess it's possible." He tried to push himself up to sitting. "I'll be fine now. I feel better already. We need to—"

Parker pushed him back down, hardly needing any force. "Nope. You need to rest. No arguments." He rose and started pacing. Adam heard his heart speed up, but only a little. Parker said, "Okay, if it's not food poisoning, it's some kind of virus or infection. We know it's not the creeper virus. Even if that virus has mutated or whatever, you'd have eaten my face way before now."

"Probably."

"And we didn't get near that dog, so—"

They stared at each other and exclaimed, "Rats!" in unison.

Adam tried to remember everything he'd learned as a child. "I always understood that rats don't get rabies."

Parker exhaled a fraction. "Okay, but they carry other shit, right? What about distemper?"

"I'm not sure."

"Fuck." Parker's pacing tempo increased. "How did people find out stuff before the internet?"

"Encyclopedias?"

"A little cumbersome in the zombie apocalypse unless Connie's dad had a set." He stopped and examined Adam. "You're not frothing at the mouth, so that's good."

Adam gave him a weak thumbs-up.

Parker paced again, muttering mostly to himself.

"You need to find Sean and the others," Adam whispered.

"Ugh. *Sean.* I mean, I'm glad he's apparently not a child molester, and I don't want him to die or anything. But if he and his pack hadn't come to our island, we'd never have had to leave and we wouldn't be here in this mess, and—" Parker broke off, swallowing thickly. "And I wouldn't know Eric was here. I wouldn't be with my brother again."

Adam prayed it would be worth it.

"God, he's so hurt from what happened to his girlfriend. I wanted to explain and get him to understand that you're not bad, but I didn't even know how to start."

"S'okay." Adam wanted to say more, but his *head*. He hadn't experienced such weight in his body since he'd been drugged at the Pines. This was different, though.

Parker ran a hand through his messy hair. "How do I tell him? I can't put you at risk. And if the others are 'neutralized,' I need to find out what that means. Damian's with them, and even though he has highly questionable taste in women, I like him. And it doesn't matter if I like any of them! I have to do what's *right*. But it feels so fucking wrong to lie to my brother over and over. Where are they? Why can't you sense them?"

"I'm not very good at—"

"Bullshit. Don't put yourself down. You *are* good at…" Parker flailed his hands and mimed sniffing. "There's something blocking you. Hmm. Do you think it has something to do with being sick?"

"Maybe?"

"Shit, sorry. I keep talking to you." Parker perched beside him and caressed Adam's face. "You're going to lie here and sleep. Stay hydrated. I'm going to line up glasses of water, and you're going to work your way through them."

"I can't." Even the little sips made his stomach roil.

"You can and you will." Parker's tone brooked no arguments, and Adam loved him so much it hurt. "Your body's fighting off the bug. You have to stay hydrated. I'm sure it's the same with wolves as with regular people. It must be. On the island, they had the same medicines humans used in the infirmary."

"There's no anti-viral for distemper, if that's what it is. It just has to run its course." Adam reached for the glass of water, swallowing with a grimace.

"There you go. Keep drinking in little sips." Parker ducked

into the bathroom and returned with a plastic garbage can he placed beside the bed. "Just in case. I'm going to see what medicine I can find, and you're going to rest. End of story."

"So bossy."

A smile danced over Parker's lips. "You love it."

He grasped Parker's hand. "Love you."

"I love you too, baby. Sleep."

Adam wanted to argue that there was no way he could. They had far too much to deal with, and Parker couldn't shoulder it all. Adam had to get up and help. But his eyes were so heavy…

Chapter Seventeen

THE ACETAMINOPHEN GEL caps Parker signed out of the infirmary cabin were obviously expired, but it wasn't like it turned to poison. Even if it wasn't as potent, it would help Adam's headache. Parker got him to drink more water, which was something.

He hated leaving Adam alone, but they didn't have time for Parker to obsessively watch him like a hawk and ask every five minutes how he was feeling. Adam had told him repeatedly to go, and Parker was just making him more tired by staying.

He smiled and nodded to people on his way to what Burton had referred to as the "communications hub," aka a windowless bunker. Parker was surprised he hadn't called it something completely random and then a word that rhymed with radio, like "pickles and flow." Plus a "guv'nor" on the end. Though *he* was the boss, that was for sure. Maybe—

"Focus," Parker muttered under his breath.

He rapped on the closed door of the hub in what he hoped was a friendly *rat-at-tat*. A young, chubby, round-faced Asian woman with dark bobbed hair and glasses answered with a quizzical frown.

"Hey! Is Eric here? I'm his brother. I don't think we've met."

She visibly relaxed. "G'day! You must be Parker. I'm Lauren."

An image of the young, doomed women he and Adam had met in the sporting goods store on the very first night flashed through his mind. One of them had been a Lauren. They'd sat in a circle and eaten bags of chips, and if only—

"Parker?"

"Yes!" He focused on this Lauren, who watched him with trepidation. "Great to meet you. Is that...an Australian accent?"

Her smile brightened. "It is! I was interning with Mr. Burton in London after uni. I'm from Perth." The brightness in her expression faded. "Long way away."

God, it was literally the other side of the world. Parker remembered how brutally far away Boston had felt from San Francisco. "I always wanted to go there. See kangaroos jumping around. And koalas! So cute."

Ugh. Stop talking.

Instead of doing that, he blurted, "Do you know anything? Heard anything from down there?"

Lauren's lips flattened. "Nah. Maybe one day, though." She motioned to the radio console. "Hoping we can strengthen the signals eventually."

"Right, yeah. What's up with that?"

She sighed. "I wish we knew. All we can do is theorize."

"Story of our lives, right?"

Ha ha. The small talk was excruciating. Adam was sick, werewolves were MIA, and Parker needed to fix it all. "Hey, did you say your name was Lauren? I think someone was looking for you. Down by the docks."

She frowned. "Really?"

"Yeah. Eric said something about it."

At the mention of Eric, Lauren's frown eased. "Oh, thanks. I'll head down there in a bit."

"I can monitor the radio for you. I've lived on a boat the past few years. I've got it covered." He stopped himself before overselling it. "If you want."

"Well..." She tapped her pen against a notebook on the desk.

"Eric always said I'm a great listener." A bald-faced lie—Eric would say he talked too much and needed to listen more—but again at the mention of Eric, Lauren visibly relaxed.

She said, "Sure. Thanks, mate."

Parker exhaled, smiling and nodding and counting to twenty once the door shut to grab the radio transmitter. He automatically switched to the emergency frequency.

"Come in, Salvation Island. Come in." He tried to think of a coded message, but what did it matter? If anyone here heard him calling the island, the jig was already up anyway. "Connie, we need you. Please help. We reached the compound. Get here as fast as you can. Does anyone copy? It's Parker. Just come here. *Now.*"

Static. Fuck, he was so sick of hearing static. What he wouldn't have given to hear Connie's smooth, soothing voice. It had never affected him the same as it had Adam, but if she'd walked through the door, Parker would have thrown himself into her arms.

"Come in, Salvation Island."

He had to check on Adam, but he also needed reinforcements. He had to at least try to get a message to Connie. Parker repeated the message a few more times before stopping. He couldn't get caught, and he couldn't be found talking to anyone. He quickly added, "Don't respond to this! Just come to the compound."

Waiting for Lauren, he scanned the empty frequencies, minutes ticking by like hours.

Finally, a confused Lauren returned, and Parker said, "Oh shit, maybe they said Liz? Or was it Diana, like that boat? I'm so bad at names! Sorry!" He escaped, trying to look casual—and smacked right into Eric in the doorway.

It felt like such a miracle to be able to reach out and hug him. God, he hated lying to his brother. There had to be a way to fix everything without jeopardizing Adam and the others.

"You okay?" Eric eased back from the hug.

"Great! I, uh, met Lauren." He waved to her, and she gave

him a smile that said she was worried about his mental health.

"One of our best!" Eric grinned at her with his perfect teeth and GQ face, and Lauren beamed.

"So cool," Parker said, and what exactly *was* he saying?

Eric said, "Good news: Mike fixed the engine on your boat. Just needed a new…engine thingy. I'm blanking on what he called it, but it's fixed."

"Seriously? That's awesome." For a moment, Parker let himself enjoy the win. Then he asked, "Hey, I was just wondering, are there cameras around the fence?" He motioned to the radio console. "Or is it just old school?"

"We have cameras, but not around the whole perimeter," Eric replied. "The fence is electrified anyway."

Shit on a stick.

"Whoa. That's hardcore. Solar power? The perimeter must be massive." No wonder they didn't have the juice for air conditioning.

"Yep. Stretches for miles. And it's amazing what solar power can do these days. As you know. You guys converted your bike, right?" Eric glanced around. "Where's Adam?"

"He's got a headache. Taking it easy." The spike of worry made it hard to smile, but Parker tried. He itched to get back to check on him. "Werewolves can't get over the fence? Even if it's electric, I thought they were all…superpowered or something."

"Nope. Not at this voltage."

Parker didn't want to know how Eric sounded so certain about that. "So, no one can sneak into the compound with that huge fence, huh? Awesome."

"Right. The only access point is the lake, and we have patrols on the water and guards blocking the river access. The other side of the lake is a swampy wasteland. There's never been an issue."

"Cool, cool. You're sure no one could get in?"

"I'm sure. Actually…" Eric glanced at Lauren, who quickly

looked away and acted busy with dials. "Promise you won't touch anything?"

Parker's heart skipped. "Of course. I would never."

Eric snorted and led him to a door that Parker hadn't even noticed in the corner of the white room. Fuck, was someone in there? Could they have heard Parker's radio broadcasts?

He followed Eric inside the dim room, where a white guy in his thirties sat at a roller desk chair in front of a bank of monitors. The guy turned as they entered, and Parker was relieved to hear the tinny music coming from wired earbuds in the guy's ears. He tugged them out and pressed a button on...

"Whoa. Is that an iPod?" Parker asked. "Blast from the past."

The guy grinned. "Yep. Found it in a junk drawer and it's still chargeable. The tunes aren't bad either. A lot of chick music, but better than nothing. I'm Scott, by the way." He spoke with a broad, harsher-sounding British accent.

"Remember when you got into Mom and Dad's iTunes account and bought Jay-Z's entire catalog?" Eric asked.

Parker groaned. "You'd think it was a Porsche. Like they couldn't afford it? Puh-lease. And they grounded me until—"

He broke off, focusing on the monitors. On the people with big guns standing by a metal fence. No, not a fence.

A cage.

"What is this?" He leaned closer, transfixed. Though they had movie nights regularly on the island using the projector, it wasn't the same as seeing live images on a screen. It had been forever, and he missed the old world fiercely.

Eric said, "This is what I wanted to show you. You really don't have to worry about werewolves getting into the compound. You just found out they exist, so it's totally reasonable to be freaked out." He squeezed Parker's shoulder. "You seem on edge."

"Do I?" He tried to laugh it off extremely unconvincingly. "Yeah, just...stressed." That was sure as hell the truth. He motioned to the screens, his eyes scanning them, trying to process the images. There was one angle from the front gate, and another on the main walkway through the compound.

Then there was the cage.

"Where is this?" Parker asked.

"The western side of the lake," Eric answered. "About a mile away. The new detainment center."

"Detainment," Parker echoed. He squinted at the camera feed that shot the angle from the top of the cage. The small barred area had metal mesh over the top, and Parker could make out maybe a dozen people crammed inside. *Naked* people. They had probably been fully shifted into wolves when they were caught.

"The monsters are neutralized," Eric continued. "They can't get out."

"Monsters," Parker repeated.

"I know it's scary." Eric slid his arm around Parker's shoulders. "Don't worry. I won't let them hurt you."

He said it so sincerely—earnestly—that it broke Parker's heart.

"Mr. Burton's been planning for this. There have been a few hiccups, and it's a work in progress. There's a constant high frequency being transmitted that paralyzes their ability to change back into werewolves."

That sounded like literal torture. Being trapped naked was bad enough, at least in Parker's book. "How did they get caught?" he asked, squinting at the monitor. Counting.

"It was ingenious. Mr. Burton researched as much as he could before we left England, and he connected with people who were developing strategies and weapons. In this case, a recording of a howling wolf to lure them in. It was a bit...messy, but we got them contained. As a bonus, the frequency makes rats run in the other direction."

The howling Adam had raced naked toward had indeed been a trap. How had Sean and his experienced pack ended up in

Burton's prison? It must have been the paralyzing frequency. Adam had to have turned back before he was in range.

Except Sean wasn't in there. Parker was almost sure. "Those are werewolves? Is there a better angle? I'm so curious." Again, not a lie. "They look like normal people." He spotted Damian and Gemma, going through his mental list of the pack.

"They're not," Eric said sharply. "Don't ever fall for that. They'll try and trick you. Play on your sympathies."

Scott nodded. "I prefer the buggers. They're just out for blood. Not trying to pull the wool over our eyes."

"Uh-huh," Parker mumbled, inching closer to the monitors. He counted again, examining faces. Damian, Gemma, and the rest of the pack looked like they were in *agony*. Naked, shaking, hands over their ears, faces contorted.

Fists clenched, Parker could hardly breathe. No Sean. Where the hell was he?

"Did any of them get killed?" Parker asked. "When you caught them?"

"No, but a few of our people were injured," Scott answered.

Eric sighed. "There's a learning curve. We'll be better prepared next time."

"What are you going to do with them?" Parker asked. "Just keep them locked up indefinitely? They must get cold at night. Do they have food and water?"

Scott laughed uneasily. "Don't stress. The Geneva Convention is toast. Doesn't apply to werewolves."

Eric didn't laugh. He said, "They're being fed. The plan is to utilize them in digging the well and new water supply system. They have incredible strength. We just need to harness it. A work in progress, as I said."

Parker counted again. And again.

No Sean.

Watching the different screens carefully, he realized there

weren't any angles that covered the harbor. "Why isn't there a camera by the water?"

"Bloody thing's broken," Scott said. "It's in the shop. We've never had a problem from the lake, though. The other side's really just an endless swamp, and we guard the river closely. That's where anyone comes from. Or the road."

"What's up?" Eric asked.

"Huh?" Parker met his gaze.

Shit, his *suspicious* gaze. Eric looked at him the way he had when Parker'd swiped Eric's ID to get into that P-town bar where the bouncer had taken one look at the blond, gorgeous guy in the photo and awkward Parker and laughed his ass off.

"You're jumpy." Eric examined him.

Burton swanned through the door, saving Parker from answering. Of course, that meant they had to listen to him talk, talk, talk. He was praising himself for some brilliant idea about the well. Parker couldn't tear his eyes away from the security monitors. How was he going to get them out?

"Lauren, darling," Burton called. "Come!"

"Oh, we shouldn't pull her away from the radio," Eric said, but Burton ignored him.

Lauren entered the inner room, her polite smile going rigid as she saw the monitors. She stared, jerking when Burton slid his arm around her shoulders, saying, "Now, tell these gentlemen what you told me yesterday about the bell peppers I planted."

Parker's mind boggled. He was bragging about vegetables while people were being held prisoner? Also, Parker seriously doubted Burton was the type to have dirt under his fingernails from planting anything.

"Uh…" She laughed nervously, her cheeks flushed, her eyes flicking back to the monitors. "That they were good?"

"Come on. You remember." Burton still held her tightly, and Parker was very tempted to shove his arm off. "She told me they were the best peppers she'd ever had! But she called them 'capsicums.' Isn't that charming?" He rubbed his hand up and down her back and addressed Parker. "I can't tell you what a privilege it is to be able to provide for my people."

"I bet," Parker managed. Eric was tense as hell beside him.

Then Eric said, "Is that a message coming in? I think I hear something."

Lauren performed a quick twist-duck maneuver that freed her from Burton's grasp, and she escaped to the radio room with a wave.

Burton barely noticed she was gone, already talking. "Once we get the new water system up and running, I've got ideas for brewing our own beer."

"Beer," Parker echoed, his gaze returning to the naked prisoners on the screen. "But they need food and water. Clothes. It's not right to keep people locked up."

"There's your mistake," Burton snapped, suddenly unsmiling, his whole demeanor going alarmingly cold. "They aren't people."

"We should let Scott get back to work," Eric said, trying to usher Parker out the door.

"Not yet." Burton scowled at Parker. "I've got a lump of ice for you."

"Like...for the beer?" Jesus, this guy was weird.

"He means advice," Eric murmured.

Burton's beady gaze shifted to Eric. "Your brother here seems to need an education. You know firsthand what these monsters are capable of!" he boomed. "Parker, I assure you I have everything under control. You're clearly still confused about werewolves, but there's really no need to concern yourself with any of it. I'm keeping all my people safe here, including you and Adam. That's all you need to know."

In the silence, Parker was tempted to ask where the actual advice was, aside from never questioning Burton and knowing his place. Then he realized Burton was waiting for a response, so he nodded and dug deep.

"Sorry. It really is confusing. It's new for me. Thank you for everything you do."

Like a switch was flipped, Burton beamed. "Of course, my boy, of course. I understand. You're forgiven. Eric, a word."

"Thanks." Parker ordered himself to smile like he meant it as he left, Burton shutting the door on his heels.

At the radio desk, Lauren gave him a shaky smile and whispered, "Are you okay? He's always been…temperamental."

He whispered back, "Dude, I'm fine. What about you? Has he always been handsy too?"

She huffed out a laugh. "You could say that. All the women know not to be alone with him."

"Ugh. This guy is the worst."

"Tell me about it." She quickly added, "Don't get me wrong. I'm grateful to him. We wouldn't be alive without him."

"Yeah, but did he help you all stay alive for *your* sake or because without you he wouldn't have an audience to stroke his ego?"

Lauren arched an eyebrow. "I shouldn't answer that." She glanced at the door, then leaned forward in her chair, her voice barely audible. "I know werewolves are evil, but I don't think this is right."

Parker dropped to his knees at her feet to whisper back, "They're not evil." He reminded himself he was supposed to have just learned of their existence. "I mean, they're half person, right? How do we know they're all bad? I've met terrible people. It doesn't mean all humans are evil, does it?"

"No." She glanced at the door again. "It was awful when Pippa was murdered. Eric was destroyed. The werewolves in London were terrifying, and I was very glad to come here. I hoped there wouldn't be any in America. But you're right. It doesn't mean we can just lock them up like that. Mr. Burton is..." She shook her head. "His power trips are getting worse. He doesn't even pretend this is a democracy anymore. I wonder how long it'll be before locked bedroom doors don't stop him."

The door to the video room opened, and Parker stood. Eric smiled tensely, and Parker followed him out with a wave to Lauren, asking, "You okay?"

Eric shrugged off the question. "What were you saying to Lauren?"

"Just making sure she was okay. Burton's a sleaze."

Glancing around, Eric jerked to a stop on the flagstone pathway. "You can't say things like that! Look, I know, okay? Trust me, I know. But we owe him our lives."

"So that means he gets to be a dictator? He gets to sexually harass Lauren and apparently plenty of other women?"

"No." Eric ran a hand through his hair, and Parker wanted to smooth it down. "I'm going to talk to him about that. We just need to get the water situation under control."

"That is not the only situation here!" Parker's voice rose and trembled.

"Hey, hey. I know this is all a lot to take in." Eric squeezed Parker's shoulders. "Don't go down an anxiety spiral. You're with me. Everything's okay."

God, Parker would have given almost anything for that to be true.

ADAM OPENED HIS eyes blearily as Parker rushed in and went straight to the bed. He felt Adam's forehead—still hot—and held one of the glasses of water he'd lined up on the side table to Adam's lips. Just seeing him again was a relief.

"Hey, baby. Keeping the water down?" Parker checked the

makeshift bucket—empty—and breathed a little easier when Adam nodded. "That's good."

"What's wrong?" Adam croaked, watching him warily.

"I found Sean's pack. Minus Sean. I guess that's a good thing?" He gave Adam the short version of what he'd seen and learned. "I mean, it's good unless Sean took off and cut his losses."

"No way." Adam shook his head, then winced. "He'd never abandon his pack."

"Wouldn't he? Didn't he leave behind the rest of the pack in England?"

"That's different. They formally separated so he could come here."

Parker went to the water cooler to refill the glasses one by one. They'd need more purified water soon, the cooler glugging as the level dropped almost to the bottom. "Why did he do that anyway? Why not stay in the UK with his full pack? Apparently, wolves are taking over."

"I don't think that's his priority. Something else is driving him."

Parker wasn't sure if Adam was being too optimistic or loyal to a fellow werewolf, but there was no point arguing since neither of them knew for sure. "If only we knew what. Okay, so if he's still around, where is he?"

"Trying to figure out the best way to get in."

"Is he a good swimmer? Because apparently the lake is the best option. 'Best' being subjective. I guess he could be across the lake waiting for his chance."

"If he's tried the perimeter and it's all electrified, then that's what I'd do."

Parker sighed. "Then I guess I need to sail over there and find him."

"I'm coming."

"Cool, cool. Okay, out of bed. Chop, chop." He clapped his

hands, channeling his mom on school mornings. He stood and waited, hands on his hips, not letting himself help as Adam slowly pushed himself to sitting with a pitiful groan.

"Are you done?" Parker asked.

Adam flopped back down, and he went so pale that Parker rushed to his side. He kissed Adam's hot cheek.

"I've got this, baby. You rest and hydrate. That's your job. Let me do mine." What was that old saying?

Fake it 'til you make it.

A couple of hours after an excruciating group dinner with Burton holding court once more, Parker strolled down to the dock. It seemed that Burton's dinner companions were a chosen few, and honestly, Parker would have been thrilled to be excluded.

He'd asked after Jacob and was told that Bethany had taken him under her wing and they were "recovering." The Scottish woman had implied that both Bethany and Jacob had been kept captive by the werewolves and tortured, and Parker had shoved a bite of admittedly delicious lemon risotto in his mouth to stop himself from saying something.

It was late, but not *so* late as to be suspicious, and he'd only passed a few people chatting on a porch on his way in the darkness. He took off his sneakers and sat on the dock with his bare feet dangling over the water, acting casual, waiting until a patrol boat chugged by, heading toward the river.

Grumbling, he pried open Mike's amateurish knots in *Bella*'s ropes to free her from the dock. The wind was strong from the north, which he could use to sail back. He'd have to rely on the motor to get across, but it had been sunny all day, so the battery should have been primed.

He flipped the switch, cringing at the noise even though *Bella*'s motor was expensive and smooth. In daylight, the other side of the lake was visible but distant. Under a quarter moon, the lake might as well have been the ocean.

"You'd better be out there, asshole."

Chapter Eighteen

THE TROUBLE WITH finding a werewolf was that Parker had no clue how to start. Adam had always been by his side, reliable and strong since the night the old world ended. When they'd been separated by creeper chaos, Adam had been the one to sniff him out.

Parker'd kept the engine on low crossing the lake, knowing the noise would carry. As he neared the shadowy cypress trees of the far shore, he switched it off and let *Bella* drift. Squinting into the darkness thirty feet from shore, he only heard the gentle splashes of water on the hull and the light breeze rustling leaves. Cicadas sang, their choruses rising and falling.

"Sean!" Parker hissed.

Only the sounds of a peaceful, humid night reached him. He walked to the bow, peering into the marshy bush, the deck cool under his bare feet. It did look swampy as hell out there, and he wasn't splashing around with gators unless he really, *really* had to.

"Sean! Come out, come out, wherever you are."

The light wind sent goosebumps over Parker's arms as he waited, tense. It was entirely possible Parker was out there with no one but the gators and birds who were trying to sleep. He wished he could at least sweep a flashlight over the dark lumps of bushes amid the trees, but the last thing he wanted to do was attract creepers. Even if the area seemed deserted, he knew too well how creepers could swarm seemingly out of nowhere.

Besides, *he* didn't need to spot Sean. If Sean was actually there, he could see Parker easily. Parker held up both his middle fingers.

"How about now? Anything?"

With a snort—of laughter?—a shadow moved. Parker's pulse thundered as the figure neared the marshy edge of the water.

"What the hell were you waiting for?" Parker demanded.

"I wanted to make sure you're alone," Sean replied in his usual silky, posh tone, coming close enough for Parker to finally see him. He was shirtless because this guy apparently really loved showing off his pecs.

"Couldn't you just count heartbeats?" He motioned to himself. "One. Uno. But I guess you're not too good at that."

It was impossible to make out Sean's face, but he went still. "What does that mean?"

"Get on board already, and I'll tell you. They have boat patrols. You're lucky I didn't get caught on the way over."

"The patrols focus much more on the river access. Foolish."

"Still. Come on."

"Aren't you going to come over in the dinghy?"

"No! It'll take too long. Swim. Why haven't you just swum over to the compound?"

"I was going to later tonight. I've been watching their routines in the prison area."

"Aren't they using some kind of high-frequency sound to stop you all from shifting?"

"Yes," Sean growled. "The range is limited, though." He bent. "Catch."

"Huh?" Parker barely dodged in time as one, then two muddy, sodden cowboy boots rocketed onto the deck. Then Sean was stripping off, his jeans flying through the air. They almost didn't make it, but Parker lunged over the rail and caught them.

Sean swam the distance in no time, pulling himself up with his super strength. Dripping and naked, he gave Parker a grim smile. "What's the plan?"

"Uh…this? I realized you weren't in the cage with the others, and Adam figured you'd be out here if you couldn't get through the fence."

"Where is he?" Sean wiped water from his face.

Parker's first instinct was to hide the truth, but Sean could help. "He's sick. He might have been bitten by a rat. Distemper, maybe? We're not sure."

"Doesn't matter anyway. He can't get any closer to the cage than I can."

"It still *matters* that he's sick," Parker sniped, even though he knew being pedantic was ridiculous. "He'll be okay, right? *Right?*"

"Should be. He's young and strong. Is he keeping down water?" At Parker's nod, Sean added, "That's a very positive sign."

Should. Adam "should" be okay.

"Can you catch it from him?" Parker asked.

"Not unless we share bodily fluids, which isn't on the agenda. Distemper's not airborne. What are his symptoms?" After Parker rattled them off, Sean nodded. "Yes, sounds like it. He should be able to fight it off. And he can't give it to you."

There was that *should* again, though. Parker didn't give a shit if he could catch it or not as long as Adam was okay.

Sean's gaze flicked around, then back to Parker. "Am I supposed to liberate my pack with just…you?"

"Yep."

"There's no other friendly ords here?"

"Bethany and Jacob, but—"

"*Jacob?* Why on Earth would you bring him? I'm not even sure how or why *you're* here."

"I'm here because *you* left with Jacob, and we chased after you to bring him back since he's an innocent kid. Also, you can put your pants on anytime."

In the dim light, Sean's gaze narrowed as he rubbed his legs briskly with his hands, water droplets flying. "*I* left with Jacob?

What the hell are you talking about?"

"He covered himself with salt and fish oil and stowed away. Allegedly, you didn't hear him in the hold. Or smell him."

Sean smiled sharply with a flash of perfect teeth. "The hold is full of preserved food. Plenty of salt and fish. Clever." He shook his head. "I suppose there were enough of us on board that we didn't pick up an extra heart." He lifted his hands. "Not my finest alpha moment, I must admit."

"Yeah, no shit." Parker hesitated. "You really didn't know he was there?"

"I truly didn't." Sean's eyes shone gold as he clenched his jaw. "Despite your disgusting accusations, my only interest in Jacob is sympathy for a miserable boy."

"Why? What's it to you?"

"It doesn't matter. My pack fell into this bloody trap even though I warned them—*commanded* them—not to, and I need to get them out. Who are these ords? You're not a prisoner. You seem to fit right in with them."

Sean picked up his jeans, then froze. Before Parker could ask, Sean jammed his hands in his pockets, exhaling audibly as he found whatever he was looking for.

"What? Your car keys?" Parker snarked.

"Just a talisman." Instead of pulling out some wolfy good luck charm, Sean withdrew a quarter, tossing it before slipping it back into his pocket. He tugged on the jeans, going commando.

Parker didn't know why a British werewolf was carrying around a quarter, but he figured they had bigger fish to fry. He filled Sean in on the compound—leaving out Eric—as he hoisted the sails. They'd be quieter than the motor, yet more visible. But if they came across a patrol boat, it was more plausible that he was out for a midnight sail. At least, it was to him.

Sean said, "I'm vaguely familiar with this man Burton. One of those insufferable billionaires who fancies himself an inventor and explorer and leader of society. He's a buffoon."

"Sounds about right."

"How did you and Adam gain entry to the compound? Connie's father did an excellent job securing the perimeter. The lake is the weak point, but I imagine in his time, it wasn't much of a concern with only swampy land on this side. Surely you didn't sneak in undetected via the river."

"We walked through the gate. Grab that rope."

Sean did, surprisingly following Parker's instructions without comment as they got under way. "They didn't blow their little whistles?" Sean sneered.

"I...distracted them." He wasn't ready to share about Eric yet. "But those whistles are probably a good detection system, aren't they? Simple but effective unless you can stop yourself from reacting to them."

"I suppose so," Sean admitted. "That's good that Adam's inside. Though he's not going to be much help if he's ill. I can't wait."

"Wait to do what, exactly?" At the wheel, Parker adjusted their heading slightly.

"Free my pack."

"Duh, yeah. But *how*?" He may not have liked the guy much, but Parker was totally ready to have someone else in charge of the plan.

Sean was silent, and Parker waited.

And waited.

Finally, he sighed. "You don't have a plan either, do you?"

"It's a work in progress," Sean replied stiffly. "I need more information first. Tell me about Bethany. Do you trust her?"

Parker had to laugh. "Hell, no." He shrugged. "Maybe? I don't know. She's pretending she was your prisoner. Which is smart, sure. But would I be surprised if she completely betrays you all and jumps ship to Burton's side in a heartbeat? Nope."

"Really? She and Damian seem very bonded."

"I'm sure Damian loves her." Parker shrugged again, trying not to think of Shorty and that day when he'd been caught alone on *Bella*.

"Why are you distressed?"

"I'm not!" Fucking werewolves and their heartbeat detection. "Is Damian in your pack now? Connie's still his alpha, right? But he defers to you when she's not around? How does that work?"

"It works exactly like that. Damian's part of my pack while he's with us as Connie's ambassador."

"And Bethany?"

"She's his mate, so yes. She's included."

"Even though she's an ord? Huh. I still say she's a question mark. Jacob's completely with us, but he's staying safe until this is all over." Whatever *this* would be. Parker gripped the wheel, his sweaty palms slick on the metal.

"We don't have that luxury. If Jacob wants to grow up and find excitement, it seems he's come to the right place."

"Nope. No way. Jacob is staying the hell out of Operation Free Howl." Parker squinted at the compound in the distance. There was only a faint red glow coming from a few buildings. "Hey, did you see any creepers over there on the other side of the lake?"

"No. There were clusters closer to the river. Along with the rats. Also, 'Free Howl'?" Sean asked with a smirk.

"You have a better name? Speaking of howling, that's how they trapped the pack? With that recording? Adam said it was really hard to resist. He took off in the middle of the night while I was sleeping to run after it."

Sean scowled. "Yes. The noise drew infected near too, though not nearly as powerfully as light. Still, I assume that's why Burton's stopped playing it. They tried for a few more nights after they caught my pack but didn't have any other takers. And their prison is full enough. They don't seem to know what to do with us."

"Yeah, I think it's one of those 'careful what you wish for' situations. Burton's grand plans apparently aren't always the most practical. Although the trap worked."

"I admit, I didn't realize it was a ruse at first. The biological instinct to protect our young…" Sean inhaled and looked away. In the pale arc of moonlight, his eyes were haunted. "It's powerful. The most powerful urge we possess."

Parker didn't say anything. There was something there—a soft underbelly exposed for the first time.

Sean went on, almost talking to himself. "When I finally did realize, it was already too late. We were too close, running too fast. When we're fully transformed, we cover ground quickly."

Perhaps that had saved Adam—his inability to fully shift.

"It's done," Sean said in a tone that didn't welcome questions.

Parker still asked, "How did you escape, though?"

Through a tight jaw, Sean gritted, "As I said, I belatedly realized it had to be a trap. It was…off. I stopped, yet my pack raced right past me. They ignored my calls, as if they were in some kind of trance. They'd never disobey me normally."

Adam came back for me.

Parker took a moment to relish that. He loved Adam so much in that moment he could barely breathe.

Sean frowned. "What?"

Parker shook his head. "Nothing." But as they sailed on in silence, more questions bubbled through his brain—and inevitably out of his mouth. "How did you get your pants and boots back? You guys get naked when you totally shift, right?"

"I went back and found them in the forest. My boat was already gone."

"Didn't you suspect Bethany of taking off?"

"It crossed my mind. But it didn't matter. My pack is what

matters."

"Fair enough." Parker adjusted the sails, his mind still bouncing around. "Seriously, why did you let Jacob hang around you so much? If you really aren't a pervert—"

Sean's growl made the hair on the nape of Parker's neck stand. "I swear, if you start that nonsense again..."

"Fine, fine, you're not a pervert." *Allegedly.* "Why let an annoying kid shadow you?"

"For his defender, you speak ill of him."

"Look, I love Jacob, but he can be a surly pain in the ass. He's family. I'm allowed to criticize."

After a moment of silence, Sean's lips lifted into a ghost of a smile. "He makes me think of my son."

Oh. *Oh.*

Parker's mouth was dry. "Who... Where is he?"

"I don't know." Sean swallowed with an audible click. "Probably dead. He and my wife were flying back to London from Dallas."

Parker's whole concept of Sean scrambled and reformed. He tried to process this new info. "I didn't know you were married. You don't wear a ring."

"Lost it after everything changed. I shifted suddenly one night, and it snapped. I searched the streets in the morning, but..." Sean fished the quarter from his jeans pocket. "Caroline's from Texas. She kept a bowl of American coins for when she visited home. More of a sentimental thing since we used cards to pay for just about everything."

Sean flipped the coin, and Parker waited.

Sean said, "She dropped this one on the rug in our bedroom, and I put it in my pocket. I was in a rush, and the cleaner was coming. I didn't want the vacuum to get clogged." He smiled sharply. "Strange, isn't it? The things we used to worry about."

Parker nodded.

"Now, this quarter feels like a tether. It's superstitious. Foolish." He slipped it back into his pocket and picked up one of his boots, running his fingers over the worn leather. "She'd taken Harry home to visit her parents. He was only a toddler. Nineteen months and seven days."

So young. "Oh." Parker scanned left and right, looking for any patrol boats. There was only the gentle fluttering of the sails and *Bella* gliding through the water. And Sean's low voice.

"Have you ever thought about what happened to all the aircraft that day the virus hit?"

"Actually, no. Huh." Parker's mind spun over the possibilities. It was a great question. "If the virus got on board…"

Sean said, as if reciting a familiar passage, "If the virus infected either of the pilots, the plane would eventually crash. Cockpit doors were always locked in flight. If the plane was on autopilot, it would fly on that heading until it ran out of gas and plummeted to the ground. Or into the ocean. It would be unsurvivable."

Parker nodded. They were about halfway across the lake, the wind dying down a few knots. After the virus hit, he and Adam could have passed plane crashes and not realized it given the fires and chaos everywhere.

Sean went on. "If the pilots were uninfected but the passengers were, the pilots could safely land the plane. Or if both passengers and pilots were uninfected, they could have landed. Assuming they found a suitable runway."

"Right. That's totally possible." Parker nodded encouragingly.

Sean stared out into nothing. "Then there's the question of air traffic control. With the speed at which the virus took hold, airports were likely overrun very quickly. So many people in a small area. Without air traffic controllers, the thousands of planes in the air would be flying blind. Airliners were equipped with collision prevention systems, but it would have been pandemonium."

Shit. It really would have been. Parker tried to think of something to contribute and came up blank.

"Their flight had a stopover in Orlando, but it likely would have taken off. That's my best guess. I've searched the UK, and I don't think they made it across the ocean. Caroline would have found me. If she's alive, she and Harry are here in America. Somewhere. If their plane landed safely."

So many ifs. Parker knew that uncertainty, but to think of having his baby lost out there in that world of ifs made his eyes burn.

"I'm sorry," he whispered.

Sean still looked into the shadowy distance. "Jacob makes me think of who Harry could be if given the chance. If he's still growing. If he and Caroline didn't simply disappear into ash."

Parker ached to check on Adam. See him and kiss him and feel him warm and alive.

After an extended silence, Sean cleared his throat. "The plan was to establish my pack here before I left to search. Leave Gemma in charge. She wants to come with me—they all do—but the best thing for my pack is a home. Security. If Caroline and Harry are out there, I'll find them. Bring them back here, or to the island. It's a good place."

They neared the harbor, and Parker lowered the sails, glad of the busy work to distract him from the ache in his chest.

Then Sean said, "Someone's waiting."

Chapter Nineteen

P ARKER GOT BEHIND the wheel to steer, turning on the engine
as they approached. He prayed he'd see Adam's silhouette
materialize out of the darkness, but it was another familiar shape
waiting on the dock.

"Shit!" He whirled around to tell Sean to hide, but Sean had
already vanished. Parker waved to Eric and called, "Hey!" As he
neared the dock, he tossed Eric a rope.

Unsmiling, Eric tied it in practiced knots, then waited. He
wore deck shoes, khakis, and a wrinkled linen shirt that made
Parker think of him sneaking back into the Cape house after a
party in the dunes.

Parker hopped on the dock and bent to tie his sneakers, his
face hot. Eric was clearly pissed, and Parker just didn't want to
deal. Finally, he stood up with a fake smile.

"What were you doing out there?" Eric asked intently.

"Getting some fresh air."

"At this time of night?"

"Couldn't sleep. Being on the water always helps. You know
how it is." He jerked his thumb toward the compound. "Time to
hit the hay. What does that even mean? Is it about farmers? Did
they sleep in barns?"

Eric's grim expression didn't waver. "I know you're lying.
What are you hiding?"

"Nothing! I went for a midnight sail. It's no big deal. Come
on."

Eric didn't budge. His gaze narrowed on *Bella*. "Whose boots are those?"

Parker looked at the cowboy boots still sitting on the deck. "Adam's. I was bringing them back to the guesthouse. Thanks for the reminder!" He jumped onto the boat and grabbed them.

"He didn't go out with you? I thought I saw someone else."

"Nope! He's fast asleep. I really need to get back." But when Parker turned, Eric had come aboard too.

"Parker, tell me."

"It's nothing!" He held up the boots. "What, you think I'm smuggling coke in these?" He tipped them upside down.

Eric's face creased. "Why are you lying to me?"

"I'm *not*. Dude, I solemnly swear I'm not smuggling coke." He tossed the boots onto a bench.

"Cut the shit. We both know you're hiding something. You've been acting weird. At first, I thought it was because we obviously live in an extremely messed-up world now. And because it's been years since I saw you. You've really grown up. You've changed."

"Uh, yeah. Living through the zombie apocalypse will do that. We've all changed. Seen things. Done things." He exhaled a shaky breath. "Lost people."

Eric watched him for a long moment. "I thought you were nervous because you found out about werewolves. That you were scared, and if I showed you that we have it all under control—"

"Do you?" Parker couldn't stop the question, his voice rising. "What I saw was naked people suffering in a cage. There's nothing under control about it."

"They're not people! They're animals! Murderers!" Eric's nostrils flared as he lifted his hands. "You don't understand. I know it's confusing, okay? Just trust me."

"I..." Parker's mouth was dry, his face hot and gut churning. He was being tugged in opposite directions, a fissure cracking through him. "Do you trust *me*?"

"Yes." Beseeching, Eric stepped closer. "Always. Please tell me. Whatever it is, tell me. I want to help you. You're my baby brother. I—" He froze, his eyes popping so wide Parker thought of creepers. Eric lunged for Parker and yanked him back, stepping in front of him with arms wide.

Sean growled, fangs visible in the pale moonlight, his bare chest covered in hair where before it had been almost smooth.

"Get back!" Eric shouted. "Parker, *run*."

"It's okay." Parker stepped out from around Eric and hissed at Sean, "Put those away!"

Lip curled, Sean did, his body rippling back to its purely human form. He said, "I'm tired of listening to this garbage. Also, you didn't mention a brother."

"It's not important. I mean, it is, actually. It's incredibly important." Parker tentatively reached for Eric's arm. "Okay, so you trust me, right? I know this seems crazy."

Eric stumbled back, tearing his arm free, looking between Parker and Sean. "You know this...*thing*?"

"Yes. You're right, okay? I was hiding something. I already knew about werewolves. I couldn't tell you. I wanted to! Please. Let's just talk."

Eric stared at him like Parker had grown three heads with dicks coming out of the ears.

Sean sneered. "This is all very touching, but—"

"Stop!" Parker snapped.

There was too much happening at once. Adam was sick, the pack was in a cage, Sean was on his last nerve—and Eric was staring at Parker like he was a stranger. The knots in Parker's stomach tightened, and he struggled to breathe.

"Are you one of them?" Eric demanded of Sean. "The same ones from London? The animals who killed my—" His voice broke.

Sean shook his head. "I'm just here for my pack. I don't agree with the wolves who want to take over."

"Why should I believe you?" Eric turned to Parker. "This isn't you," he whispered. "You'd never associate with killers. With *monsters*." He looked to Sean in clear disgust. In horror.

"Exactly!" Parker tried to find the right words in the hurricane in his brain. "I wouldn't. Doesn't that tell you werewolves aren't all monsters? Hear me out."

Tears shone in Eric's eyes. "This can't be you." He shook his head, backing up.

"Wait." Parker held up his hands. "Don't run away. Please."

"No one's running anywhere," Sean said. The threat was matter of fact, but it still sent a chill down Parker's spine.

"You're not hurting my brother." Parker was proud that his voice didn't crack. "I won't let you."

"Who the hell is he?" Eric asked. "What's happening?"

"What's happening is y'all are going to lower your fuckin' voices," said Bethany, appearing out of the darkness on the dock with a gun in her hand.

Parker yanked Eric behind him.

Eric stared in disbelief. "You're one of them?"

Bethany climbed onto the boat, *Bella*'s deck creaking. She wore dark jeans, tennis shoes, and a hoodie, her hair in a tight ponytail. She looked ready for a fight.

"Sugar, if I were a wolf, I wouldn't need a gun. Sorry, but I can't let you raise the alarm." To Parker, she said, "Why don't the two of you get down into the hold and hash it out?"

"No way," Parker automatically argued. "And leave you to do what, exactly?" He eyed her gun closely. It looked like his, though he couldn't be sure. Had Adam given it to her? Or had she stolen it? Was Adam okay?

Bethany pressed her lips into a thin line. "Really? You still don't trust me?"

"Why should I trust you?" Parker hissed. "For all we know,

you're Burton's spy."

Her lip curled. "That jackass? Are you for real? What, I've forgotten about Damian overnight?" She shook her head. "It doesn't matter. I get why you don't like me, but you're stuck with me. And I need your help." Though her gun hand didn't, her voice wavered. "Please. I need to get Damian out."

Was it possible she really did love Damian? Could Parker actually trust her? While part of him still wanted to shout in denial, he had to take the chance. "Where's Jacob?"

"I jimmied the door and locked him the bathroom," Bethany said. "He insisted on coming along, and I thought it was for the best that he stayed put."

Parker nodded. "Definitely." To Eric, he said, "Come on. Let's talk."

Eric seemed shell-shocked as he followed Parker down into the galley. "This can't be happening. You can't be with them. They've brainwashed you."

Breathe. Stay calm.

Parker flipped on a solar-powered lamp and held out his hands. "I understand why you feel that way."

"They're sneaking in here now? Do they know the last one?"

"The last...who?"

Eric paced a few steps back and forth, the low lamplight casting shadows as he moved. "One of them showed up at the gate before we crafted the whistles. Acted friendly and helpful. He was a liar."

Parker braced. "What did he do?"

"Luckily, we found out the truth about what he was before he had a chance to put his plan into action."

"Wait, how do you know he had a plan?"

"Of course he had a plan! He infiltrated our community, and he was waiting until the time was right." Eric sputtered, his face red. "A-a sleeper agent—"

"What, like a Russian spy? Do you hear yourself? Maybe he was just looking for a safe place. For a home." *A pack.* "Isn't that what we all want?"

"*We* do. We're humans. They're monsters!"

"They're not! They have feelings and families. They laugh and grieve and love and just want to live their lives in peace."

Eric opened his mouth, then snapped it shut. His eyes were wild, his chest rising and falling. He stared at Parker. "How would you know that?" His voice was a hoarse whisper.

Parker could hear his own heart thudding in his ears, tasting acid in his mouth as he tried to breathe. He'd already given it away, but even if he hadn't, he couldn't look his brother in the face and lie anymore. Not standing in one of the homes he shared with Adam. Not on *Bella*, where they'd made love and laughed and cried and *lived.*

Before Parker could speak, Eric gasped. "Adam's actually one of them?" He looked around like he expected him to burst out.

Parker reached for his brother but let his hand drop as horror creased Eric's face. Parker kept his tone steady with a fuckton of effort. "Yes, Adam's a wolf. I know it must be hard to believe, but werewolves are just like us. I promise."

"That's insane. That's a lie! You must be..." Eric shook his head. "What did he do to you? Oh, Jesus." He jerked forward and pulled Parker into his arms. "Did he hurt you? It's okay. You're safe now."

Parker hugged him back tightly. "He would never. It's not like that. I'm not brainwashed. Please listen."

"You were so young when you met. You don't know what you're saying. I won't let him hurt you again."

Part of Parker wanted nothing more than to hug his big brother, cling to him and impart this knowledge like some kind of osmosis. Make Eric *see.* Make him understand.

Taking a deep breath, Parker stepped back. "Adam has never

hurt me. Adam *will never hurt me.* He loves me, and I love him. Yes, he's a werewolf. I don't care. No, actually. That's not right." He echoed Eric's own words about Parker being queer. "I do care. I love every part of him. Just the way he is. Human and wolf. He's my ride or die."

Shaking his head, Eric gaped. "It's not possible. They can't *love.*"

"They *can.* Just because some of them are bad doesn't mean they all are. It's the same with people. Some people are rapists and killers and monsters. Not all of us, though. I'm so, so sorry for what happened to Pippa. That was wrong and horrible, but it wasn't Adam." He motioned up with his chin. "It wasn't Sean. He's here trying to find his wife and son. He wants to be with his family. Just like we do. Let his pack go, and no one needs to get hurt."

"They're killers."

"Who have they killed? Who? They didn't do anything! You're keeping them locked up, naked and suffering. It's not right. So they can dig Burton's well? You're using them as forced labor, and then what?"

"We'll have an endless supply of clean water. It's necessary for the community."

Parker exhaled sharply. "I mean, what happens to the were-wolves?"

"I don't know!" Eric's brow furrowed, and he sputtered. "They'll, they'll—" He waved a hand in the air.

"What?" Parker raised his eyebrows. "Be released into the wild hundreds of miles away like bears being a nuisance at a campground? What's going to happen when Burton doesn't need them anymore? What happened to the werewolf who came here alone?"

Red-faced, Eric opened and closed his mouth. "I don't know."

Parker could tell Eric hadn't considered it. He hadn't allowed himself to face it. "You've been blinded by your pain. You haven't let yourself really *think* about what's going on here. It's wrong."

Eric swallowed hard. "It's not my decision."

"How can you willingly follow Burton? God, how can you stand that guy?"

"I don't!" Eric exploded, gesturing wildly. "I fucking hate him! But he's the reason I'm alive. He's the reason Pippa was in the bomb shelter. I had the chance to love her, to—" He broke off raggedly. "To be loved. I owe him for that."

"I get it. I do. But that doesn't mean you have to bow down to him forever."

"I don't—"

"You do!"

"What am I supposed to do? Mr. Burton's in charge! This is his world. We just live in it."

"Spare me the 'I was only following orders' crap. That's not good enough. You're better than that! You've been my hero as long as I can remember." Parker rubbed his face. "It's bad enough you trapped them using a kid."

"What? That godawful howling? Mr. Burton got the recording from one of his contacts before we left England. It's some call to arms. A way to attack us."

"You're wrong. Do you know what that sound actually is? A baby werewolf in distress. That's why it works. That's why they all come running when they hear it. Because they want to help a child in pain."

Eric blinked. "Is that…" He shook his head. "That can't be true."

"It is. It almost caught Adam too, but he wouldn't leave me alone. He had to fight it with all his strength to come back to me. He loves me. How could a *monster* love me?"

Eric muttered something under his breath, his brain clearly overloaded. "How can you—" He cringed. "You actually let him touch you?"

"I don't *let* him. I want it. I want him. I don't have Stockholm Syndrome. I know exactly what I'm doing. You're wrong about them, Eric. Please listen to me."

"You have to listen to *me*! They're dangerous. You don't know what you're doing. You're too young—"

"I'm not a child! I grew up. I grew up with Adam at my side, loving me and protecting me and laughing at my jokes. Hanging up my wet towels. Sharing his last orange with me."

Eric shook his head. "I know what I saw in London. Not just—" His throat bobbed. "Not just Pippa being murdered. Werewolves and humans are at war."

"That's just so fucking *typical*. The world was decimated by a virus that turned people who were infected into creepers who are still roaming the Earth trying to eat our faces. Our infrastructure was destroyed overnight. So instead of banding together, humans and werewolves go to war. Terrific. Just fucking fantastic."

"*We* didn't start it!" Eric shouted. "They killed Pippa without a second thought for the crime of being human!"

"But *you* started it here. You set a trap. The wolves in that cage weren't out to hurt you. Two wrongs don't make a right! Mom and Dad taught us that a long time ago."

"God, what would they think? You and a *werewolf*?"

Parker jerked like he'd been slapped. "Well, they were never too thrilled with me being queer, so I don't think they'd like Adam either way."

Eric's brow furrowed. "That's not true. They came around. Dad was very tolerant of—"

"Fuck tolerance. Tolerance isn't acceptance. He never really accepted me. You were the perfect golden boy, and I was the fuckup." Parker shrugged. "Maybe he would have come around eventually."

Eric's gaze softened, his tone imploring. "Mom and Dad loved you. You have to know that."

"I'm not saying they didn't love me. But they liked you a lot more after I came out."

Eric shook his head. "Parker..."

"They tried. I know they loved me, okay? Mom said it when she called that day. The last day. 'We love you.' I know it was true, and I'm sure they would have gotten used to it—me being gay. They never got the chance, though. I never got the chance for things to be normal again. It was awkward the last time I saw them. That fucking *hurts*."

Eyes glistening, Eric whispered, "I'm sorry."

Parker rubbed his face. "It doesn't matter. They're gone. This isn't therapy. The only thing that matters is now. What we do next. What kind of future we want in this fucked-up world. You're my brother, and I love you. I want a future with you. But werewolves are part of my life. Adam is non-negotiable."

Sean and Bethany suddenly came down, Bethany saying, "You'll have to work out your issues later. We're wasting time."

Parker realized Sean held a rope. "You're not tying up my brother!"

"We're not going to hurt him," Sean said. "If I wanted to, he'd be dead already, and there wouldn't be anything you could do to stop me. But I. Don't. Want. To. Hurt. Him. That said, we need him out of our way."

Parker stepped in front of Eric. "I know I can make him understand. I just need a bit more time."

Bethany shook her head, ponytail swishing. "I'm not leaving my boyfriend in that fucked-up prison another night." She laughed humorlessly. "Jesus, that sounds juvenile. 'Boyfriend.' He's my partner, my husband, my whole fuckin' world. We're tying up your brother, and we're going to get Damian and the others out." She motioned at Eric with the gun. "Into the bathroom."

Eric didn't move, and Parker desperately tried to think of another way.

Bethany leveled Parker with a gaze that bored into his soul. "What would you do if it were Adam?"

He thought of the security footage—of Damian and Gemma and the others in agony in that cage. Parker could only look his brother in the eye and say, "I'm sorry."

Chapter Twenty

HAD IT BEEN a dream?

Adam blinked into the darkness. His hair was drenched in sweat, and he shivered, but he was able to truly focus for the first time since he'd vomited all over the floor that…morning? What time was it?

He missed the little battery-powered owl clock that hung on the wall of their kitchen at home. The owl sat on a branch, the clock situated in its belly. Parker had dubbed it "Theodore" because "*it looks like a Theodore.*" Adam could hear Theodore ticking from anywhere in the cabin.

He pushed out of bed with a groan, stretching and gulping tepid water. He tried to piss in the bathroom, though hardly anything came out. Then he checked under the bed. The gun was gone.

Bethany *had* been there. When she'd realized he was sick, her heart had jumped into double time even as she'd assured him not to worry. He'd let her take the gun since she said she was going to find Parker. Had Sean been on the other side of the lake?

At the window, Adam peered out. Aside from the low, eerie red light glowing from a couple of buildings that made him think of developing photos in a dark room on campus in his undergrad days, the compound was shrouded in shadow. No one moved, which indicated it was very late or very early, depending on your perspective.

The fever had apparently broken, but Adam felt as though he

was in a twilight zone. He got out the door before realizing he was naked, and he returned to tug on pajama bottoms. His bare feet were silent on the dirt path. Should he have put on boots? And a shirt? Probably, but he wasn't going back now.

He could have easily crawled back into bed and slept for days, but not while Parker was out there alone. Adam didn't encounter anyone as he found his way down to the lake, past fields of peppers and zucchini. His mouth was painfully dry, his lips cracking in the corners and then healing.

Walking along the shore path, pebbles and twigs under his feet, he peered out at the water, inhaling deeply. A hint of Parker, but fading. When Adam rounded a bend, *Bella* came into sight tied to a dock, and his heart leapt. *Diana* was there as well.

There was a single heartbeat on *Bella*, and Adam knew it had to be Parker. Who else would it be? As he jumped aboard, shaking off a wave of dizziness, he belatedly realized the scent wasn't quite right. Similar, but definitely not Parker. He wondered again if this was a dream as he went below deck.

He didn't need a light, the shapes of the galley familiar as he approached the bathroom—no, the head. The heartbeat accelerated, and Adam opened the door. He stood blinking down as Eric squirmed back against the toilet, the whites of his eyes stark in Adam's vision.

Eric's feet were bound with a long rope that looped around his wrists in the back. He mumbled around a gag of cotton that Adam distantly recognized as one of Parker's old T-shirts. Bending, Adam loosened the gag until it hung under Eric's chin.

"Please don't kill me!"

On his knees, Adam tried to make sense of it. "I'm not going to kill you." His voice sounded rough and distant. *Had* his fever broken?

"Adam?"

He realized Eric couldn't see in the dark and switched on a

light. They both blinked in the sudden glow. Adam's eyes were dry and crusty in the mirror. He should have washed his face.

"Where's Parker?" Eric demanded.

"I don't know." Adam reached for the rope, but Eric wrenched away from him, his breathing shallow and pulse thundering. He had nowhere to go. Adam said, "I'm not going to hurt you."

"You're one of them," Eric whispered.

There was no sense in playing dumb. Whatever was happening, it was clear there was no going back. "I am."

"You killed her."

"I haven't killed anyone." Was that true? Was he awake? Why was Eric bound and gagged?

"How can I believe that?" A sob tore out of Eric. He shook, and Adam grasped his rigid shoulders gently. Eric froze.

"Parker's missed you so much. You have no idea. He loves you with all his heart. And I love him. You can hate me—hate what I am—and I'll live with it for him. Parker is what matters."

"How?"

Adam sat back on his heels, dropping his hands. "How what?" He felt as though he was underwater, swimming deep, the pressure strong in his ears.

"How do you love?" Eric whispered.

"The same way you do."

"You really care about my baby brother?"

"More than anything in this world."

Eric exhaled, shuddering. *Sobbing.* "If you can love, then... God, I don't know what to do."

As Eric gasped and froze, Adam reached behind him and untied the ropes. "You get up and help me find Parker."

After Adam gulped a warm bottle of water from the stash in the galley, Eric led the way through the compound, glancing behind at Adam nervously, his heart jumping. The compound was still and silent, sunrise a couple of hours away judging by the time on Eric's watch.

"Are you sick or something?" Eric asked.

"I'm fine," Adam lied.

Suddenly, Eric spun around and stopped dead. "You're actually a werewolf?"

"Do you want me to show you?"

When Eric said nothing and only stared at him as if waiting, Adam let his fangs and claws extend, hair thickening and spreading over him, his body shifting. As Eric struggled to breathe, the sharp salt sweat of terror emanating from him, Adam returned to his human form.

Holding out his arms, Adam said, "I was born this way. We all are. I grew up with parents and sisters. We went to school. We argued over whose turn it was to do the dishes. I was grounded when my friend Jimmy Bell dared me to steal a pack of gum from the corner store. I did, and I felt so guilty about it I told my mom and dad as soon as I got home."

Adam wanted more water. He still felt off. He needed more sleep. What had he been saying?

Eric sounded like he needed water too. "They told us you were different. Mr. Burton said…"

"I was ashamed of who I am for a long time. I kept it hidden from almost everyone." He thought of Tina with a pang of sorrow. "Parker changed everything. He accepted me. He wasn't afraid. He's the bravest man I've ever known, and I'll do anything to protect him."

A tremor rippled through Eric. "Is that a threat?"

"Only a fact."

Footsteps hurried toward them, and Adam spotted a young woman approaching in a tank top, sweatpants, and sneakers. She called softly, "Eric! Is that you?"

He faced her. "Lauren? What are you doing up?"

"Something's going on. We have to—" She halted and stared at Adam. "Who are you?"

"This is Adam," Eric said. He hesitated. "Parker's boyfriend."

Lauren pushed up her glasses. "Did you wake up and realize he's not there?"

"How do you know that?" Adam wished his mind was sharper.

"Uh, you're out here with Eric in your pajamas."

"I meant how do you know Parker's not in bed?"

"I saw him on the monitors. He was with that new woman, Bethany, and a man I've never seen before."

Adam exhaled. He'd found Sean. That was good.

"What were you doing looking at the monitors?" Eric asked.

She bit her lip. "I know I'm not supposed to, but... I couldn't stop thinking about those people locked up. Joanna's on the night shift, and it was easy to convince her to take off to screw her boyfriend. I was just going to watch the feed, I swear."

Adam asked, "How can you see anything on the cameras in the dark?"

"They have night vision mode," she said. "I just wanted to look. I've never really seen werewolves before. Just once when we came out of the bunker, but mostly I heard stories about them. Parker told me they're not all bad."

Adam waited for Eric to argue with her, but he didn't. He didn't out Adam either. That was progress.

"We need to get to wherever this cage is," Adam said. "Now." A wave of dizziness crashed through him, and he squeezed his eyes shut.

"Are you okay?" Lauren asked, her voice faint beyond a growing buzz in Adam's head.

He inhaled deeply, thinking of Parker in danger. A rush of adrenaline banished the brain fog. They had to catch up with Parker before they were in range of the frequency, or Adam would be useless. Sean was an alpha—he had to have a plan.

Ignoring Lauren's question, Adam said, "Let's go."

Now he just had to stay on his feet.

Chapter Twenty-One

"**D**UDE, ARE YOU okay?"

"*No*," Sean gritted out. He was in his human form, hands in fists, the cords in his neck bulging. He'd been fine until he suddenly staggered. He dropped to his knees in the dead leaves and twigs between the trees.

"Whoever created that weapon sure as shit knew what they were doing," Bethany said, kneeling beside Sean.

Parker couldn't hear anything, though of course he wouldn't. They had to be close, but he couldn't see the cage—or "detainment center" as Eric had called it. How could his brother be okay with torture?

Because he doesn't see them as human.

But that still didn't track. When Parker had bought a pet store guppy for fifty cents and it had died overnight, Eric had helped him dig a hole in the backyard to bury it. Eric had ridden horses and spent countless hours in the barn rubbing down his mount and feeding her carrots. He'd never, ever been cruel to creatures that weren't human.

Of course, those animals hadn't been so-called *monsters*. It was easier to ignore suffering if you thought it was deserved. And now Eric was stuck in the head on *Bella*, bound and gagged. Sean had tied the knots. Sloppy as hell, but they'd definitely hold.

Parker's head throbbed. He wanted to run back and free his brother and beg for forgiveness. But Bethany was right—and wow, that was a weird sentence to even think. If it was Adam in that cage being tortured, Parker would do anything to free him. He had to get the others out. He had to do what was right, although that concept had never been more complicated or confusing.

"Earth to Parker!" Bethany snapped her fingers in his face.

He shoved her hand away. "Jesus, *what*?"

"We're trying to finalize the plan if you're interested." She jerked a thumb at Sean writhing on the ground. "He can't do anything until we turn off whatever's making that noise."

"On the security feed earlier there were multiple guards with multiple big-ass guns. Speaking of which, is that mine? Did you see Adam?"

"Yeah." Bethany's brows met. "He was pretty out of it. What's wrong with him?"

"He's sick. Distemper, maybe? There's no way to know for sure. As long as he was in bed resting, that's good."

"He was, don't worry. He's strong. He'll be fine." She looked over her shoulder. "Where'd Sean go?"

Parker peered around in the darkness, seeing only branches and leaves. "Sean?" he hissed.

"Over here, for the love of God."

Parker and Bethany crouched and followed Sean's voice twenty feet to the back of a tree. Parker said, "I guess you're out of range of the frequency here."

"Well spotted," Sean replied dryly. "Glad you two are here to save the day."

"Hey, the *ords* are the only ones who can get close enough to disable the frequency," Parker said.

"Touché."

"What if you shift here, then get closer?" Parker asked. "I know it stops you from shifting once you're in range, but what if you already have?"

"I tried that yesterday. I'll try again. If I can just muscle through it…"

He transformed into his werewolf form, his body still half human, and ran forward. As soon as he was in range, he jerked and dropped to the ground. For a wild second, Parker thought he'd been shot. Sean writhed, and Bethany lunged forward to drag him back.

Panting, Sean lay on the dirt, shaking his head. "It's so much worse when I'm shifted," he rasped. "Impossible."

It stood to reason that in full wolf form, the frequency would be even stronger still. Well, there went that idea. Parker and Bethany shared a glance.

Bethany's lips were a thin line. "Looks like this is our show."

Terrific.

Through shallow gasps, Sean said, "They change shifts just before dawn. They could be distracted."

"How do you know if you can't get close?" Bethany asked.

"I scouted the trail to the compound. Watched them coming and going the last few days."

"Yeah, but there'll be double the guards there when they do a handover," Parker said.

Sean growled, "If you can turn it off, there could be a hundred guards."

"Okay, but no killing people. Not unless you really, really have to."

Sean saluted sardonically, which didn't fill Parker with confidence.

They left Sean under a tree, keeping low as they ran on until Bethany tugged Parker behind a bush and whispered, "See that red light?"

He pulled his arm free. Squinting, he could barely make it out. "We're close. So, what do we do now?" He peered up. "It's still dark, but I think it's a little grayer? The day shift should be coming soon."

"I could use my tits. Pull a helpless routine."

"I'm sure you're very skilled," Parker muttered.

"I'm alive, ain't I?" she snapped.

He couldn't argue with that.

"I guess we wait," Bethany said. After a silence, she snorted. "You know what I thought when I first saw you?"

The memory of that day slammed through him. Parker could imagine Bethany on the deck of *The Good Life* approaching him silently from behind while he watched for Adam on land, waiting for him to return.

Heart in his throat, Parker didn't answer.

"I thought, this dumb kid's dead meat. Mick was gonna make your last minutes pure hell, and I couldn't stop him."

Shorty. Parker remembered turning to find the boat bearing down on him. The terrible screech as their hulls met. He'd buffed out the mark and repainted it, but that sound would live in his mind forever.

Parker grated out, "And you just watched."

She exhaled, her cheeks puffing. "Yep. I was outnumbered. I didn't think you would be any goddamned help. So, it sucked to be you, and at least it wasn't me. But here you are. Mick's at the bottom of the ocean where he belongs, and you're alive and kickin'. I never woulda thought it."

"Is that a compliment?"

"Damn right it is. You're a badass motherfucker."

"Am I?" He didn't feel like one at the moment. Not even a little bit. Also, this was the longest conversation he'd had with Bethany since he'd pulled a gun on her.

"Are you kidding?" Her eyebrows shot up. "You're way tougher than I ever expected. And you know what? So am I. My momma never believed I'd amount to much. Said I was too fancy. Had too many ideas in my head. Always out when I should have been home doin' my chores. Don't know if Momma's alive. I hope so. I know she wanted the best for me."

Bethany suddenly sucked in a breath, her eyes shining in the night. Parker watched, frozen.

"I got a second chance on that island. Hell, fourth or fifth is more like it. When you and Adam showed up, I was so damn jealous."

Parker's throat felt like he'd swallowed sand. "Jealous of what?"

"Whaddya think? Of the two of you. You're crazy about each other. I'd watch you in the mess hall and *burn*. I never thought anyone would look at me the way Adam looks at you."

Warmth rushed through Parker, calming his racing heart. "He's the greatest."

She nodded. "Then, one day, Damian sat with me at breakfast. That's how it started. Over scrambled eggs and fish cakes. Damian loves me, and I love him more than I thought I ever could. He makes me so fuckin' happy." Bethany clenched her jaw. "I have to get him out of there."

Then she lifted the gun in her hand, and Parker was suddenly back on the boat that awful day, naked and helpless. That persistent, cruel little voice in Parker's head that fueled his anxiety hissed, "*See?*"

Panic stole his breath. His whole body tingled, and he was going to puke. He scrambled back, hands slipping on leaves. Bethany was saying something, but he couldn't make it out over the blood rushing in his ears. She was going to kill him. He was weak and useless and—

Squeezing his eyes shut, he imagined drawing a line upward, the chalk squeaking on the blackboard. Then it crossed to the right, then down, then back to the left, the box complete. He gasped, drawing another, and another, and another until he'd synced his breathing, slow and steady.

When he could open his eyes, Bethany knelt a few feet away,

watching him warily. She still held the gun, lowered against her thigh. "I ain't gonna shoot you!" she hissed.

"I know." His voice was painfully hoarse.

"Why didn't you freak out before when I had the gun?"

"PTSD isn't always linear." Sweat dampened Parker's hair, and he brushed it off his face. "What were you saying about me being a badass? As if."

Bethany looked him dead in the eyes, leaning forward. "You're. Still. Here."

Parker blew out a long, shuddering breath. He *was* still here. More than that, he was *here* at the compound when he'd been terrified to leave the island. He'd done it.

He could do this.

Bethany turned the gun and offered him the handle, but Parker shook his head. "You're better with guns than I am."

Looking up at the sky, she said, "It's almost time." She met Parker's gaze. "Let's do this."

Keeping low, he followed her. The red light grew stronger but wasn't bright. Parker saw motion ahead, and he stopped Bethany, grabbing her hand.

"There," he breathed.

She squinted, then nodded, her sweaty palm clasping his.

Parker finally had a chance to see the entire "detainment center." The barred cage was surrounded by four guards with assault rifles, along with a fifth in a windowless wooden shack. The shack had to be where the frequency came from. It was the only structure other than the cage. The camera sat atop the shack along with its dim red light.

The frequency was supposed to be undetectable to humans, but a noise vibrated through Parker's bones. Bethany's fingers dug into his hand. He was about to ask what they were hearing when he understood it was the pack.

In the cage, they whimpered and cried and *suffered*. The torture had been continuous for days. The guards nearby laughed and talked, ignoring their prisoners completely.

Between the recording of the child that lured in the werewolves and whatever emanated this frequency that kept them powerless, Burton had certainly come up with an effective system.

Bethany made a small sound, her gaze locked on Damian curled in the fetal position near the bars. Parker squeezed her hand, profoundly grateful that Adam wasn't trapped in the cage too. Lips at her ear, he asked, "Operation Tits is a go?"

She nodded and unzipped her hoodie to strip off her T-shirt before zipping the hoodie back up over her bra. The gun was snug in the back of her jeans.

Only a few minutes passed before the day shift ambled along the path to the right. The electrified fence loomed to the left, and Bethany and Parker stayed huddled in the bushes. Once the five replacement guards passed, Bethany stole across the path, disappearing into the foliage.

Parker waited for her to sneak around and come at the guards, who were indeed milling and chatting. His legs cramped, and he wished Adam was beside him. Though if he was, he'd be in agony, so Parker was thankful Adam was fast asleep in bed.

"Hello? Is anyone there? Oh my god, help me!"

Every head swiveled north at the sound of Bethany's cries, and Parker sprang forward. His heart pounded in his ears as he reached the shack. Flattened against the side, he listened. He'd caught a flash of someone in the doorway, and he waited.

"Where the fuck did she come from?" the guard from the shack asked. He was inches away from Parker around the front of the structure. Parker didn't move a muscle.

"Please, Lord, help me!"

"Jesus, is she okay?" the voice asked, growing fainter on the last word.

Parker had to look.

Ducking down, he peeked around the side of the shack. A mess of guards had moved about twenty feet away. Bethany's pale skin and white bra flashed, her hoodie unzipped down to her bellybutton, red hair streaming loose. In the cage, Damian screamed. The shack guard was maybe five feet from the door.

Now or never.

Holding his breath, Parker ducked around the shack and inside the open door. He squinted in the faint red glow from outside. It was bare bones: a small table and wooden chair. Several battered coffee mugs sat on the table along with a large thermos and a flashlight. Without windows, Parker supposed it was safe enough for the guards to use the flashlight inside the shack. Keys hung from hooks on the wall. A roll of toilet paper from an old-world hoard jutted out from another hook.

Crawling, Parker searched. If the frequency wasn't coming from the shack, they were fucked. But he couldn't see any electronic equipment.

Outside, Bethany was shrieking some story about outrunning a gang of men. The wolves were rattling the cage, guards yelling for them to stop. There was so much noise.

As Parker went up on his knees, fumbling around the mugs on the table, his fingers touched smooth, cool metal. It was another iPod. No, wait. This was a no-name MP3 player.

No headphones were connected. He could feel the tiny holes of an external speaker below the small screen, and a black charger cable snaked from the bottom to a rectangular power bank. On the island, they'd rigged power banks to solar energy, so surely that was possible here too. He ripped out the cord, and the narrow screen across the top lit up.

On the iPod he'd had as a kid, the screen had displayed the song title and album cover. This player simply said:

Control

White text on a blue background. The play, stop, rewind, and fast-forward were physical buttons between the screen and speaker. Parker's thumb moved to jab stop when the hard barrel of a gun jammed into the back of his head. A hand snatched away the MP3 player.

"Well, if it isn't a queer little traitor," Mike drawled.

Chapter Twenty-Two

A DAM'S HEAD THROBBED.

He was aware of Eric still watching him nervously as they made their way along the wooded path. Lauren's peeks were more curious, though of course she didn't know he was a werewolf yet. All that mattered was finding Parker, getting the pack out of the cage, and...

Then what?

"What is this paralyzing frequency?" Adam asked. "Where did you get it? How is it broadcast?"

Lauren looked to Eric, who said, "I'm not sure exactly where Mr. Burton got it. The black market in London. I do know it cost us more than half our food supply. It's on an old MP3 player. That's why the range is limited. And there's no auxiliary function to hook it up to an external speaker."

Speaking of limited range, as they got closer, Adam could finally sense the presence of wolves. Perhaps it had been the incubating distemper virus that had dulled his senses? It didn't matter now. He could sniff out Parker—determination, anxiety, adrenaline. If only he could haul Parker into his arms and inhale the scent from every pore.

What if I made him sick? What if this virus can *be passed to humans?*

Logically, Adam knew there was nothing he could do about it. Still, just pondering it deepened the ache in his skull.

"So, there's only one copy of the frequency?" Lauren asked.

"On this player?"

"Correct," Eric said. "It's locked. It'll play, stop, and charge. The woman Mr. Burton acquired it from warned that if we tried plugging it into a computer to copy the file, it would erase."

"I'm surprised he didn't try anyway," Lauren said.

"Oh, he did. Put his best tech guy on it. Apparently, this woman's tech was better. The player was toast."

Lauren said, "But if the goal is to stop werewolves, why not make it replicable far and wide?"

"Because the goal is capitalism," Eric replied grimly. "The Dow Jones is dead and the currency's changed, but capitalism is alive and well."

"God, that's depressing," Lauren muttered. "Wait, how does he have the frequency then?"

"This is the second player he had to buy from the same seller. That's why it cost more than half our food stock in the end, and that was a huge factor in coming here. Resources in London were scarce."

Lauren laughed sardonically. "That's the real story, huh? I should've known. Also, what's the plan here? Are we just going to rock up to the detainment center and ask them nicely to turn off the frequency?"

"What about the howling?" Adam asked. "How is that broadcast?"

"Howling?" Lauren echoed, clearly puzzled.

"That recording was from another seller," Eric said. "It's played a few miles away on a boom box out of earshot from the compound. Out of earshot for humans, at least." He hesitated. "Parker said it was a child in distress?"

Adam shuddered at the memory. He nodded. "It was unbearable."

"Wait, how do you know?" Lauren asked before her eyebrows shot up. She adjusted her glasses. "Oh. Oh! Wow."

A low whir and vibration reached Adam, and he spun to face the way they'd come. In the distance, he could just make out the top of the main house beyond the tree branches and rustling leaves. "Something's coming."

"What?" Eric asked, he and Lauren whipping their heads around. "I don't see—" He strained, listening. "Shit. Golf cart."

"Oh, crap." Lauren nudged Adam. "Hide!"

He was incredibly tired of hiding, but he ducked into the undergrowth of bushes amid the trees. Unsurprisingly, it was Burton driving the cart, which had a large solar panel attached. Actually, maybe it was surprising he didn't have a chauffeur.

"Eric!" Burton snapped. "What has your brother gotten up to? I was fast asleep, but Mike called me on the walkie-talkie. This is unacceptable behavior."

"I'm so sorry, Mr. Burton." Eric raised his hands. "We were on our way to stop him. I'm afraid, uh, he…"

"Oh, Mr. Burton, it's my fault." Lauren's voice had risen multiple octaves. "He was so curious after seeing the detainment center in the communications hub. I told him where it was, but I didn't realize he was going to see it for himself until it was too late. I woke Eric, and we ran after him. I just wasn't thinking."

Burton's nostrils flared. "I expected better. I thought you were a smart girl. You'll lose points for this. You too!" he yelled at Eric. "He's your brother, and you'd better make sure he doesn't step a toe out of line again."

Adam could only imagine what the points system of a petty tyrant entailed.

"Of course, sir." Eric nodded to the cart. "May we get a lift?"

"Only because it's an emergency," Burton replied petulantly, zooming away before they'd even sat in the back of the cart, almost toppling them out. Hopefully, Eric could manage Burton.

In the meantime, Adam veered through the trees, picking up Parker's scent. A familiar woman had been with him, surely

Bethany. He couldn't smell Jacob, which was a relief. They'd been with Sean, whose scent grew stronger, Adam's senses overwhelmed as he spotted Sean ahead.

Naked and pacing, Sean could have been the one in the cage. "It's still broadcasting," he snarled in greeting. "I'm ready to shift, but…" He took a long stride forward and jerked back as though he'd touched an invisible electric fence. His eyes narrowed on Adam. "I thought you were ill."

"I'm better." At Sean's arched brow, Adam added, "Better than I was."

"They got caught," Sean muttered flatly.

"Seems that way." Not knowing what was happening tortured Adam more than any frequency could.

"You released the brother, I see."

"I'm surprised Parker let you tie him up."

Sean shrugged. "He didn't want to, but your ord—*Parker*—is a feisty one. I understand what you see in him." He lifted a hand. "Don't worry, I'm not into men."

"I'm not worried."

"Besides, I'm married," Sean said quietly.

Adam blinked. "Oh. I didn't realize."

Sean shrugged. "It's been a long time since I've talked about her. Caroline. And our son, Harry. My pack know better than to speak of them. I told Connie and Theresa, but…"

Adam wasn't sure how to respond.

"Now they're on my mind, I suppose. They always are. But speaking their names has a different weight."

"I know what you mean."

Abruptly, Sean turned and strode forward again with the same result. This time, he dropped to his knees, holding his head.

Adam rushed to his side even though there was nothing he could do. "What happens when the frequency is shut off?"

"We take over. This is Connie's compound. Her father's creation. Squatter's rights don't apply, I'm afraid." Sean smiled humorlessly. "Don't fret. I promised Parker I'd only kill if I have to. Most of the humans here are innocent."

"Make sure Parker's brother and the woman he's with aren't harmed. They're trying to help."

Sean's eyebrows rose. "Eric's had a change of heart? He and Parker had quite a heated exchange. I suppose he's had some time to ponder. Also, it's interesting that you said 'when' the frequency's shut off. You're terribly confident."

Adam thought of waking in Dr. Yamaguchi's lab. The despair of knowing he'd never make it out. Parker urging him on, refusing to leave him to save himself.

"Yes," Adam said simply.

Chapter Twenty-Three

A S MIKE SHOVED Parker to his knees beside Bethany in the
dirt outside the cage, the asshole was really enjoying it. In the
red-lit cage, trapped in his human form, Damian screamed in a
furious, impotent rebellion.

This close, Parker could see the pack were thinner already.
Even if they were being given food and water, how could they get
anything down while being tortured?

"Listen, mister, I need your help!" Bethany tried.

Mike shone the flashlight in her face. "Look who we have
here. The uppity bitch who said she'd been their prisoner. Their
whore is more like it."

As Damian rattled the metal bars, Bethany knocked the flashlight up, the beam slashing wildly through the treetops. "Get that
out of my face."

She received a *whack* on the side of the head from the butt of
Mike's shotgun. She wavered but stayed conscious, Parker
automatically reaching for her. He brushed the gun still tucked
into the back of her jeans before Mike snarled, "Hands up."

They somehow hadn't checked Bethany for weapons. Did
they really underestimate a pretty woman that much? Mike had
roughly patted down Parker, making noises to be clear that
touching Parker disgusted him. Parker had barely managed to stop
himself from responding that the feeling was mutual, which was a
good thing since the last thing they needed was both he and
Bethany sidelined with head injuries.

"It's the bootlicker's brother," a male guard with an American accent said.

"Yep." Mike sucked his teeth and spat in the dirt. "Knew he was trouble the minute I saw him. What the fuck do ya think you're doing, huh?"

"It was just a dare," Parker tried. "A joke." He kept his hands in the hair, adrenaline coursing through him.

"Sure, sure." Mike curled his lip. "I bet youse were those Greenpeace types, huh? Vegan motherfuckers."

No, but I am a badass motherfucker, Parker reminded himself. God, he'd been half an inch away from the button. Now, the MP3 player was tucked into Mike's denim pocket, the top sticking out.

Something was approaching, and it took Parker a minute to realize it was a golf cart carrying Burton and—his heart leapt— Eric and Lauren. Burton was shouting, Damian and the wolves were basically howling in human voices, and Eric rushed toward Parker in the chaos.

Who had let Eric out? Lauren? It didn't matter. Eric was reaching out when Mike blocked him with the shotgun, yelling at Eric and spewing the other F-word, blaming Parker for everything, which was fine with Parker. He'd take full responsibility for doing what was right.

Burton loomed over him. He wore jeans and loafers, but his shirt was silk polka dots that were clearly pajamas. "Young man, what do you have to say for yourself?" His gaze slid to Bethany, who had managed to lift her hands and keep her head up. Blood trickled down her cheek, her hoodie now hanging open to completely expose her bra. "And involving this poor girl. What kind of penny-come-quick is this?"

"A...what?" Parker puzzled it out. "Just say trick! Jesus, you're obnoxious."

"Parker!" Eric raised his hands. "I'm sorry, Mr. Burton. I don't know what's gotten into him. If I can just take him back to my room, I'm sure we can work out this misunderstanding."

Misunderstanding.

That's what Parker had tried to convince himself was going on with Eric. Was his brother really taking Burton's side with suffering people crammed into a cage ten feet away?

"I'm afraid it's too late for that." Burton was positively fuming. "This is beyond the pale. This is treason. You know the punishment."

"He's my brother!" Eric insisted, "He doesn't know anything about werewolves. He doesn't know what he's doing!"

Parker wanted to argue, the words fighting to trip off his tongue. He tasted blood as he bit the inside of his cheek. Noise thundered from the wolves and the guards in turn yelling at them to be quiet.

"Can I do it?" Mike asked with a feral grin, pointing his shotgun in Parker's face.

The fear was weirdly distant as Parker realized this might actually be it. He met Eric's panicked, familiar eyes. Parker purposefully looked to the MP3 player sticking out of Mike's front pocket.

"Don't be uncivilized," Burton scolded. "We have procedures. Don't we, Eric? You understand. Listen to this cacophony! This is why we have rules. This is why *I'm* in charge. What would any of you do without me? You'd never have survived a day! And this is the thanks I get?"

Eric stood frozen in place.

Tears flooded Parker's eyes as grief punched him. Had time and loss and the brutal new world changed his brother so much? Would he stand by and do nothing? Parker's pulse galloped in his ears. If he was going to die, he wasn't sure he could survive his heart breaking first.

Eric lunged.

As he yanked the MP3 player from Mike's pocket, Parker grabbed the gun from Bethany's waistband. Lauren thrust Mike's shotgun to the sky, and as Eric pushed the stop button on the MP3 player before crushing it under his heel, the cries in the cage transformed to *roars.*

Parker only enjoyed a split second of satisfaction before the creepers spilled over the wall.

Chapter Twenty-Four

A DAM AND SEAN knew the moment the frequency ceased. They would have heard the pack's escape from the prison even if it were miles away. Sensed the rage and release as they were finally able to shift.

Sean immediately shifted fully and was gone, disappearing into the fading night.

A howl choked Adam, and he almost called after Sean to wait.

He tried with all his might, tensed from head to toe, his fangs and claws free, but the final change forever out of reach.

He ran, his mouth achingly dry. He could hear absolute chaos ahead, and with a jolt, he realized the chatter of creepers vibrated through the air and across the ground, the wall shaking. Why wasn't the electricity affecting them? How were they indestructible?

Adam ran.

If anything happened to Parker because of Adam's weakness, he wouldn't be able to survive. He had to get there, had to be faster—

Adam stumbled and kept going. If he could just be better. Be good enough, *strong* enough.

His knees crashed into the dirt, his head spinning.

He couldn't breathe. Braced on his hands, his jaw was clenched so hard it might snap. He was going to shatter into endless pieces. It wouldn't work. He couldn't go on another step. If only he could shift fully and access that deep well of power...

Racked by a sob, he closed his eyes and collapsed to the ground, stones and twigs digging into his skin. "Parker!" His cry was barely a whisper as memories of Parker filled his mind. Images of smiling, laughing, crying, coming. His beautiful lover. His love. His *mate*.

A strange peace washed over Adam.

His lungs expanded. His bones were melting and reforming. There was no struggle or strain—his body had become water, and he *flowed*.

Distantly, he heard fabric tear.

Beyond the leaves and dirt, the scent of Parker filled his senses completely. Adam opened his eyes, and the world was the purest gold he'd ever seen.

He ran—no, *bounded*—forward. Not on two legs.

On four.

He experienced the transformation both from within and a distance. As if watching footage on his camera while deeply inside the fur and tendons and muscle and bone and lifeblood of the wolf.

Through a golden lens, Adam saw the mass of chaos ahead, wolves and humans battling each other and dozens of chattering infected. He closed the distance in a heartbeat. The golf cart rocketed past him back toward the main compound, carrying only Burton, though it would have held three more.

The commotion faded away as Adam zeroed in on Parker. Parker and Eric wrestled with the man named Mike, who gripped the barrel of a shotgun. Parker was screaming something in the tug of war.

Then, Mike struck Parker across the face, sending him stagger-ing to the ground, blood spraying from Parker's beautiful mouth.

Adam charged, his four legs giving him more power than he even could have dreamed of as he leapt and ripped into Mike's throat, metallic blood coating his fangs.

Parker spun and fired the handgun at the creepers swarming close, shoving Bethany behind him as a wolf Adam knew to be Damian jumped over them, crashing into the infected.

The creepers chattered, their eyes almost out of their sockets, bony fingers reaching, reaching. One of them clawed at Parker's foot, and he kicked wildly, Eric tugging his arms.

Adam lunged. The creeper's spine cracked into pieces in his jaw, its head flopping back, barely attached with sinew and skin.

"Jesus!" Eric screamed, still dragging Parker away.

But Parker dug in his heels, staring at Adam. In the midst of the madness, a smile bloomed over his bloody face. "*Baby.*"

Parker knew him without hesitation, and Adam's howl was triumph and joy and love that would never die.

"What are you doing?" Eric shouted, yanking Parker's arm. "Run!"

More creepers swarmed over the wall, the chatter of hundreds on the other side. Adam tore into them, Parker on his feet with the gun, helping Bethany up. Adam's senses were full of blood and death and the scent of Parker's terror.

Adam kept a safe perimeter around Parker, Eric, and Lauren, Damian half shifting back to carry Bethany down the trail, running faster than a human ever could. Sean and the other wolves cut off the surge of creepers.

There were still too many, and Parker blasted at them with a shotgun now, yelling at Eric and Lauren to run. The creepers lurched forward, the vibrations from their throats growing so high and strong Adam thought the frequency was back on. With a roar, he knocked them down and tasted more blood, the spurting red sepia-toned through the golden veil of his wolf's eyes.

"Fuck, fuck, fuck!" Parker's words were punctuated with shotgun blasts.

Even though Adam tore through the creepers, there were too many. The shack had been toppled, and Parker was trapped near the wreckage. Adam had to shift back. Had to carry Parker away like Damian had Bethany. He concentrated, growling, his claws digging into the earth. He'd shifted part way thousands of times before, but now, he remained on four legs.

His fangs tore through creepers, keeping Parker close. He tried to shift again and again. If only he could carry Parker on his back. Parker was clubbing a creeper's head with the shotgun, shouting something.

The sound of the engine was achingly, wonderfully familiar, jolting Adam with energy as he spotted the red chrome. Mariah screeched to a stop, Jacob on her back.

"Get on!" Jacob held out his hand to Parker.

Adam shoved him with his snout, and Parker clambered onto Mariah, looking back as he disappeared to safety, shouting Adam's name, his hand outstretched.

Adam howled to his mate, then wheeled around to face the onslaught.

His job wasn't finished.

Chapter Twenty-Five

"WE HAVE TO go back!" Parker cried, hanging on as Jacob veered around what was either a dead body or an injured guard. "That was Adam!"

"He can handle it!"

"But..."

Parker looked back even though he could only see trees. Adam had fully shifted, and the pride that swelled Parker's chest made it tough to breathe. He thought of that awful night in the desert, driving away on Mariah's back alone as Adam died for him.

This wasn't that empty highway. Adam had returned to him, and he would again. Parker wasn't alone. He was surrounded by family. Breathing through the whirlwind of worry and anxiety, he hugged Jacob around the middle harder than necessary.

"Slow down!" Parker shouted. "You can barely see without the headlight."

"Yeah, yeah," Jacob muttered, but he eased off the throttle.

"How did you get out?"

"Picked the lock. It was the one useful thing my father ever taught me."

Parker glanced back, hoping to glimpse Adam even though they were too far away. When he looked forward, he pointed to Eric and Lauren shuffling down the trail, and Jacob slowed.

"Are you okay?" Parker asked, jumping off. No one chased them, the wolves apparently keeping the creepers at bay.

Lauren's laugh was tinged with mania. "Not really, mate!" She gripped her side, blood seeping between her fingers, her other arm over Eric's shoulders.

Parker's stomach dropped, and he jerked back. "Bitten?" If she was, they didn't have much longer. Only minutes.

"Shot," she said with a grimace.

"Jacob, take her back," Parker ordered. "Straight to the infirmary."

No one argued, least of all Lauren, who hung on to Jacob as they zoomed away. Parker and Eric started running, and as the sun rose over the horizon, blinding beams winking through the trees, Parker almost shouted that they needed to turn off the lights.

Eric panted. "That wolf—the dark brown one with the white patch on its head? That was Adam?"

Pride filled Parker with a warm, sweet glow, and he could have run for hours. "Yep. He saved us. They all did. They could have let the creepers eat our faces, and I wouldn't have blamed them."

"That was *Adam*," Eric mumbled like he was talking to himself.

"Yes. That was my Adam. If you can't accept that..." Parker trailed off, still not wanting to say it out loud even though his meaning was clear.

"I'm sorry," Eric said, gasping for air as they ran on.

Parker's stomach clenched, and he stumbled on a root before righting himself. "You're sorry?" For never talking to Parker again?

Stopping with hands on knees, Eric sucked in air. "For...not...listening." He straightened and faced Parker, face and golden hair blood splattered. "For being too afraid to listen to you. For believing Mr. Burton knew anything. For standing by while they suffered."

Sweat and blood and dirt coated Parker's skin, but he hugged Eric fiercely. "I'm sorry Pippa died. I'm so sorry. But I promise there's a way to live with them. To thrive. Together. I'm going to bring you to our island, and you'll see."

"Island?" Eric pulled back, brow creased.

"Salvation Island. Surprise! It's not a creepy cult after all. It's—" He broke off as another roar filled the air. But this one was coming from the mansion.

"Mr—" Eric shook his head as he started running again. "That was Burton."

Parker fell into step beside his brother. "He doesn't sound too happy."

They encountered stressed people milling around the main house entrance. Eric said, "I've got to make sure no infected got through." He called, "Peter! Suzanna!"

While Eric gave instructions on setting up an armed perimeter, Parker pushed his way inside. It was a disaster—furniture overturned, vases shattered. People stood in shocked clusters, looking up at Burton holding court at the top of the stairs.

"We have been betrayed by our own! He let the werewolf prisoners loose!" Burton shouted, face so red Parker thought his head might pop off his neck.

Parker couldn't keep in a bark of laughter. Burton was absolutely ridiculous.

Burton's beady gaze swiveled to Parker. "*You!* There he is! The Judas in our midst!"

A circle formed around Parker, people edging away, their eyes widening at the state he was in.

"You're responsible for this. I welcomed you into my home." Burton beat his chest. "My compound! You'll pay for this. Seize him!"

Everyone looked around at each other. Scott cleared his throat. "Er, who?"

"Him!" Burton stomped halfway down the stairs, jabbing his finger in the air toward Parker. "The traitorous poof."

"No one's laying a finger on my brother," Eric said, stepping to Parker's side, his voice loud and unwavering.

"I meant who's supposed to be doing the seizing?" Scott asked. "I don't see any of your usual muscle around."

Burton sputtered. "I don't care! Anyone!"

No one moved.

The Scottish woman Parker remembered from dinner said, "Just so I'm understanding, you captured a pack of werewolves and have been keeping them on the premises without telling us, let alone asking us?"

"Asking you?" Burton echoed, seeming genuinely confused.

The woman continued. "Instead of keeping them far away, you actually brought them here. You risked our lives. For what?"

Burton huffed impatiently. "To build our water system! For the good of our community. They're animals. We can utilize them the way we would any beast of burden."

"Except they're people just like us," Parker said. "Only a little hairier." He strode forward, Eric at his side. They mounted the stairs, stopping a few below Burton, who positively seethed.

Parker announced, "You were torturing them in a cage. You could have lived here in peace. We could have worked together on a new well. Instead, you were so concerned with exerting control over the werewolves, you drew the creepers in. They came right over the wall. So many of them the electricity didn't matter. They piled up on each other and jumped over."

Alarm rippled through the crowd, voices rising in panicked unison.

Eric turned to them, raising his hands. "It's all right. The werewolves are keeping us safe. I saw them killing the infected. Despite what Burton did to them, they helped us."

"The threat's been contained," a woman's familiar voice announced. "Almost."

Parker turned to see Connie strolling in, and he could have wept with relief. "How?" he breathed. His emergency call had only been yesterday. If Connie had somehow learned to fly, he'd believe it.

"Hello, Atticus," Connie said. She wore her tennis shoes, capri jeans, and a pink sweatshirt that read in flowing white script:

Believe you can and you're halfway there.

Jaw dropping, Burton stared. Then he sputtered. "I, I— Connie?" He opened his arms, smiling too widely. "My god, what a sight for sore eyes! You're alive! It's a miracle."

"What have you done to my daddy's compound?" she asked calmly.

"Oh, well, you see—I thought you were gone! That the worst had happened." Burton hurried down the stairs, pushing past Parker and Eric. "I came here hoping you'd welcome my band of weary travelers. Come in, come in! We've had a spot of trouble, but—"

Eyes glowing gold, fangs and claws extending, Connie lifted him by the throat. Her expression was still placid, and as Burton thrashed, his face red and eyes like a creeper's, she held him off the floor.

The word barely scraped out of him. "*You?*"

"That's right, Atticus. I'm a werewolf. So were my parents. My useless husband wasn't, and I guess he's the reason you're here. You caged my people. Tortured them."

She dropped him, and he sprawled back on the floor.

"Do you deserve mercy?" Connie asked, her claws tipped red, pinprick wounds on Burton's neck.

"I, I—of course! Connie, you know me. I never meant harm. Ask anyone!"

Connie gazed around at the hushed circle around them. "Speak up if he deserves mercy."

The silence said it all.

"You'll pay for this!" Burton shouted, shooting glares around the room. "After everything I did for you! After all I sacrificed!

This is the thanks I get!" He narrowed his gaze on Connie, pushing to his feet. "You bitch. I should have known you were a filthy animal."

A gasp rippled through the crowd.

Connie only smiled, her fangs gleaming. "I'll give you food and water, and then you'll be escorted to the gate. Any of your people are free to join you." She nodded, and three wolves from the island appeared in the crowd to drag Burton away, kicking and swearing, his wild eyes darting around.

"Well?" Burton screeched. "*Well?*" His gaze landed on Eric. "You were always weak! Pathetic! Moping over that dead cunt. You'd be nothing without me! Nothing!"

Burton's ravings died away, and Connie announced calmly, "As you heard, this is my compound. As you can see, I'm a werewolf. There'll be a change in leadership style here. You're all welcome to stay as we find a way to move forward together. Or you're free to go with as many supplies as you can carry. You don't need to decide today." Connie's gaze found Parker, and she smiled, wrinkles fanning out from her eyes as she shifted back into human form. "I need to check in with my people."

She opened her arms, and Parker practically jumped from the stairs to hug her. She smelled like the island somehow—oranges and sea salt and family.

"Did you see Adam?" Parker asked, searching her kind, tired face. "Is he okay?"

"He's just fine. Don't you worry."

"Is he still—did you see?" Despite everything, Parker couldn't stop a grin.

Connie's matched his. "I sure did."

Parker sagged against her again, not ready to let go yet. "How are you here?" he asked. "I only radioed yesterday. Did you hear it?"

"No, but Bethany called days ago."

259

"Oh, thank God." It must have been after she was left alone on *Diana*. "Did you come up the river? What about the patrol boats?"

"They took some convincing. Good thing bullets don't hurt us." Connie squeezed him. "Just breathe. You don't need to worry about anything. You're safe." She glanced around. "Where's Bethany?"

"I'll take you." Parker led Connie over to where Eric still stood on the stairs watching them. "Eric?" He took Eric's hand, glad when he didn't flinch or pull away. Eric only clutched Parker like a lifeline. "This is Connie. She took in me and Adam on Salvation Island. Connie, this is my brother."

"It's a pleasure to meet you, Eric." She extended her small, work-worn hand.

Still gripping Parker with his left, Eric shook Connie's hand. "You didn't kill him. He deserves it."

"I admit I was sorely tempted. But that's no way to build bridges."

Eric nodded, seeming to shake himself out of his daze. "I'll make sure everything's okay here and follow in a minute to check on Lauren. You're sure the infected aren't a threat? An imminent one, I mean?"

"I'm sure," Connie said. "There had to be hundreds of them to pile up high enough to get over the wall, and I guess now we know they can apparently survive electrocution. Resilient, to say the least. But most went to ground as the sun came up. We took care of the rest."

Parker shuddered. "What if they come back tonight?"

"We'll be watching, but as long as there isn't a ruckus, nothing should attract them."

"Right. Okay. Yeah, there was a ton of noise, and stupid Mike had that flashlight..." But Mike couldn't hurt him now. Parker's palms were sweaty, and he focused on a deep breath as Eric left and Connie nodded encouragingly.

On the way to the infirmary, Parker asked her, "Do you think Burton will make it out there?"

Connie flashed a wicked grin. "I wouldn't bet on him making it to noon."

"Is it wrong that I wanted you to gut him like a fish?"

"Nope. But it wouldn't be smart. At least, not in front of his people." She shrugged nonchalantly. "Who knows? Maybe I'll go for a run later. Been cooped up on a boat, and I need to stretch my legs. You know, I just might bump into Atticus."

Parker couldn't find it in himself to be sorry. Not even a little bit. "Well, you know what they say. Today only happens once. Make it amazing."

Connie grinned. "That's a good one. I'll get Devon to make me a sign so I can put it up in my office."

Again, Parker waited to feel guilt or regret for Burton, but all he could think about was how much the captured pack had suffered. Nope. He had more important people to worry about.

Someone had given Damian sweatpants, so he was no longer naked at Bethany's side. Still, Parker could see how much weight he'd lost, his ribs jutting out.

Parker asked Bethany, "How's your head?"

"Hard as ever." She winked, though she was pale, blood staining her hair. "You good?"

"I will be when Adam's back."

"I hear that." She kissed Damian's hand. "Connie, will you make him eat something?"

Connie was already bustling around, going into nurse mode. "I sure will. Let me just check on this young lady."

On another cot, Lauren winced. Her shirt had been cut away, and the bandaged wound on her side oozed blood. After disinfecting her hands, Connie snapped on gloves and examined it.

"I think it's mostly a flesh wound. Nothing to worry about."

She asked the man who was treating Lauren, "Ever taken out a bullet?"

He held up his hands as if she'd pulled a gun on him. "Not even close. I give out Tylenol and Band-Aids."

Rolling up her sleeves, Connie said, "Ready to learn?"

In the doorway, Eric answered, "I am."

Lauren's smile transformed her sweaty, pale face. "Hey, Eric."

Parker asked, "Do you need more help, or...?"

"No, you go find Adam," Connie said with a shooing motion. "Isn't he beautiful? Worth the wait."

Chapter Twenty-Six

"FINALLY!" PARKER EXCLAIMED, rocketing forward as Adam trudged into the guesthouse.

Adam clutched him, inhaling deeply. Parker was filthy with dirt and blood, his sweat spiked with anxiety. "Sorry."

"S'okay," Parker mumbled into Adam's neck. "I figured you were doing wolf stuff. Is everyone all right?"

Adam nodded. "Sean took care of us."

"Got you some pants too, so that's good. But you need a shower."

"So do you."

Parker shepherded Adam to the bathroom. He had a glass of water waiting, and Adam gulped it down gratefully. They squeezed into the glass cubicle under the tepid shower. Adam dropped his head, enjoying the sensation of Parker's fingers shampooing his hair.

"Hmm," Parker murmured.

"Hmm?"

"I thought maybe you'd have grown a white patch. In your hair. You have one as a wolf."

His breath caught. "I do?"

"Yeah. Close to your neck."

"My father had a patch on his head."

"No shit? Rinse."

Adam closed his eyes under the stream of water, then took his turn shampooing Parker's hair.

"That's so cool that your dad had a patch too." Parker rinsed, then wrapped around Adam from behind, his lips moving against Adam's shoulder blade. "I couldn't believe it when I saw you. You were…"

Adam held his breath.

"So fucking beautiful."

The exhale punched out of Adam's lungs.

"What is it?" Parker squirmed and squeezed in front of Adam, taking his face in his hands. "You did it. I knew you could. How did it feel? Was it amazing?"

"Yes." He brushed his fingers over Parker's swollen cheek.

"I'm fine." Parker took Adam's fingers and kissed them. "We're still here. You should sleep. Let's sleep."

Adam didn't think he could, but it was late afternoon when he woke judging by the sun. Parker's heart beat steadily as he spoke to Eric outside. Sometimes, Adam wondered if Parker was developing a sixth sense from being around werewolves so much, because Adam had only swung his legs around to sit on the side of the bed when Parker rushed in.

"You're awake! How do you feel? Drink." He pushed a cup into Adam's hand.

"Good. Better."

Eric hovered in the doorway. "Hey." He lifted a hand awkwardly. "I just wanted to say… Thank you. And I'm sorry. This has all been…"

"I can imagine." Adam nodded. "I'm sorry too."

Eric said, "I need to check on Lauren again. Connie says she's doing well, but I just want to make sure."

"Cool." Parker nodded. "Um, see you in the morning?"

"I'll be here." Eric smiled tightly.

Parker closed the door and puffed out his cheeks. "It's so weird. To not really know what to say to my brother. I mean, I said sorry for letting Sean tie him up. And gag him. *Awkward.*

Eric'll get over it, right?"

"Absolutely. You're family." Adam stood and stretched.

"You up for a walk?"

Adam tugged on shorts, and they strolled down to the lake and along the path away from the harbor, fingers entwined. The day was humid, birds trilling and insects buzzing lazily. After the madness of the night before—the *screaming*—it seemed impossible the world could be so peaceful.

"Can you do it any time now?" Parker asked.

Adam's stomach tightened. What if he couldn't? What if he'd never experience the freedom of running on four legs again? What if—

"I can hear you worrying. I'm the one who's supposed to go down anxiety spirals."

Adam laughed softly. "I suppose the answer is that I'm not sure."

"Let's try."

"Here?" Adam gazed around the empty trail. No boats passed on the lake. Still. "Anyone could come by."

"So? Let them see." Parker's smile faltered. "No pressure, though."

"I know. That was the problem. I was trying too hard. Forcing it. I think being sick actually helped me...surrender to it. I even had a hard time changing back after. I can't overthink it."

"Is it... Can I watch?"

Desire flared in Adam's veins. He nodded, then took off the shorts, folding them carefully, his camera in the pocket. He closed his eyes.

Surrender. Don't force it. Flow like water.

It was when he heard Parker's soft gasp that he realized he was closer to the ground, his perspective new. He was reshaped, reformed, and he ran ahead on the trail in that golden world. When he returned, Parker dropped to his knees, reaching for him.

Adam rubbed against him, nuzzling. Even in wolf form, the desire to kiss burned in him, and he shifted back, flowing into his human self, still in Parker's arms. Tangled together on the earth, they kissed until they panted.

"That was incredible." Parker grinned. "Holy shit. You're a full-on wolf, but it's *you*. It's still all you. I wish you could see it. Oh!" He lunged for Adam's shorts. "Do it again. I'll film you."

"What?" The idea seemed strangely shocking. "I'm not sure."

"Why not?"

Adam couldn't think of a single reason.

"Come on, you need to be in your movie too. A director cameo."

So, Adam shifted again, and Parker filmed him. Then again from another angle. And another. Until the urge to kiss Parker was too strong, and the camera was forgotten.

"LETTING HIM DO all the work?" Connie asked cheerfully as she kicked off her Birkenstocks and joined Adam sitting on the end of the dock.

Adam glanced behind at Parker on *Bella*'s deck getting her ready to sail, humming along to the Dolly Parton CD.

"He says it's easier if I just let him do it. And that I should be resting."

"Well, I won't argue with that."

"I'm not sick. I feel totally back to normal. It's been weeks."

"I know. But a little R and R never hurt anyone." Connie elbowed him playfully.

"Parker should rest too."

"For him, working on the boat is relaxing."

Adam had to smile. "True." He watched a bird circle, then pluck a fish from the water, flapping its wings desperately as it carried off its prize. "It'll be good to get home."

"That it will."

"How long are you going to stay here?"

Connie closed her eyes, tipping back her face in the sunshine. "Just a bit longer to make sure everyone's settled. Damian, Bethany, and Eric are in charge. I thought Gemma might object, but it turns out she's happy as a clam not to be the boss."

"And Sean?"

"Sean left last night."

Adam didn't know what to feel. Surprise. Sadness. Regret. "Do you think he'll find them?"

Connie met his gaze. "No. But stranger things have happened. Look at Parker and his brother."

"I wish he were coming with us."

"I made it clear the invitation is open. I think we'll see him on the island when he's ready."

"Is Sean still the alpha of his pack?"

"Officially. I don't see the need for another rite of separation. He'll always be an alpha, but his pack is mine while he's away. Ours."

After a time, Adam said, "Can I ask you a question?"

"Always."

"Why do you think my parents kept us isolated from other wolves?"

Connie swung her bare feet, contemplating. "I didn't know them, of course, but my guess is they thought they were protecting you and your sisters. It was what they knew. It's amazing they found each other. With modern life, packs splintered and we became isolated. It happened slowly. That was one of the reasons my daddy bought the island—so we'd have a place to reconnect."

They were silent for a time. Then Adam asked, "Do you think we'll ever really know what caused the virus?"

"Son, I may be an alpha, but I'm not a magic eight ball."

Adam laughed. "I should ask again later?"

"Signs point to yes." Her smile faded. "But no. Whether it was the phantom Zechariahs, a freak of nature, or something else entirely, I don't think we'll find out in our lifetime. Certainly not mine." She elbowed him again. "Don't look so downcast. I'm not going anywhere yet. And before I forget, there was so much kerfuffle when I arrived that I'm not sure if I told you."

"What?"

"How proud I am. I knew you could do it when the time was right. You were ready."

Adam's heart sang, and he could only nod, eyes burning.

"Hey!" Jacob called. "Wanna help me load her on?"

Adam turned to find him wheeling Mariah to the dock. "I'll be right there!" He pulled out his camera. "Is it... Do you mind saying that again?"

"How's my hair?" Connie finger-combed it. "I'm ready for my close-up."

Adam moved to the edge of the dock so he wasn't filming up Connie's nose. He brought her into focus and nodded. She spoke right into the lens.

"Adam, I'm so proud of you. I knew you could do it when the time was right. You were ready."

He pressed stop and carefully tucked his camera away. Even if he lost the footage one day, the memory would always be his.

"I'M SICK OF fish," Jacob grumbled from where he sprawled on the bench. "I miss Big Macs. Don't you guys miss Big Macs?"

"Obviously we miss Big Macs," Parker said as he trimmed the sail.

The wind had finally pointed north, and they passed Cape Canaveral. Adam had gone there with his family when they drove down to Disney World one summer. He filmed it now as they passed. Where space shuttles had once blasted off, only ghostly metal towers remained.

After a few minutes of silence, Jacob asked, "Do you think Devon, like, misses me?"

Adam and Parker shared a glance, and Adam tried to hide his smile. Parker did a better job, casually saying, "Yeah, probably."

"Do you think Craig's mad?"

Parker snorted. "Definitely." He softened. "Only because he's worried."

"I know," Jacob mumbled. "And in case I never said it, thanks for coming after me." He eyed Parker. "I know it was a big deal for you to leave."

Parker stepped back to the wheel, adjusting their heading. "It was. But I'm glad I did. It wasn't so scary after all." The sail luffed, and he tightened the rope. "Still, let's, you know. Not leave again for a while."

"That actually sounds good," Jacob agreed. "Okay, what was better? Big Macs or McChickens?"

"Filet-O-Fish," Adam said.

As Jacob squawked his disapproval, Parker grinned, then snapped back into captain mode, adjusting the sails.

Adam closed his eyes, inhaling the sea air deeply as Parker charted their course for home.

Epilogue

Five Years Later

"LAST CHANCE, LIL. Sure you don't want to come on an adventure?" Jacob gave her a devilish grin. His skin had cleared, and he'd somehow grown up when Parker wasn't looking.

Lilly laughed. "Oh, I'm sure. You're all crazy, for the record. I'm staying right here where I don't have to worry about creepers and jerks and sometimes *rats*." She shuddered.

"You'll get bored eventually," Jacob said.

Lilly raised a brow. "Do you know how many books we have on this island? I won't get bored. But you'd better bring me back something cool."

"The pressure's on," Craig said with a brave smile, clearly trying not to cry. "Be good," he said to Jacob. "I'm proud of you. Your mom is too. I know she's watching over you."

Jacob nodded, swallowing thickly. He hugged Craig hard, and Parker heard him whisper, "Thanks for being an awesome dad."

Blinking away tears, Parker took a long breath, sharing a smile with Adam, who squeezed his hand. Nearby, Chris and Heather and a few others said their goodbyes to friends and family. The expedition of ten people would visit the compound first before heading north to another colony. Parker still didn't like that little shithead Chris, though Chris and Jacob had buried the hatchet ages ago.

Devon asked, "Any messages for the compound crew?"

After a few moments, Parker said, "Tell Bethany hi. I hope she and Damian and the baby are doing good, and that the well's working, uh…well. Oh, and if Sean's back, tell him hi too."

Sean had come and gone over the years. Still searching.

Devon nodded. "Will do."

"I guess this is it," Jacob said.

He was really leaving, and Parker couldn't make him stay. He'd tried, but… It was time. Jacob had to explore and live his life. Even if it meant they might never see him again.

Parker supposed it had always been that way. There'd never been any guarantees in the old world either. Danger had always lurked around every corner. And young people had always needed to find their own path.

Parker cleared his throat and ordered, "Be careful."

"Hold on, I should be *careful*? This is groundbreaking." Jacob grinned. "And I will, but only because you said so. Adam, any sage words of wisdom?"

Parker slugged Jacob's arm as Adam cleared his throat. "It's a big world out there, but you have each other. Stick together."

They'd heard snatches of news from the odd working radio transmission and from boats that appeared on the horizon. Creepers still owned the night in most places. There were a few more colonies they'd established trade with along with the compound. Werewolves and humans warred in some areas. Made truces. Warred again.

But they had peace on Salvation Island.

"We will," Jacob said confidently. "And Devon will protect me."

Even though he still looked like an actual angel with his golden curls and delicate features, Devon let his eyes flash gold as he grinned and growled. Parker had no doubt he'd eviscerate anyone or anything that threatened his boyfriend.

Devon and Jacob shared a secret, tender smile that made Parker's heart sing.

"Got everything?" Parker asked. His gaze flicked to the silver dove at Jacob's throat.

Jacob fingered the necklace with a little smile. "Yeah. I'm good."

Parker kept his voice steady. "I'm really, really going to miss you. You'd better come back."

Eyes glistening, Jacob nodded. "I know you'll chase after me if I don't."

"Damn right I will. Which means Adam will have to come with me because he's my big, bad, protective wolf, and it'll be a whole thing. So just come back before too long."

They hugged, and Parker realized Jacob was as tall as him now and had more muscles. He hadn't quite noticed the transformation seeing him every day.

"Thanks for being my friend," Jacob whispered.

Parker managed to smile. "We're family."

It was Adam's turn to hug Jacob, and there were more folks who wanted to say goodbye. Theresa and Connie squeezed both boys—young men now—fiercely, and Yolanda and others lined up. Eric was there, hugging Jacob and Devon and giving them one of his most reassuring smiles.

Drawing a box on his mind's blackboard, Parker breathed steadily. Adam filmed the farewells with his camera, still going strong due to his careful tending.

Parker listened to the slosh of water against the dock, glad of Adam's strong arm around him. He slid his hand around Adam's waist, and they stood with Craig and Lilly, watching until the boat was only a speck on the horizon.

Then the day went on like any other before or after.

Parker kissed Adam goodbye for the morning and picked oranges with Lauren while Adam joined the building crew constructing the latest block of cabins. Eric strolled up the path to the grove and snatched an orange from Parker's basket.

"Hey!" Parker grabbed it back. "I have a quota."

"What about you?" Eric asked Lauren, pulling her into a kiss. "Do you have a quota?"

"Preggo people get off the hook." She passed him an orange with a wink.

"I don't see why uncles don't get special dispensation," Parker grumbled.

Eric raised an eyebrow. "I don't see Adam asking for it."

"Ugh, his work ethic." Parker sighed dramatically as he climbed the ladder to reach higher branches. "Hey, are you two still coming for dinner tomorrow before the movie? You three, I should say. Unless you're having twins. Or triplets. There could be five of you along with Lilly and Craig. We're going to have to cook more food."

They ate in the mess hall most days, but once in a while a family dinner was nice. Knowing Jacob was leaving, Parker had planned a meal for the next day. He wasn't the greatest cook, but Adam wasn't bad. They made it work.

Lauren gave him a withering glare. "One baby will be plenty, thank you very much. At least to start. Oh, I keep forgetting to say thank you! I have pregnancy brain, I swear."

"For what?" Parker asked, pulling on an orange and getting the satisfying release of fruit that's ready to be picked.

"The shell from the Bahamas. It's perfect for my collection in the nursery. I don't know how you and Adam found a purple one."

"I'd like to say skill, but it was dumb luck." He knew Lauren loved beachcombing for little treasures, and the purple clam shell was a keeper.

They'd cruised south on *Bella*, venturing to the white sand beaches on small, uninhabited cays as they'd toured around.

"Still, thank you for thinking of us," Lauren said.

Eric clasped Parker's shoulder. "That's my baby brother for

you. He was always so good at presents. I mean, what kid buys good presents for other people?"

"You bought everyone gift cards, didn't you?" Lauren asked, narrowing her gaze at Eric.

"What's wrong with that?" Eric protested. "Then you could get exactly what you wanted. Justice for gift cards!"

At lunchtime, Parker picked up fish tacos for two from the mess hall and made his way back to the cabin, knowing Adam would be engrossed in his other work.

He called, "Hey, baby!" and kicked off his shoes, the floor creaking in the same old spots as he joined Adam in the kitchen.

Adam sat at the round table, his camera plugged into an ancient laptop loaded with editing software that kept launching a pop-up to run an update that would never come. The island's solar power battery chargers were better than ever, so at least they could run old tech.

Sometimes, Parker wondered if he'd be downloading texts straight into his brain by now if the world hadn't ended and then begun again. Then he'd go for a swim and think about the sun and the ocean swells and how lucky he was.

Parker kissed the top of Adam's head and combed his fingers through his hair.

Clicking at a frame and clipping the video, Adam asked, "Any sign?"

"Not yet. But mark my words, you're going to develop a patch of white hair one day." He ran his fingers behind Adam's left ear. "Back here, I bet."

"Mm. I guess time will tell."

Parker took an orange from his pocket. Even though he should have saved it for dessert, he peeled it, the fresh, powdery scent filling the kitchen. Theodore ticked faithfully on the wall.

Parker separated an orange segment and passed it to Adam. Juice dribbled onto Adam's beard, and they laughed as he licked his fingers, a drop of juice running down over the small tattoo on the inside of his right wrist.

Damian had inked Adam's drawing of the circular wolf with its tail curving up. An identical tattoo marked the same spot on Parker's wrist. Unbroken.

Standing behind Adam, Parker passed over another segment. Adam drew him down for a kiss. His fangs extended, and Parker licked them clean of fresh, sweet-tart juice.

When Parker straightened, he smiled at the footage on the screen. It was him on a deserted white-sand beach a few days earlier in the golden hour, caramel light on his sun-kissed skin, laughing as he tried to skip rocks on the clear water.

How had he grown so much older? That prickly, anxious freshman who'd thought a C-minus was the end of the world wouldn't even recognize himself.

"Your movie must be almost finished," Parker murmured, resting his chin on Adam's head.

"This is only the beginning."

The End

About the Author

Keira aims for the perfect mix of character, plot, and heat in her M/M romances. She writes everything from swashbuckling pirates to heartwarming holiday escapism. Her fave tropes are enemies to lovers, age gaps, forced proximity, and passionate virgins. Although she loves delicious angst along the way, Keira guarantees happy endings!

Discover more at:

keiraandrews.com

Made in the USA
Las Vegas, NV
19 August 2024

94040476R00173